Abby loves chatting to readers and reading reviews, so please do get in touch/share on Amazon, Instagram, Twitter and Goodreads.

Find out more about Abby and her books at

www.abbydavies.com
Twitter: @Abby13Richards
Instagram: @abbydaviesauthor

By Abby Davies

Mother Loves Me

The Cult

Arrietty

Her No.1 Fan

THE GIRL WHO HEARD MAGGOTS

Abby Davies

Apple Loft Press

The Girl Who Heard Maggots

Published worldwide by Apple Loft Press.
This edition published in 2023.

www.abbydavies.com

For Aunty Spoiler and Uncle Smee

The Haunted House

Oh, very gloomy is the house of woe,
Where tears are falling while the bell is knelling,
With all the dark solemnities that show
That Death is in the dwelling!

Oh, very, very dreary is the room
Where Love, domestic Love, no longer nestles,
But smitten by the common stroke of doom,
The corpse lies on the trestles!

But house of woe, and hearse, and sable pall,
The narrow home of the departed mortal,
Ne'er looked so gloomy as that Ghostly Hall,
With its deserted portal!

The centipede along the threshold crept,
The cobweb hung across in mazy tangle,
And in its winding sheet the maggot slept
At every nook and angle.

Thomas Hood, 1798-1845

Chapter One

The sky was clear and black, and speckled with stars. Beyond an iron gate, the moor lay silent. My skin crawled. I shifted my weight, told myself everything was going to be okay. A woman generous enough to overlook my past must be decent. What I'd done was bad. Unforgivable in most people's eyes.

I glanced over my shoulder. "Can't you get closer?"

The taxi driver shook his head, wound up the window and reversed, leaving me alone in the dark. I cursed and fumbled in my bag for my phone. An enormous man lumbered out of the gloom towards me, a lantern gripped in one huge fist. I tried not to stare as he wrestled a ring of keys out of his pocket and unlocked the iron gate. He had a crooked eye that made it hard to know where to look. Squints always made me uncomfortable – I never knew which eye to choose and usually flitted between the two, which probably made my indecision all the more obvious to the squinter.

I stared some more.

His body was more fat than muscle and a scorpion tattoo curled across his neck. Think: World's Strongest Man crossed with Uncle Fester. I stifled a giggle.

"Ivy Smith?" His voice had a gritty voiceover quality, like he'd been munching glass.

I chose his right eye. "Yep. That's me. Nice to meet you –"

He cleared his throat and thumped his chest, rattling a lump of phlegm. He took my case and locked the fence behind us. "Maddock."

For a huge man, he moved quickly. I sped up and tottered after him like a toddler, watching open-mouthed as Fairwood House emerged from the gloom like a beast in a dream, its size intimidating, its appearance uncanny in the barren landscape. My heart jittered; the building was huge, blurred by mist and darkness - deliciously weird.

I jerked to a halt. We'd reached another iron gate. My guide unlocked a second padlock and ushered me through, following so closely I felt his body heat on my skin. Heaving the gate closed, he pocketed the key ring and exhaled a beery breath before striding across a fenced-off area.

My excitement ebbed. I glanced back, wondering at the need for not one but two iron gates.

"Miss?"

Maddock was waiting for me. I hurried along the path and joined him at an oak door. I glanced at a silver plaque that announced FAIRWOOD HOUSE, and saw my face staring back at me. I looked deranged. Like a Picasso gone wrong.

My escort unlocked the door and dragged my case into an entrance hall lit by one lantern. I hurried in after him and he locked the door behind me. I tried to speak but he was already moving away, taking his light with him.

"Wait here, Miss."

"But –"

He pretended not to hear me and dragged my case up the dark stairway without a backward glance.

Irked by his rudeness, I watched him ascend, steps muffled by a blue carpet that licked the centre of the steps like a giraffe's tongue. Halfway up, he snatched off his hat, stuffed it in his pocket and used the banister to climb. His head resembled a boiled egg. He disappeared at the top of the stairway where there was no light at all.

I looked around and shivered. The house was warmer than outside but not warm enough. I smelt smoke but heard no fire.

I felt twitchy, evermore the stranger in someone else's home. I watched the interplay of light and dark. Dark was clearly winning; light leaked from the lantern but vast shadows snaked up the wall and across the high ceiling like outstretched fingers. I glanced to the right and flinched. An umbrella stood in a silver bucket. My tummy hardened. I clenched my fists and shook my head, willing the memory to stay buried. A cold sweat spread across my back. I tried but couldn't fight them. The demons of my past would not be tamed. They wouldn't stay buried because I had buried them alive.

Inside my mind, the maggots twitched, and the past crawled out of its grave.

I'm upstairs digging around in my school bag for my certificate. It's the highest award imaginable: a Headteacher's Commendation. The message on the glossy card reads 'for producing a super piece of writing entitled 'What I Want To Be When I Grow Up'.

I've written about my dream of being a police lady. I'm the only one in Year Three to get a certificate. I'm so excited to show Mummy I feel sick.

I giggle at the sound of the door opening and shutting. I hear the rumbling voices of Mummy and the childminder talking, then the door opening, Mrs Sprig leaving, the front door shutting.

Knowing I'm alone with Mummy, I go to grab the certificate but not before wiping my sticky fingers on my school cardigan. With the certificate in one hand, I dash out of my bedroom onto the landing and stop.

The back door slams shooting terror into my lungs.

He's home early.

Shaking, I turned away from the bucket. The maggots retreated with a spiteful hiss.

Chapter Two

For a while, nothing stirred. It was like the walls roared with silence. Like the silence was fake.

Like me.

Then, from behind the staircase, a door groaned and a tall figure emerged.

I tried not to stare, but it was impossible not to.

The woman's face was pale, her hair silver before its time. She wore a black Victorian-style dress and a scarlet shawl. Weird with a capital W, but she greeted me with a smile that made her eyes glow and, though she stood a head taller than me, my shoulders dropped and I returned her smile.

She removed a velvet glove and gave me her hand. As I took her palm, I smelt lavender and coal smoke.

"Ivy, I am so *very* pleased to meet you. My, what a beauty you are. And so young. You look far younger than your twenty-six years, which is a rare blessing indeed."

"Lovely to meet you too," I said in a posher voice than normal, feeling like an idiot.

I'd read somewhere that in the first thirty seconds of meeting a new person you formed opinions of them mainly based on their body language and tone of voice. I wondered what impressions she was forming of me. Did she see a fraud trying too hard to seem like the real deal?

I stood up straighter and took her hand, which made mine feel measly. Her grip was strong. I gripped back.

"Maddock took your luggage at the gate?" she said.

"He did, yes."

"Good, good."

She frowned and leant down, bringing our faces close, "You didn't see the Weirlock Hill ghost on your way up then?"

Before I could respond, she threw her head back and laughed.

I smiled, relieved she had a good - if random - sense of humour. Random was my middle name. *Along with Messed Up and Paranoid and -*

"The child is in bed," she said, "so you'll meet him tomorrow. Let's move into the living room, shall we? It's snug as a bugaboo in there."

"Your home's incredible," I said as she led me through the door behind the stairs.

"It is isn't it? I'm dreadfully lucky, of course."

We entered a vast lounge that was every bit as cluttered and beautiful as the entrance hall wasn't. Several linen tapestries adorned the walls. I was drawn to one depicting a woodpecker against an ornate backdrop of autumn trees. Below this lazed a cream chaise lounge draped with a plum blanket, its arm warmed by a thriving log fire whose flames frolicked beneath a mantel piece lined with china ballerinas.

"Please, sit wherever you like," Mrs Waters said, settling into a leather armchair that sucked her in like quicksand.

She crossed her legs. Patted her hair. Smiling at me, she picked up a china bell and gave it a shake. I noticed her not-so-little little finger poking out, and smiled. The bell tinkled and in dashed a Thai woman about my age wearing the sort of clothes a Victorian maid might have worn. I raised an eyebrow. Weird again, but I told myself not to judge.

I sat on the armchair's larger cousin, felt myself swallowed up in its squishy folds.

"This is Ping. She's *fabulous*. Elderflower please, my sweet. Ping, meet Ivy, our new nanny."

Ping offered a furtive glance as she poured tea. The nails of her pinkie fingers were so long they'd begun to curl. I smiled at her. She ignored me.

"She's shy," Mrs Waters said as Ping scurried out of the room, "Poor lamb speaks barely any English."

I nodded. Wondered how long the Thai woman had worked there, but didn't ask. I was too busy gaping at the room. There was no technology of any kind. Everything was an antique. I felt like I'd been transported back to the nineteenth century, which was bizarre but exciting. Like I'd been sucked into a period drama. Then I thought about *The Turn of the Screw*. Told myself not to go there.

I pulled my phone out of my pocket to check for service. Decided to ask if it was okay to take a picture.

Mrs Waters looked up from her tea. "Ivy, I don't like modern technology. I'd really rather you didn't use it when here. I'm sorry to be a pain."

She looked so uncomfortable that I apologised and pocketed the phone.

An awkward silence followed and I sipped tea, scalding my lip. The maggots giggled manically.

No. Each to their own. Each to their own. Try not to judge. I'm not exactly perfect. And Mrs Waters is so generous to overlook what I've done.

"Do Ping and Maddock live here?" I said.

"Why yes, of course. They and Wren use rooms upstairs, just as you will. The old servants' quarters are down below but with so few of us living here, it makes sense for the help to have more comfortable rooms. Each bedroom has a fireplace. We don't have electricity out here so Maddock regularly goes to the wood to chop logs for the fires. He's such a useful man. I don't know what I'd do without him."

"So, it's just the four of you?"

"Not quite."

I saw her jaw tighten. She smiled at me and sipped her tea, pinkie finger out.

"I expect you'd like to unpack, have a bath perhaps

before our evening meal?"

"That would be lovely, thank you."

"Excellent. I'll have Ping draw you a bath. Dinner will be at seven. Please don't be late. Tepid food is such a rotten affair."

She dabbed her lips with a serviette then rang the china bell. Ping appeared and Mrs Waters instructed her to run me a bath then prepare the evening meal. The maid nodded and tidied away the tea things before exiting the room at a speed walk. I noticed she never made eye contact with Mrs Waters. If it wasn't for the fact that she was so lovely, I'd have thought Ping was scared of her.

"Come," Mrs Waters said, "Let me show you your rooms."

Her pluralisation of 'room' didn't go amiss. *"Rooms?"*

"We can't very well have the most important person in the house living in squalor, can we?" she said, eyes twinkling.

She trailed one gloved hand over the banister as she climbed, her low heels clip-clopping the carpeted steps. At the top of the stairs the corridor glowed with lantern-flame. Mrs Waters turned right and I followed her, eyes on the walls which were hung with oil paintings of the same girl at various stages of youth. She was dressed in Victorian clothing like Mrs Waters, but waif-like with dark hair and bovine eyes.

"Who's that?" I said, but Mrs Waters didn't hear me.

She led me past three doors. At the fourth she stopped and withdrew a key from her sleeve. She unlocked the door and held it open. "You first."

"Thank you," I said, walking past her. "Wow."

"I'm so glad you like it. This used to be – well, I shan't bore you with that now."

Fire billowed in the grate. White church candles lined every surface. I walked over to the four-poster bed and touched a gold satin pillow, wishing I could take a picture and send it to Grandma. The room was so romantic, decorated in pale pinks and golds, the bed piled high with velvet blankets.

"There's more," Mrs Waters said, chuckling at me.

I followed her into an adjoining room that appeared to be a lounge. This too was luxurious, the palette cream and sage. A collection of ancient books filled the shelves of an oak bookcase. My inner bookworm wriggled. This was too good for me. I didn't deserve it, and yet here I was, lapping it up and counting my lucky stars - thanking myself for following my instinct and ignoring Grandma.

"And this," she said, leading me to another door, "is your ensuite."

"Wow," I said, fingering the rim of a bath tub that stood on four gold lion's paws in the centre of the bathroom which, thankfully, contained a modern-day toilet. I almost made a joke, but didn't want to risk offending her. Toilet humour probably wasn't her bag.

"Adorable, isn't it?" She threw back her head and laughed long and hard.

I joined in with her laughter, doing one of those 'Ha ha ha' laughs that sound a lot faker than they're supposed to.

She stopped laughing and glanced at a gold pocket-watch. "Duty calls. Please make yourself comfortable. I'll see you in the dining hall at seven."

I walked through the lounge into the bedroom and threw myself face-first onto the bed. For a while, I lay there running through everything I'd seen and heard since I'd stepped inside the house. Things were a bit odd but Mrs Waters was nice and my rooms were incredible. As long as the little boy wasn't a monster, I could see myself liking it here. I'd miss Grandma, yes, and modern things – TV especially - but since I'd done what I'd done, going on FB, Insta and Twitter made me feel even worse about myself. Turned out, being the subject of everyone's gossip wasn't all it was cracked up to be. And Annalise, my best friend (and only one, truth-be-told – I was an acquired taste, like Roquefort), had moved to Australia, so she wouldn't be around to miss.

I turned onto my back and closed my eyes, allowed my body to sink into the marshmallow bed, felt myself drift.

I opened my eyes as Grandma's parting words rang in my head and the maggots slithered upward.

She didn't ask for any references, Ivy. I don't know about you but that strikes me as rather odd. Makes me think this Mrs Waters might be a tad off her rocker.

Chapter Three

A knock on the door made me jerk upright. "Hello?"

"Bath, Miss."

I stood up. Ping appeared, struggling to keep the door open with her foot while holding a bucket of steaming water in each hand. I flinched at the sight of the buckets. The memory leaked into the front of my mind like a bloody puddle.

"Let me take one," I said, darting forward. I needed to face my fears but more than that, I needed to come across as normal.

"No," she said, staring at the floor.

I wrinkled my nose and stood back to let her pass, wondering what her problem was. She shuffled through the bedroom into the adjoining room.

I opened my case and put my underwear in the top drawer of an ornate chest. I'd only brought one evening dress and a couple of shirts so I hung those up in the wardrobe then laid out my make up on the dressing table. I put my shoes at the bottom of the wardrobe, grabbed my toiletries and wandered through the lounge into the bathroom.

Ping scurried out of the room, closing the door with a clunk.

The tub steamed. There were no bubbles but lavender scented the air, reminding me of Mrs Waters. I took off my clothes and sank into the water. Ping had lit candles. I felt like on was holiday not at work. Of course, I wouldn't start until tomorrow, so to all intents and purposes I was on holiday. Having a bath run for me wasn't something I'd experienced since I was a little girl when my mum was still okay.

The bath was shallow and my shoulders weren't warm enough. I dunked my head under the water, squeezing my nose to stop it being flooded. Sometimes I liked to see how long I could hold my breath, holding until my lungs tightened and panic set in. There was something about gasping in air after having none for so long that gave me a rush.

I shot out of the water and sucked in a breath. Pushing my hair back, I almost screamed at the sight of Ping standing over me. She held a towel out, her face turned away.

I stood up and took the towel. "Thanks."

She left the room without a word and I frowned after her. Couldn't she knock?

I wrapped the towel around myself, went to the sink and brushed my teeth. The mirror above the sink was steamed up. I rubbed it with the towel and stared at myself, pulled a stupid face then turned and left the bathroom.

In the bedroom I found Ping standing beside the bed, which had been smoothed from where I'd wrinkled it. On top of a blush-pink blanket lay a black dress similar to the one Mrs Waters had worn. On the floor were a pair of brown leather ankle boots, true vintage. Pretty cool. I opened my mouth to ask, but Ping said, "You wear. Mrs Water order."

She scurried out of the room and shut the door with a loud snap, leaving me to stare at the dress.

This was weird to the power of ten. I bit back a laugh, picked up the dress and held it against myself. It looked about the right size, almost like it had been made specially for me, but that was impossible. There was no way Mrs Waters could have known my size, unless...

No. Don't be ridiculous.

I swallowed a nasty idea and tried to work out why Mrs Waters insisted on fancy dress for everyone in the house, including herself. It wasn't as if Fairwood House was a theme park or a tourist attraction.

A memory came unbidden like oil on water. When I lived with my mum, before I went into Grandma's care, there'd been a strange couple who'd lived near the local Tesco. At the time, the couple had seemed ancient to me, but thinking about it now, they must have only been about Mrs Waters' age, early forties or so. This bizarre couple dressed as though they were from the 1950s. Like they'd been frozen in time. The woman always wore a swing dress with a full skirt, and the man, a bowling shirt and chunky glasses, hair styled like Elvis. Rumour had it that their entire house was decked out that way too. They even drove a pale pink Morris Minor.

Passion for the era, for the fashion and fittings, must have been their motive. The same must be true for Mrs Waters. And there was nothing wrong with pursuing your passion, even if it marked you out as weird. I actually found it kind of cool. It took guts to do your own thing.

I held up the dress again and nodded. If Mrs Waters wanted me to wear it I would. The whole thing was strange but exciting, like I was dressing up or playing a role. And I didn't want to disobey or upset her.

The clock on the dressing table told me I had to hurry. Mrs Waters had told me not to be late.

I pulled the dress over my head. It fitted like a glove. The material was soft and warm against my skin. I slipped on a pair of red velvet gloves and tugged on the boots. Outfit complete, I hurried to the full-length mirror beside the dressing table. I looked silly. There weren't any plugs for my hairdryer so I combed it through and tied it back with a scrunchie.

I left the room and made my way back along the dimly lit corridor, intentionally not looking at the portraits of the girl because it felt like she was staring at me. I did, however, glance at every door I passed and listen in case I could hear the little boy, but the rooms were silent. I wondered why he went to bed so early. At my old job, Liam had gone to bed at seven o'clock and he was three. Wren was six. Maybe I was wrong. It certainly wouldn't be a first. I could write a dissertation about getting things wrong.

I didn't want to start thinking about everything that had happened at Liam's house, so I thought about the girl in the pictures and wondered who she was.

Ping appeared at the bottom of the stairs. She didn't say anything so I didn't either, but I gave her a smile, which she chose not to reciprocate. I was beginning to find her quite rude. Even if she didn't speak much English, she could at least smile at me. I hated non-smilers. Always made me wonder what they were thinking – or hiding.

Avoiding eye contact, she turned. I followed her across the entrance hall towards the door on the left. She opened the door and held it for me and I entered another amazing room where Mrs Waters sat at a huge round table laid for two. My place was not next to her but the one next to that, which was good because I hated bumping elbows when I ate. Hated being touched at all when I ate, just like when I slept – or when I tried to sleep, at least.

"Ivy, you look simply splendid. Do you like your dress? I made it specially for you."

"You made this?" I said, "You're so talented."

"Why thank you. I am rather, aren't I?" she laughed and patted her hair. "Of course, it's not difficult to make such a garment look good on a pretty girl like yourself."

I blushed and laid my serviette across my lap like Mrs Waters had.

"You got my size just right," I said.

"I know."

I started to ask what she meant but Ping arrived with a tray and placed soup bowls in front of us.

"French onion soup, how scrummy," Mrs Waters said. "Let's eat."

The soup was good but the bread – I'd never tasted anything like it. We ate in silence, which felt uncomfortable to me, but I let her take the lead. I knew some people liked to eat in silence and really focus on the taste. Given the noises she made while she ate, she loved her food more than most. I was surprised she wasn't fat.

Ping cleared away the plates the moment Mrs Waters finished.

"And so, to business," my employer said, dabbing her lips with a serviette.

I sat up straighter.

Her voice was colder than before. "There are certain rules you must abide by if you are to fulfil this role adequately. I expect this was so in your last employ?"

I nodded, tense.

"Good, good. There will be rules that will surprise you, but as you will have already gathered, the way we live here is exceptional."

"Yes. It's lovely," I said, not sure what else to say.

"I am so glad you think so," she said, "Now, there are only three rules, you'll be relieved to learn. The first is the most important, of course, and that is that no technological devices are to be used in the grounds. I've had Ping remove your mobile phone and computer from your room so that you're not tempted." She smiled and patted her hair.

Too shocked to speak, I forced anger out of my eyes, but failed to control the goldfish-like motion of my mouth. The fact she'd had Ping go into my things and take my phone and computer was a lot to wrap my head around. It wasn't just an invasion of privacy, but a robbery of my personal freedom. And it was so calculated.

"You wouldn't get any reception out here besides," she said, watching me. "You are, of course, permitted to take your devices with you should you journey into town on your day off."

I relaxed a little, relieved she understood my need to use technology, even if she couldn't tolerate it. "That's good, it's just I'll need to contact my grandma from time to time or she'll worry. She's a real worry-bot."

Mrs Waters winced at my use of the word 'worry-bot'. She recovered quickly and patted her hair, smiling in what I worried was a forced way. "Of course you will, Ivy. I wouldn't expect anything less from a lovely young girl like yourself. You are free, of course, to write to her by hand. Maddock regularly takes my letters to the posting office for me and I have a vast collection of stamps that you are welcome to use."

"Thank you," I said, feeling lighter.

"You're welcome. Now, onto the second rule. You must never set foot in the wood that lies to the east of the house. It's simply not safe."

I wanted to ask why but she moved on. "And last, but not least: you must never leave the child unattended when he is awake. I do not want him to cross paths with my daughter unless absolutely necessary."

"Your daughter?" I said, smiling to hide my unease.

Mrs Waters nodded. "Yes, my daughter lives here also. He can, I'm afraid, be rather disruptive at times. Indeed, I intend to send him to boarding school when he turns eight. The school won't accept full boarders until then."

Ping delivered the main course: roast chicken with all of the trimmings.

"What's the child's name?" I said.

"Wren," she said, slicing into her chicken with a harsh squeal, "He was an accident."

I sipped water, feeling sorry for Wren. To be referred to as an accident in such a flippant way was mean, but Mrs Waters didn't seem mean. *All cruelty springs from weakness* the maggots murmured. I jumped at their intrusion and silently snapped at them to be quiet. I glanced at Mrs Waters and fought the urge to ask more questions, sensing she wouldn't like it if I did.

"So, Ivy, those are the three main rules that you need to follow. Follow these and we'll have a wonderful time. The child needs to be watched and guided in his studies, that is all. Nothing more, nothing less. His books are in his room as are his writing implements. His last nanny taught him to read so all I ask is that you listen to him read every day and check his work. He is to have an hour of exercise outside daily, regardless of the weather. I have plenty of warm clothes for you to wear should the mood turn sour. His meals will be provided by Ping so you won't need to worry about that. Please keep him out of trouble."

"I understand," I said, not sure I did.

Ping cleared away the dirty plates and Mrs Waters thanked her then stood abruptly, making me jump.

"Well I never. Look at the time. I'm afraid I shall have to say good night now, Ivy. It's time for my daughter's bedtime story. She turned twenty-one last week," Mrs Waters said with a shake of her head, "My, how time flies."

I watched her leave the room with a weird feeling in my gut. Was something wrong with Mrs Waters' daughter?

I thought about asking Ping but there was something about the sly sideways glance she gave me as she tidied away the plates that told me she couldn't be trusted. Also, maybe, that she was hiding something.

Chapter Four

Nerves made me feel sick, but I wasn't a fraud - I'd made a mistake at my last job, that was all – a huge mistake, yes, but everyone deserved a second chance. This was mine. No matter how awfully Wren behaved, I'd cope. And I'd follow Mrs Waters' rules as much as possible, no matter how annoying I found the first one.

But no technology, really? What was that about?

My fingers itched. I wanted to ring Grandma and let her know I'd arrived safely. I wondered where Ping had put my phone and laptop. Told myself not to wonder - Grandma would understand if I didn't call straight away. She'd think I was busy settling in.

I went downstairs in another Victorian dress, this one burgundy. Around my shoulders lay a black shrug which kept off the morning chill.

In the dining hall the table was set for two, but Mrs Waters wasn't there. In her place the table was laid, the chair vacant. In the seat I'd used the previous evening sat a little boy fiddling with his serviette. Wren. I found it odd that his mother wasn't here to introduce us and considered waiting for her, but decided against it. If she wasn't here it was because she'd chosen not to be.

For a few moments I watched him. He didn't resemble my employer at all; he had thick auburn hair for starters.

"Hello, Wren. I'm Ivy, your new nanny."

Wren didn't look up from his serviette. I knew he'd heard me because his body stiffened. I watched him play with the napkin and waited for curiosity to get the better of him. He appeared engrossed, folding it in places, twisting in others.

"What are you making there?" I said unable to stop myself.

He shrugged.

Good. Any kind of communication was good.

"Is it an aeroplane?" I said.

He glanced up then down. Glanced up again. He stared at me in the unabandoned way only children can. I smiled at him but his small, pale face remained serious. He was sussing me out. I began to find his scrutiny uncomfortable. His fingers stilled on the napkin and he narrowed his eyes and cocked his head.

"What's an aeroplane?" he said.

I explained as best I could, determined to hide my surprise. Had nobody ever pointed up at the sky and told him what one of those white flying things was?

He remained unsmiling during my explanation.

"Can you draw one?" he said.

"What's the magic word?" I teased.

He frowned. "I don't know."

Huh.

"Yes, I can draw one for you, if you like?"

He nodded. "I'll get a bit of paper and a pencil."

He got up, pushed the chair in and walked out of the room. Quite the little grandad. He plodded away in his brown trousers, braces and white shirt. He didn't seem dressed properly for the time of year. Even though a fire roared in the grate the air was chilly, the space too vast to heat with one fire.

Ping walked in carrying two bowls. Without a glance in my direction she placed one in front of me and one where Wren had been sitting.

"Where boy?" she said sharply.

"He'll be back in a second," I said.

She nodded and hurried away, heels clicking on the floor, arms motionless.

Fear gripped me as I realised what I'd done; I'd broken one of Mrs Waters' rules – how could I be so careless? Would Ping tell on me? What if Wren ran off or got up to mischief? What if he disturbed Mrs Waters' daughter?

I got to my feet to go searching for him and he walked into the room. I exhaled and told myself not to break her rules again, knowing I probably would. Impulse control wasn't my strong point and I wasn't a fan of pointless rules.

Thanking him for fetching the paper and pencil, I tried to forget the mistake I'd made and began to draw. Wren gaped at me for a few seconds then devoured his porridge like Oliver Twist, looking up every now and then to watch. I drew the best I could and somehow the aeroplane ended up resembling one. I handed him the sketch and he stared at it, expression grave.

"It has wings like a bird so it can fly," he said.

"Yes, but it's made of metal. It's used to carry people from country to country."

"Is it big?"

"Yes. There are different types of aeroplanes and some are larger than others but on the whole they're very big."

"And men made these?"

"Women too." I smiled.

The entire time I ate breakfast Wren stared at my sketch. He traced the outline with his index finger, his mouth an 'o'. I wondered what else he didn't know about the world beyond Fairwood House.

"We'd better go to your room now and begin studying."

I half-expected him to fight me on this, but he pushed his chair in and led the way into the entrance hall and up the stairs. So far, he seemed like an obedient little boy. I hoped this remained the case. Liam had been a lovely child. Easy to look after, always eager to please. It was his parents who'd presented problems.

Wren's room was, it turned out, opposite mine. I paused

in the doorway to his bedroom, stunned. Every surface was covered with models. Models of animals mostly, made out of paper, sticks, coal, twigs, stones, moss and leaves. They were incredible. I couldn't believe a six-year-old could make such life-like figures.

"Did you make these?" I said.

He nodded, eyes solemn.

"They're wonderful." I moved to the only model that wasn't of an animal. It was Fairwood House. The model stood in the back-left corner of the room and was half as tall as Wren. On top of the roof sat two odd creatures made out of pebbles and coal.

"This must've taken you ages," I said.

"My old nanny helped me with it," he said sitting at a Victorian school desk.

"Did she? What was she like?"

He turned away and began to write in a Maths book. "It doesn't matter. She left."

He said the words robotically but his forehead scrunched and he exhaled a shaky breath.

I hovered my hand over his shoulder wanting to comfort him, but something told me he wouldn't welcome the physical contact. Not yet. Perhaps not ever.

Chapter Five

Wren worked hard all morning.

I studied his room while he worked. Unlike my bedroom, where Mrs Waters had spared no expense, Wren's bedroom was basic. He had a single bed with a thin mattress, a battered-looking wardrobe, a small chest of drawers and a wooden desk and chair. Light came from a lantern on his desk and one on the chest so the room was dim. It would have been brighter had the day been better, but the window revealed an overcast sky. The view exposed the Exmoor Hills, the open moorland too vast and remote for me. My hands started to go clammy so I moved away from the window and sat on the bed, turning my back on the view.

A fire burned keeping the room fairly warm. There were no pictures on the walls. If not for Wren's models there would be no sign a child lived there.

A lump formed in my throat. There were no toys. No teddy bears. No comforters of any kind. But I noticed something. Around his neck Wren wore a bumble bee pendant on a gold chain. He had a habit of holding the bumble bee and stroking it with his thumb. I suspected his old nanny had given it to him but didn't ask. She was a sore subject. Curiosity bit - I wanted to know why she'd left.

At eleven I asked Wren if he'd like a break. He shook his head.

"Are you sure? We could go outside? Go hunting for bits and bobs for your models?"

That got his attention. I could almost see his ears perk up.

He turned around and stared at me. "But I'm supposed to work until noon then have lunch then work until four then do my exercises from four to five. I'm only supposed to have breaks on Sunday. That's when I work on my models."

My employer hadn't said no to breaks when she'd told me the rules.

"It'll be fine. I make the rules now!"

"No, you don't. Mother does."

"Mrs Waters told me to make sure I guided you in your studies and I can only guide you properly if I've had some fresh air, so that means you have to have some too," I said heading for the bedroom door. I glanced back. His little face was scrunched up, his fingers toying with the bumble bee pendant. His frown vanished.

"Wait," he said leaping up from his chair. He dashed over to the wardrobe and pulled out a black coat and a red scarf.

I led the way along the gloomy corridor down the stairs to the front door where I found my coat, my gloves stuffed in the pockets. Ping had been nosing around my stuff again. I reached out for the front door and found it locked.

"There's a key under the umbrella bucket," Wren said.

I stooped down and tipped up the bucket, shivering the moment my fingers made contact with the cold metal. I swallowed. Heard the grubs clear their throats. The memory's icy fingers spidered upward. I grabbed the key, dropped the bucket and stood up. A wail broke the quiet of the house.

I turned in the direction of the sound. "What was that?"

"Odette," Wren said, a frown crinkling his forehead.

"Who?"

"Mrs Waters' daughter."

"Your sister? Oh. Right. Do you think she's okay?"

"No," Wren said looking at the floor.

"Really? What's wrong with her?"

He said something I couldn't hear.

"What did you say?"

He looked up and I noticed he'd paled. His fingers found the pendant.

"Wren, what did you say?"

He looked away. "She's not okay."

He shifted his weight, looked up at me.

"Wren?"

He held the bumble bee pendant so tightly that the tips of his fingers were white.

I waited.

He looked at the front door and whispered, "She's mad."

"What do you mean?"

The wailing came again, this time more angry-sounding. Wren's shoulders twitched. He stared at the front door.

"Wren?"

"Lucinda told me she's not well. Lucinda told me to stay away from Odette or something bad would happen."

Mrs Waters had told me to keep Wren away from her daughter so that *he* wouldn't upset *her*. I wondered if she actually meant it wasn't safe for Wren to be around Odette. My spine tingled and I opened the front door.

"Was Lucinda your nanny?" I said.

He nodded.

"What else did Lucinda say about Odette?"

"I don't want to talk about it," he said, leaving the house.

I frowned, wanting to know more.

I watched him walk outside; pictured Liam sprinting out - shouting and jumping and racing around like a child should. But Wren was a different sort of kid. He plodded with his hands in his pockets as if going for an evening stroll, steps slow and measured, eyes on the ground.

I followed him out and closed the door behind me. The air was crisp, the sky the colour of pig's swill, turning the wild heather a muted shade of purple.

Wren took the stone path I'd followed Maddock along the previous night, but he didn't jump from step to step; his footsteps remained slow and careful, arms limp by his sides. I followed him at a distance inhaling the clean air and stopping halfway along the path to stare at the army of oak trees Mrs Waters had banned me from entering. Even from a distance their thick trunks and meaty foliage made me think of *Macbeth* and Birnam Wood, and maggot-pies. *Understood relations have maggot-pies.* I would never forget the line. Of course, I'd seen it a different way to everyone else in class.

Feeling queasy I turned my attention to the house, which was forged from large blocks of dark grey stone and would have been quite ordinary-looking if not for the roof. The building's dimensions were square and linear, the windows evenly spaced and latticed with black iron. There were no carvings, columns, turrets, towers or clever structural angles - nothing to indicate the architect had had any artistic intention other than to produce a sturdy, functional structure capable of housing a lot of people.

But the roof told a different story, like an entirely different person had designed it.

Two grotesque creatures - the likes of which I'd never seen - lunged out of the corners of the roof. One looked east and one looked west, but both were one and the same hideous creature. A creature I couldn't name. A hybridised beast that appeared to be half-wolf, half-gargoyle. Each was as large as a bull; each so life-like I feared it would come to life, leap down from the roof and rip me and Wren to shreds.

A presence behind me made me spin around. Wren stared up at me. "Lucinda used to look at them too."

"Really? Oh. What've you got there?" I said noticing he held something close to his chest.

"Lucinda called them the Stone Demons. She said they're there to frighten bad people away but they aren't very good at their job."

"What do you think she meant by that?" I said.

He frowned and opened his mouth to say something then stopped. He held out his hands to me. Fragments of snail shell covered his palms. "Look what I found."

I picked up a piece of shell and smiled. "Well done. That'll be an interesting new material to use, won't it?"

He nodded but didn't smile. Carefully, he transferred the pieces from his hands into his pockets.

"Can we go inside now?" he said, looking past me at the house, "I'm cold."

I followed his gaze, saw and heard the front door slam. Someone had been watching us.

"Sure. You can do a bit more work then we'll stop for lunch," I said, trying to sound more relaxed than I felt.

Chapter Six

I hurried to the front door, opened it. Saw Ping. She was the one who'd been watching us.

She scurried away, opened the dining room door and hurried through. I followed her, letting Wren close the front door.

"I'll just be a minute," I said, glancing back at him.

I strode after Ping, catching the door before it shut. She was rushing through the vast room toward the door that I presumed led to the kitchen. I followed her across the room, catching the door again before it closed. This time she heard me and turned around.

"You," she said, "no be here."

"I'm sorry," I said feeling rash, but hot around the collar all the same, "Why were you watching us?"

"What you mean? I no watch," she said folding her arms.

"Okay. Whatever, but look, is everything okay? Have I done something to annoy you?"

She frowned. "Don't understand."

"Is it because you preferred Lucinda?"

A frightened look entered her eyes. She stepped back and bumped into the large table in the centre of the kitchen.

"Lucinda," I repeated, "Wren's last nanny?"

She shook her head. "No want talk about."

"Talk about what? Lucinda?"

Her jaw set and she turned her back on me. Her voice softened. "I sorry Miss."

I stepped back, surprised by her apology, worried I'd overreacted. I walked back to the entrance hall to find Wren but he wasn't there. The vast space was empty. Mrs Waters' words rang in my head. I was to watch him, make sure he didn't disturb Odette. Oh god - I'd done it again.

I dashed up the stairs two at a time, jogged to Wren's room and yanked open the door. He wasn't there. My stomach squirmed. The grubs writhed. Where the hell was he? Had he gone back outside? What if he'd squeezed through the fence and gone to the woods? The woods I was forbidden to enter.

I jumped as Wren came out of the bedroom next to his cradling a bumble bee cuddly toy. His eyes looked huge in his face. His skin was ghost-white.

"I found this," he whispered. "In Lucinda's room."

I walked up to him and bent over, bringing our eyes level. "Is something wrong?"

"This is Lucinda's," he said looking down at the toy.

"Oh. She must have forgotten it when she left. Maybe we can send it to her in the post."

He shook his head. "This was her *prized possession*. She told me. She took it with her everywhere."

"Did she leave in a rush? Sometimes when I leave in a rush, I forget really important things, like my purse or my phone."

"I didn't see her leave."

"What? She didn't say goodbye?"

"No."

I thought quickly. He needed me to say the right thing. He was on the edge of tears. "How long was she your nanny?"

"Since I was a baby."

The lump in my throat grew. I smiled. "Bet you any money she did say goodbye then. You were probably asleep. I bet she crept into your room and gave you a goodbye kiss. She might have found it too upsetting to say goodbye to you when you were awake."

"But if you're here, why did she have to go? I still need a nanny so why didn't she stay?"

What he said made sense – why did she leave? I paused, thought. "Maybe a member of her family was in an accident and she had to leave very quickly."

"She should have said goodbye."

"Did she love you?"

He shrugged. Looked down at the toy. "She used to tell me she did when she tucked me in bed."

"Exactly," I said, "She loved you so there's no way on earth she'd have left unless an emergency came up."

Wren wiped his hand over his eyes. He looked so tired.

"I miss her. I want her back."

"I know, sweetie, I know. You know what? I've just had a great idea. Why don't you write her a letter?"

Wren's eyes brightened then clouded. "Will you help me?"

"Of course I will."

"Okay," he said hurrying into his room. He sat down at his desk and grabbed some paper and a pencil. The cuddly bee rested on his lap. His fingers toyed with the pendant and his little legs jigged up and down.

He looked up. "How shall I start?"

"With 'Dear Lucinda'."

"How do you spell that?" he said hunching over the desk.

I sat on the bed and began to spell the words, glad to be able to help him. The entire time alarm bells blared in my head and one question repeated itself over and over and over again.

Why didn't she say goodbye? Why didn't she say goodbye? Why didn't she say goodbye?

Chapter Seven

After lunch, which consisted of cucumber sandwiches that Ping - with all the friendliness of a rattlesnake - delivered to Wren's bedroom, I made sure Wren was set up with *Black Beauty* then left to find Maddock.

I knew I wasn't supposed to leave Wren on his own but he'd promised to stay put and was so excited about the letter that I wanted to make sure it was sent as soon as possible. I'd asked him if he wanted to send the cuddly bee too but he'd hugged it to his chest and shaken his head. I didn't have the heart to make him part with it. Now he had two things to remind him of his former nanny.

I descended the stairs thinking of Grandma. I had a photo in my purse, nothing else. If I had my phone, I'd have her words, but that had been taken away from me. Then again, with no reception out here I couldn't call or text her anyway. I could write to her though and Maddock could take both letters tomorrow.

As if conjured by a spell, the big man slipped out of the dining hall and hurried toward the front door. His steps echoed through the space and the shadows seemed to cling to his bulk giving the uncanny impression that the entrance hall was some kind of unearthly portal.

Feeling spooked, I hurried after him, but he was out of the door before I reached the bottom step. I thought about calling his name but didn't want to make a racket and potentially upset Odette, not to mention annoy Mrs Waters.

I opened the front door and looked out onto the enclosure. Maddock was already on the other side of the iron fence heading, by the look of it, for the wood. He held a large crate under one burly arm and an axe in his free hand. I considered following him, but Mrs Waters' second rule stopped me. According to her, the wood was too dangerous to enter. I wanted to know why and tried to work it out, but a plausible answer escaped me. I wasn't a fool; I could safely navigate some trees on my own without risking injury, which made me think for a second that there was something in there she didn't want me to know about. The maggots began to murmur dark ideas and I pushed them away. I couldn't give in to paranoia, not this time. Not again. Mrs Waters was a good woman. I wouldn't let the crawlers wheedle their way into my thoughts and make me make another huge mistake.

Shaking my head, I headed for the stairs.

On the landing, I paused outside Lucinda's old room. Why hadn't she taken the bee with her? Why hadn't she said goodbye to Wren? Neither action made sense. I'd only known Wren for a bit and there was no way I'd leave him without saying goodbye, even in an emergency.

So, why? I couldn't exactly ask Mrs Waters about it. Or Ping. Maybe Maddock would tell me...

The grubs muttered again. I licked my lips. Tried to fight them; didn't succeed. Something told me their fears were more well-founded this time.

I knew I shouldn't have done it but I did. Impulse control was a skill I didn't possess.

Running my tongue over my front teeth, I found myself reaching for the door, opening it, walking into Lucinda's old room. I closed the door behind me, cringing as it creaked.

The room, as I'd expected, was dark and cold. Over the other side of a four-poster bed scarlet curtains bordered an iron-latticed window through which yawned the moor, vast and blue-grey in the morose afternoon light. The air inside the room was chilly and tinged with a faint scent of vinegar. Like my bedroom, the room was beautifully furnished, but the palette was scarlet and gold. Brighter and harsher. The bed was made, the cover unruffled. No personal items lined the shelves and the dressing table was bare.

I walked up to the bed and scanned the room again. A full-length mirror stood in the corner near the window. I moved to stand in front of the mirror. I was a dark figure, my face indistinct in the gloom. I touched the cool glass and wondered what Lucinda had looked like when she'd last stood here. How often had she stared out of the window at the vastness of the moor? Had she felt overwhelmed by it too? Was that why she left? Or had she never left at all?

A faceless woman dripping with blood sprang to my mind's eye. I shook my head to dispel the image and heard rattling inside my skull as if the maggots were beads in a box. In the mirror's reflection, I caught a glimpse of something poking out from under the bed. It looked like a strap. I swivelled and made for it but the sound of someone climbing the stairs froze my blood. I dashed toward the bedroom door, bashing my knee on the bed-post. Grabbing the door, I opened it and slipped out of the room. As I took a step in the direction of Wren's room, I heard Mrs Waters' voice.

"Ivy?"

I turned, heart in my throat. She was at the top of the stairs, cloaked by shadows.

"Hi - I thought I heard something so came out to check. Wren's in his room reading."

She smiled. "Of course. No need to explain. I hardly expect you to remain in his room with him for the entire day. You'll need to pop out to spend a penny at some point."

I joined in with her laughter, relieved. She hadn't seen me, hadn't clocked the fact I'd been snooping.

"Wren's been such a good boy," I said.

"So far, so good. But be careful. He's got bad blood in him."

I gave an awkward smile.

"It would be lovely if you'd join me for dinner and

drinks this evening. Wren's bedtime is six o' clock so if you put him to sleep then come down at seven, that would be wonderful. I intend to put Odette to bed early tonight. She's not had one of her best days."

"Oh, really? That's a shame."

She sighed and rubbed her face. "Yes. Some days are harder than others. Perhaps that's why I fancy a tipple tonight."

She gave me a wink and headed back downstairs.

I returned to Wren's room and found him lying on his front spreading out the pieces of snail shell he'd collected earlier. He jumped when he heard me and gathered up the pieces.

"I'm sorry," he said.

"That's okay. When I was your age, I'd have leapt at the chance to play with my toys if my nanny had gone walkabout. It's normal for children your age to break the rules every now and then."

"I'm not normal."

"Yes, you are, Wren. Don't say that."

"Mother doesn't think I'm normal."

"What makes you say that?"

He shrugged and placed the shells on the end of his book shelf. His little shoulders sloped like teardrops. I moved forward to hug him then changed my mind. He wasn't ready. His fingers found the bee pendant.

"Why don't I read you a few more chapters of *Black Beauty* then we'll go outside for your exercise?"

His eyes lit up.

I plucked the book off his desk, sat on the bed and patted the space beside me. "Come on. Let's get comfy."

He sat on the bed, leaving a healthy space between us, but gave me the smallest of smiles. I read to him for an hour. By four 'o clock, his body was nestled close to mine and he was stroking the back of my hand.

Chapter Eight

Wren followed an exercise regime that Lucinda had designed for him so all I had to do was sit and watch. I perched on a stone bench and wrapped my arms around myself for warmth, wishing I had my phone to keep me entertained. The bench was directly opposite the house which meant I had a choice of four views: the house, with its disturbing creatures poised on top; the hilly moor to my right; the wood to my left; or Wren jogging around the inside of the iron fence like a prison inmate. If I watched Wren, I'd see the wood behind him or the moor or the house, so I stared at my gloved hands and let myself daydream about meeting the man of my dreams. The daydream started with me bumping into a young Tom Cruise lookalike in a pub then him offering to buy me a drink, but as soon as I imagined my response, the dream turned into a disaster. I opened my mouth to speak and dream man couldn't understand what I was saying because strange, unintelligible noises streamed out of my throat. Dream man gave me a weird look and left me alone in the pub, sobbing hysterically.

I rolled my eyes at myself. This was usually how this daydream went. So far, I'd been unlucky with men. My first boyfriend had cheated on me and my second had dumped me because he decided he was too young to be in a 'serious relationship'. I'd been single for three years. Grandma said the right man would come along when I least expected it, but I doubted any man would be understanding enough to be with me, especially if he knew about the maggots. Grandma knew about them and was unbelievably sympathetic. She always said they'd go away when I *found myself*, but she didn't know where they came from, because I'd never told her.

I looked up and scanned my dismal surroundings. It wasn't very likely I'd find myself out here, in the middle of nowhere.

Wren was still jogging. He seemed to be enjoying the exercise, which made me feel happier. If I could make his life better, it was worth it. From what I'd seen so far, the poor kid had little to be happy about. Mrs Waters' attitude toward him was odd. I wondered if I could get to the bottom of it this evening when we were alone together. I'd have to tread carefully. Make sure I didn't offend her in any way.

Wren stopped running and turned to face the wood. Gripping the iron railings, he pressed his face against the cold bars and watched Maddock lumber out of the trees carrying a crate of logs. Light was fading fast so it was just as well Maddock had returned to the house because he didn't have a lantern with him. I wondered if he had a torch – if he was permitted by Mrs Waters to use one - she couldn't be against something like that as well. A torch wasn't exactly high-tech.

I leapt up from the bench; this was the perfect moment to ask Maddock about posting the letters.

He unlocked the gate and carried the crate through. He walked on then cursed, went back and locked the padlock.

So much security. How odd.

I hurried across to him and Wren joined me, pink and breathless.

"Maddock?"

He stopped and glanced over his shoulder. "Yes, Miss?"

He placed the crate on the ground and cracked his neck. There was a nasty scratch on his cheek.

"How did you get that?"

He shrugged his massive shoulders.

"Hi Maddock," Wren said.

"Alright, kid," Maddock said with a softness in his voice

I'd not heard before.

"Would it be possible for you to post two letters tomorrow? One from me and one from Wren?"

"Course. Who's the little chap writin' to?"

"Lucinda," Wren said.

Maddock hesitated then said, "Oh, right. Got her address, have you?"

Wren looked up at me.

"We'll get it from Mrs Waters. Where shall I put them when they're ready to send?"

"Just pop 'em on the round table in the entrance hall."

"Okay. Great. Thanks," I said as he bent to pick up the crate. "Oh, one more question."

He raised an eyebrow.

"Why is Mrs Waters so against technology?"

"Technophobia."

"What – fear of technology?"

"Yup. Everyone's scared of something."

Too true.

"Huh. I didn't even know that was a thing."

"There are a lot of things you don't know," he muttered.

I frowned, not sure whether to take offence.

"Maddock?" Wren said, "What happened to your face?"

Maddock stopped and smiled at Wren displaying two rows of straight, white teeth. He coughed and touched his cheek. "That old thing? Oh, that's nothin'. Just a grumpy old tree gettin' testy with me."

Wren looked confused. I stared at Maddock's retreating back. A tree hadn't done that to his face. I was as sure of that as I was that the big man in black was lying through his perfect pearly whites.

Chapter Nine

I read Wren a story then tucked him up in bed and went downstairs to join Mrs Waters for dinner. The dining hall glowed with candle and fire light, creating a rich softness I wouldn't have imagined possible in such a vast room. Mrs Waters looked stunning in a lilac dress that was less severe than her other dresses. Her silvery hair tumbled around her shoulders making her look ten years younger. She smiled when she saw me. I relaxed and sat down, stomach grumbling. Ping dashed in and put plates of smoked salmon and watercress on our table mats. I thanked her and to my surprise, she answered, "Welcome, Miss." I glanced at her face but her eyes were downcast, her mouth a tight line.

"Wine?" Mrs Waters said, raising a decanter.

"Yes please."

"To the start of a wonderful life together," she said.

I smiled. "I'll drink to that."

We clinked glasses. I took a healthy swig and tucked in to the starter, but Mrs Waters didn't touch her food. I looked up. She smiled and sipped her wine, a thoughtful look on her face. I tensed, the food sticky on my tongue.

"I understand you gave the child some time outside this morning?" she said.

"I thought the fresh air would do him good. Me too, to be honest."

"That makes sense. Is it something you intend to do on a daily basis?"

"If that's okay with you, yes. When I was at school, we had a morning break, a break for lunch and an afternoon break. I loved playtime. I think it's a really good way of tiring kids out so they sleep well at night."

Mrs Waters smiled. "Quite right. I entirely agree. It's just that I don't particularly worry about whether the child loves things or not. All I care about is making sure he doesn't become a burden to society. I've never known him to be violent, for example, but if he ever raises a hand to you, you need to tell me. I'll deliver the punishment, which will be swift but harsh. We can't have him becoming a bully when he grows up."

"Wren seems like a lovely little boy to me. He's a bit standoffish but he's polite and hardworking," I said carefully.

"Yes, but don't let him fool you. It won't be long before the devil in him shows its face. Mark my words, Ivy, he's not as innocent as he seems. You must watch him carefully."

"I will. But he seems to have a lot of love to give. Did you know he misses his old nanny?"

"Such a shame about Lucinda. Poor girl. She suffered a terrible loss, had to leave so quickly. I had Maddock arrange a taxi for her. She was here one day, gone the next," she snapped her fingers, "just like that."

"Poor Wren," I said.

"Yes, well, he's the sort who likes to pretend. I wouldn't place too much belief in what he tells you."

I opened my mouth to defend him, but stopped. There was no point. For some inexplicable reason, Mrs Waters seemed determined to criticise her son.

"Let's talk about more pleasant affairs, shall we?" she said, patting her hair.

Ping dashed in and cleared away the plates. She appeared moments later with two steaming plates of sausage and mash.

"Scrummy. My favourite," Mrs Waters said.

I looked at my wine glass, shocked to see I'd nearly finished it already. As if reading my mind, Mrs Waters topped up our glasses. I took a sip, telling myself to be careful. If I drank too much my tongue would get loose and I could be tactless when drunk.

"So, I hear you plan to send a letter tomorrow?" she said.

"Yes. To my grandma."

"And who is she to you?"

"Everything. She's looked after me for years. Since I was ten. She's amazing."

"May I ask why?"

"Why what?"

"Why your grandma needed to take you into her care?"

I stiffened at the personal question and chewed my food slowly, trying to work out what to tell her. I usually lied, but had a feeling Mrs Waters would know if I did.

"My mum got ill. She wasn't well enough to look after me, so Grandma took me."

"Mentally?" she said, her voice soft.

My stomach knotted. I nodded.

"I'm so sorry, Ivy," she said, reaching out to hold my hand, "I have a little experience in that regard too. It's terribly difficult to wrap your head around, isn't it?"

"It's okay. Grandma made the rest of my childhood amazing."

"And so, what went wrong in your last employ?" she said, still holding my hand.

I tensed. Looked at her. Her eyes were kind. In my head I ran through the various responses I could give and settled on the vaguest.

Forcing myself to meet her gaze, I said, "I thought something was going on that wasn't. I got it in my head and thought I was doing the right thing, but I made a mistake. A huge mistake."

She released my hand. "I thought as much. My first impressions of people are nearly always correct and the first time I set eyes on you I knew you were a good soul. Did you know good people have a tendency to be the most self-critical? It's true," she said, sipping more wine, "And you, Ivy, are trapped in that mindset. I can tell. You need to stop being so hard on yourself. Everyone makes mistakes. I know I certainly have."

"Thank you. That means a lot."

Not mistakes like the one you made.

She grinned and laughed. "The whole of humanity makes mistakes. No-one's infallible. Especially not those odious technologists who seem intent on bringing mankind to apocalypse."

Bit extreme.

I placed my knife and fork together and smiled uneasily.

"What's Odette like?' I said, trying to change the subject.

She stiffened. "She has her problems. Night terrors, the like. As do we all."

We do indeed.

Despite wanting to know more about her daughter, I sensed the subject was a no-go area, so bit my tongue.

Mrs Waters filled our glasses, picked up my glass and got up from the table. She beckoned for me to follow. I did, noticing as I walked after her that she was unsteady on her feet. She led me out of the dining hall, across the entrance hall, whose icy chill nipped at my skin, and into the living room where the fire roared. Closing the door behind us, she tottered across the room, tossed the plum blanket on the floor and stretched out on the chaise longue. I sat where I had the previous evening and sipped my wine. For a while, we sat in silence. A secretive smile played at her lips as she gazed at the crackling flames. Following her gaze, I watched the fire, taking comfort in the heat. A wavy sensation drifted behind my eyes, giving me respite from the tension that always grizzled away in my mind.

"Do you know what I think, Ivy?" she said, finishing her second glass and pouring herself a third before topping up mine, "I think God is a heap of mumbo-jumbo dreamed up by terrified humans."

"Hmm," I said, non-committal.

She ploughed on as if I hadn't spoken.

"If there was a God, he wouldn't let people get away with such evil."

I nodded. She downed her drink.

"Acts like creating the shitternet, for example."

"The *what?*"

"Shitternet," she slurred. She was pouring her fourth glass, "Come on, drink up."

I sipped more wine, felt the world tilt. It was incredibly strong.

"What are your views?" she said, leaning forward. Angry spots flushed her cheeks.

"On the…internet?"

"Yes. Monstrous, isn't it?"

"It's got it's bad points, sure, but there're good ones too."

"How so?" she said, voice harder.

I swallowed more wine. I needed Dutch courage to get through this night. "It's packed full of information. One click and you can find out practically anything, which obviously saves a lot of time and energy and -"

"Voila! Mankind is reduced to a pack of simple-minded sloths incapable of hard work," she said, thrusting her glass in the air and sploshing some on the chaise longue. She seemed not to notice the blossoming red stain and eye-balled me. "Go on."

"There is that," I agreed, gulping more wine, "but what with today being such a rat race and everyone so busy, I think we need to have information more quickly than ever."

"Information like where to go if you want to watch unscrupulous material or purchase vicious technological devices like machine guns?" she said, lip curling.

I could see this was a no-win situation. She had a

comeback for everything and her hostility was growing. Another glass of wine and she might make it personal. My grandma was a lovely woman but one sweet wine too many and she could turn into a fire-breathing dragon in seconds.

She stood up and tilted her face to the ceiling. In a quivery voice she said, "But they did not listen to Moses, and some left part of it until morning, and it bred worms and became foul; and Moses was angry with them."

I stared into my wine, felt the alcohol swirling behind my eyes. *Worms? What?*

"It needs to be destroyed," she said, raising her voice. To my surprise, tears glittered in her eyes. She sat back down and glared at her hands. Her fingers were trembling.

I raised my glass and said, "To the destruction of the shitternet."

She blinked at me then grinned and raised her glass. I got up and joined her on the chaise longue. We clinked.

"Bottoms up," she said downing her wine. I followed suit and felt ill. Another glass of this stuff and my dinner would be all over the rug.

A terrible wail pierced the air. Mrs Waters jerked and muttered something under breath. She looked at me, pushed herself to her feet and swayed. "Duty calls, dear Ivy. Until tomorrow."

"Night," I said as she staggered from the room.

I got up thinking I'd had a lucky escape, and jumped at the sight of Ping hovering in the doorway. She glared at me then marched in and tidied away our glasses. She tutted when she saw the stain on the chaise longue and gave me another look.

"What?" I said.

"Stupid English woman drink too much," she snapped.

I watched her leave, wanting to shout a clever retort but realising in all honesty she was probably right.

Chapter Ten

I was woken by a sound outside my bedroom. A creak, like someone was hovering by the door listening to me sleep. I lay still, heart clanging. My head hurt like hell. The maggots writhed as though I was Medusa but the snakes were inside my skull not outside of it.

I squinted around the dark space. Fortunately, the grubs had retired and no noise came, so I began to think I'd imagined the sound outside the door. Either that or it was just the sound an old house made at night. Like people, houses needed to settle their bones and this house was older and more arthritic than most.

Feeling better, I let my head drop back onto the pillow. I wondered about Mrs Waters' daughter. Why hadn't I seen her yet? And why did Mrs Waters read bedtime stories to her when she was twenty-one years old?

I jerked up at the sound of someone rattling the door handle. My heart banged. The handle continued to rattle. Someone was trying to get in and the door wasn't locked.

"Who is it?" I said.

No answer, more rattling.

"Answer me!"

"Ivy, let me in," Wren whispered.

I threw back the covers, swung my legs down from the bed and whipped open the curtains to let moonlight into the room then hurried to the door. Wren ran in and threw his arms around my waist. His body trembled. I shut the door and crouched in front of him.

"What's wrong?" I said.

"There was someone in my room," he whispered into

my neck.

I lifted him up and carried him over to the bed. Sitting him on my lap, I covered us with blankets and stroked his hair. He continued to tremble.

"I'm sure it was just a nightmare," I said.

He shook his head. "No. It was real. *She* was real."

"*She?*"

"She was standing at the end of my bed, staring at me."

"Who? Who was standing at the end of your bed?"

"I think it was Lucinda, but she looked different."

"Lucinda? Different? Different how?"

He hiccupped and began to cry.

"Wren? Speak to me. Please."

He sniffed and wiped his nose with his nightshirt. "Her hair was covering up her face and her feet…"

"What about her feet?"

"Her feet were dirty. Like she'd been walking outside in the mud."

"Did she say anything?"

Wren shivered and buried his head in my chest.

"Wren? Did she say anything?"

"Sort of," he mumbled.

"What was it?"

His head went still. He kept his face against my chest and said, "I don't want to talk about it anymore. Please don't make me."

"Okay. You can sleep in here with me tonight if you want to?"

He nodded. I tucked him into the bed, drew the curtains and slipped in next to him. He was asleep within minutes. I wasn't so lucky.

*

I was sitting up in bed reading when Ping marched into the room and ripped open the curtains.

"Boy need bath," she said pointing at Wren who was curled up next to me.

"It's only six," I said, "and he's still asleep. Can't he have his bath when he wakes up?"

I tried to keep my tone civil but it was difficult.

Ping shook her head. "Mrs Water order. Six, on the dot."

I sighed and shook Wren's shoulders. He stirred and opened his eyes, which were heavy with sleep.

"Time to wake up, sleepyhead."

He gave me a sleepy smile and I smiled back. Ping walked over, grabbed Wren's arm and hauled him off the bed.

"Hey!" I launched myself out of bed and hurried after her as she dragged Wren out of the room.

"There's no need to manhandle him like that," I said.

"Boy bad. Need firm hand."

"No he doesn't. He's a good boy."

Ping's face softened a touch. She let go of Wren's arm and stepped back. "Go. Bath."

Wren obediently opened his bedroom door and went inside. Ping turned to follow him.

"Why are you treating him like he's some kind of criminal?" I blurted.

Ping met my eyes for the first time. I was shocked to see a mixture of emotions in her dark eyes, one of which seemed to be fear. She shivered. "Boy got bad blood."

"Why? What do you mean?"

She opened her mouth to speak then seemed to think better. She dashed into Wren's bedroom and slammed the door behind her. I stared at the closed door, an icy chill spreading across my shoulders. A wail pierced the air and I looked down the corridor and waited for it to come again, but silence filled the house. The walls pulsed with it. Was Odette having a night terror again?

I shivered and hugged myself, ran through all of the weirdness I'd experienced since arriving here. Something wasn't right. I felt it deep in my bones. I wasn't being paranoid, not this time.

No. Something strange was going on in this house and I was going to find out what.

Chapter Eleven

A few days later, despite my decision to poke around and find out what was going on, I relented, worried that my old friend Little Miss Paranoia was rearing her ugly head again.

For three whole days nothing out-of-the-ordinary happened. I enjoyed my days with Wren, hearing him read and marking his answers, and playing chase with him outside in the enclosure. The weather was cold but fair, which meant we had a great time collecting sticks and stones for his models and spent one incredible afternoon making an aeroplane from scratch which, given Wren had never seen a real one and I wasn't in any way artistically gifted, somehow ended up looking like the real deal. My fingers itched to snap a picture of Wren and me with our creation, but my phone was locked up again, safe from prying eyes, safe from me.

To my relief no other strange night-time incidents occurred and I spent three fun, drink-free evenings with Mrs Waters chatting about trivial things like the weather and food while playing scrabble or chess. I even managed to find time to sit in my lounge area and read half of *The Turn of the Screw*.

But it was too good to be true.

The next day a car pulled up outside the iron fence. Wren and I were outside having our morning break. The day was bright and fresh and I'd convinced Ping to give us an apple every day for our morning snack, so we were sitting side by side on the stone bench munching away when Wren stood up and pointed.

"A car."

I stood up too. Beyond the grounds where I'd been dropped off by the taxi, I could just make out the white nose of a car. Maddock appeared outside the house and hurried across the enclosure. He unlocked the padlock then hurried to the next iron gate, unlocking the second padlock with the speed of a man who'd done it thousands of times before.

"It's a police car," I said, shielding my eyes.

"Wow," said Wren, dashing over to grip the railings.

I stayed where I was, not wanting to seem nosy but desperate to know what was going on.

A short man got out of the police car and shook hands with Maddock. They talked for a couple of minutes but were too far away for me to hear anything. Maddock opened the gate and walked through, ushering the policeman ahead of him. They walked side by side across the moor, a rather comical sight with one so big compared to the other, the officer taking two steps to Maddock's one. By the time they reached the second fence, Maddock was drenched in sweat. He had a coughing fit while opening the gate and the officer asked him if he was okay. Maddock grunted and the officer tipped his hat to me as he followed Maddock along the stepping stone path up to the house.

"Why's a police come?" Wren said.

"A police officer. I don't know. Let's see if we can find out."

Maddock closed the front door and I waited a minute then led Wren inside the house. The officer stood in the entrance hall looking around. Up close, I noticed that his hair was thinning on top.

"Hi," I said, walking over, "I'm Ivy, the new nanny."

"Hi. Sergeant Zachery from Avon and Somerset Police. And who's this little rascal?"

"Wren. Mrs Waters' son. Can I ask what's brought you out here, Officer?" I tried to sound casual.

Zachery scratched his chin. "I'm trying to track down a young woman by the name of Beatrice Giles. Word is she worked here. You know who I'm talking about?"

I shook my head. "I only started on Sunday. I know a woman called Lucinda was the nanny here before me but that's it. Why're you looking for her?"

"Unfortunately, I'm not permitted to reveal that information to the public, Miss -"

"Smith."

He nodded and scribbled my name down in a notebook. He withdrew a photograph of an attractive young woman with long, strawberry-blonde hair. "Recognise her?"

I shook my head. Wren slipped his hand into mine and made a strange popping sound with his tongue. I smiled down at him but he was staring at the officer intently, a frown wrinkling his small forehead.

Mrs Waters came downstairs dressed in a scarlet dress, hair loose. She smiled warmly at Sergeant Zachery and introduced herself. I could see the officer's emotions flash through his eyes – surprise, probably at her outfit, attraction and embarrassment. Mrs Waters slipped off her glove and gave him her hand. They shook, holding a bit longer than necessary and Mrs Waters threw her head back and gave a girly laugh.

"Why don't you come through to the living room, Officer? We'll be much more comfortable in there."

She smiled at me then led him away. I hovered where I was and stared after them, wanting to eavesdrop.

Wren pulled on my sleeve. "Can we go study now, Ivy?"

"You go upstairs and make a start. I'll join you in a sec."

Wren ran upstairs and I crept over to the living room door. I heard Sergeant Zachery laugh and strained to hear their conversation.

I jumped at a tap on my shoulder. Maddock loomed over me like a mountain, stinking of sweat. He raised an eyebrow and waggled his finger at me. "I don't reckon Mrs Waters'd be too happy if she saw you right now, do you?"

Heat flooded my cheeks. "Sorry, I was just curious."

"Me too. Don't mean I have to go nosin' in."

I mumbled another apology. "You won't tell, will you?"

"Depends," he said, "My Mrs don't trust you."

"Your *Mrs*?"

He rolled his eyes as if to say I was an idiot then looked pointedly at the stairs. I sighed, turned my back on him and joined Wren.

Chapter Twelve

That night I changed my mind and decided to look around. Something was going on and I needed to find out what, not only for my sanity but for Wren's safety. As I tied my dressing gown cord around my waist I told myself I was being responsible by investigating. I wasn't paranoid - I was only doing what any other normal person would do if they found themselves in my situation. But the maggots came to life the second I stepped outside my bedroom, hinting that I was about to make another mistake.

Too stubborn for my own good, I ignored them. Making my footsteps light, I dashed across the corridor holding a candle and slipped inside Lucinda's old room. I placed the candle on the bedside table, lay on my front and reached under the bed frame. Bingo. My fingers made contact with something. I pulled it out. It was a backpack.

In the weak candlelight I inspected the bag. It was grey with pink lining. It felt light.

I unzipped it, looked inside, dug my hand in and felt around. Nothing but crumbs. I tried the front pocket and found something. A card. I moved the card closer to the candle. It was a Boots card with the name Lucinda Hastings on. My heart spasmed. I ran my fingers over the raised letters. Even if she'd left in a hurry, she wouldn't forget an entire bag. I knew I wouldn't. Unless…unless I was panicking. Or scared.

I began to picture scenario after scenario, each more violent than the last. The maggots began to sing. *Round and round the garden like a teddy bear, one step, two step, stab you under there*. I reasoned with myself. Mrs Waters was lovely. There was no way she'd done anything to Lucinda. No way she'd hurt a fly. I couldn't lose control and start thinking she was guilty of something she wasn't. I couldn't let paranoia slip under my skin like last time.

But there were others in the house. Maybe Maddock or Ping did something to Lucinda Hastings…

I slipped the Boots card into my pyjama pocket and pushed the bag back under the bed. If someone knew it was there, they'd be suspicious if it was gone come morning.

Using the candle for light, I searched every drawer in the room, but found nothing. I tried the wardrobe. Empty. I sighed. There was nothing in this room, but what about the one next door?

I knew I was pushing my luck, but couldn't stop myself. I picked up the candle and left the room. Closed the door gently. I turned to walk up the corridor and bit back a scream.

A figure stood on the landing a few feet away. It was a naked woman with her back to me. Because of the dark, she was barely visible, her skin colourless. I only saw her because of my candle, which I quickly shielded with my free hand. I gawped as she started to sway, her slim hips moving back and forth slowly like she was dancing to a sad song only she could hear. Black hair pooled around her shoulders like wet tar. Beneath her hair, hideous white scars criss-crossed the length of her spine. I wondered how she'd got them. Car accident? No. They were too precise. Too symmetrical. Intentional.

I shrank back as she raised her arms and positioned them above her head. Ever-so-slowly, she pirouetted, humming Twinkle Twinkle Little Star.

Unable to look away, I watched. She turned so slowly with such control. Her ear - cheekbone – the corner of her eye – she was about to see me.

I blew out the candle and held my breath. If I couldn't

see her, she couldn't see me. I hoped.

Her humming grew louder and, by the sound of it, her twirling sped up, but I was blind. I couldn't tell if she was rooted to the spot or moving closer. My heart thumped and I held my breath, unsure what to do, unsure whether to creep back to my room and pretend I'd never seen her or go and see if she was okay. The naked woman had to be Mrs Waters' daughter and, unless she was sleepwalking, there was clearly something wrong with her.

The door at the end of the corridor opened. Mrs Waters snapped, "Get in here. Now."

The woman's humming stopped. The floorboards creaked and the door slammed.

I stayed where I was, heart jabbering like a crazed monkey, thinking I'd had a lucky escape. Neither the young woman nor Mrs Waters had seen me.

I dashed across the corridor cringing at every creak, and slipped into my room. Thankful for the glow of fire and candlelight, I opened my handbag and hid Lucinda's Boots card in the small inner pocket. When I stood up, I caught movement on the edge of my vision and jumped, but it was just my own reflection in the full-length mirror. I stared at myself for a moment, transfixed by the paleness of my face. I didn't look like me. I looked like a ghost.

I slipped under the blankets and curled up in a ball. I put my hands over my ears and tried to picture good times with Grandma and happy moments with my friends, but my mind conjured images of the naked woman with scars on her back. There was no way I could sleep. The maggots were screaming warning after warning and nothing would make them stop.

Chapter Thirteen

The next day I was a zombie. Time seemed to move more slowly with every hour I remained on my feet, so when Mrs Waters invited me to eat with her that evening it was with reluctance that I accepted.

As soon as I joined her at the round table, she instructed Ping to pour two large glasses of wine.

"So, dear Ivy, tell me about your week."

I chewed my first mouthful, stalling for time. The right words weren't coming. I sipped wine. Racked my brain. Tried not to think about the naked girl and the way the crawlers had rampaged through my mind all night, whispering insidious ideas that pulled at my nerves – nerves that were already beginning to fray.

"Wren's been a model student. Polite, hardworking, bright. He's a pleasure to look after."

"Hmm. And your rooms? Are they to your liking?"

I forced a smile. "They're wonderful. And my dresses are amazing. I love wearing them. It feels like I'm playing dress up every day."

"So much more civilised than the clothes young people wear these days, don't you think?" she said.

I didn't respond. She watched me with intense eyes. "Tell me what you really think. I prize honesty above all else, Ivy, and I can tell you don't fully agree with me."

I forced down another bite of liver pate. "I think people should be free to wear what they like and not be judged for it."

She applauded and laughed, "Well said. However, I find it hard to believe you wouldn't judge a parent who dressed their little girl in a thong and high heels?"

"True. But I don't think there are many people who would do that."

"When I found Ping, she was loitering in the doorway of a bar in Soho in a dress that barely covered her behind. She'd been doing that for three years. She was fifteen."

The leap in conversation didn't make much sense. I almost choked on a piece of toast.

"That's terrible. I had no idea."

Mrs Waters' face twisted. "I only wish I could have saved more of them."

"How did you get her away?" I wanted to ask other questions too, like why Mrs Waters had been in Soho in the first place. It was hard to imagine her anywhere other than here at Fairwood House.

"I basically kidnapped her. She was terrified of running in case she got caught, but once I got her back here, she saw sense."

"So, she's been here for what, ten, twelve years?"

"Thirteen now. She's like a second daughter to me."

"And Maddock? How long's he been here?"

She thought for a moment. "Twenty years. No-one else would have him, so I did."

A bit like with me. "Why?"

"He's an ex-convict."

"He's been in prison?"

She nodded.

"What did he do?" I said unable to stop myself.

Mrs Waters opened her mouth to speak than stopped when she saw Ping enter the room. She waited for Ping to leave then said, "I'll let him tell you in his own time. But trust me, he's fully reformed. I'd trust him with Odette's life."

She finished her first glass and poured herself a second. She looked at my glass which was still half-full. "Aren't you enjoying the wine?"

I heard tension in her voice and took a sip. "It's delicious. I'm just taking it a bit more slowly this time. I felt a bit groggy the other day."

She laughed and clinked my glass with hers. "To over-indulging."

Ping delivered the mains, shooting me an evil that Mrs Waters missed. Was jealousy driving Ping to hate me? Or was it something else?

"I expect you're curious," Mrs Waters said between mouthfuls of pie, "as to Officer Zachery's visit."

"He told me he was looking for someone called Beatrice Giles."

"Yes, he was. He only wanted to talk to me because he's visiting everyone in the village. Apparently, she went missing a few days ago and someone saw her in the area. I expect she's simply run away from home, poor girl, but Officer Zachery clearly thinks something more sinister's afoot."

"Did he speak to Maddock and Ping too?"

"Yes. Obviously neither of them have heard of this girl either."

I wanted to ask how she could be so sure they hadn't, but kept my mouth shut and drank more wine. I had a feeling this was going to be a long night. At least tomorrow was my day off. I could go into Weirlock, call Grandma and get a much-needed breather from Fairwood House and the frightening idea that everyone here knew something I didn't.

Chapter Fourteen

Maddock was waiting for me at the front door when I walked out of the dining hall. Ping was on Wren-watch while I went into Weirlock for my day off. I felt guilty about leaving Wren, especially with Ping, who'd acted like I didn't exist all morning.

I hugged Wren goodbye and told him I'd see him later. He tried to put on a brave face but his smile vanished the instant Ping appeared.

"Be good for Ping and I know she'll make sure you have a fun morning break," I called earning a glare from her as she marched him away.

Maddock unlocked the front door and held it open for me. "Your first trip to the village. Excited?"

"Not really. Relieved to go somewhere different though."

To my surprise he laughed. "Know what you mean. Me and the Mrs only get every other Sunday off and the second we get off the grounds it's like we're in Florida."

"That's not much holiday."

"We also get a couple of weeks off in the summer. That's when we go away for real."

"And Ping, *she's* your Mrs?"

"Blimey, she's got it," he laughed. He seemed to be in a good mood today. He had a booming laugh that was infectious. I smiled to hide my surprise. He was double Ping's age. I'd have never put them together in a million years.

"I know what you're thinking," he said unlocking the padlock on the first gate, "what's a pretty young thing like her doin' with an ugly mug like me?"

I began to protest but he held up his hand. "No, it's fine. Everyone's surprised when they realise. Let me just tell you this, we're like two peas in a pod, me and her. I've got her back and she's got mine. Always have, always will."

"You're lucky to have each other," I said.

He nodded and unlocked the second padlock, locking it behind us and pocketing the key. He handed me my phone and I immediately turned it on but there was no service.

The wind picked up and attacked my hair. Ahead of us, the moor grew blurry, the heather wild.

The taxi appeared in the distance, growling its way up the hill too fast for my liking.

In the car, I checked my phone again and this time there was service. Five messages from Grandma. I decided not to call her yet because I didn't want Maddock listening in.

*

It felt like I'd been asleep for seconds when the engine stopped and I heard a door slam. I got out of the taxi to see Maddock paying the driver in cash. The driver sped away leaving us outside a row of stone cottages. The wind was stronger and sleet slashed the air, forcing back my hood and drenching my face.

"I've got errands to run. Heading back at midday. You can meet me here then or I'll arrange a taxi to get you later."

I looked at my watch. It was early. I had all day here if I wanted it. I thought about Wren, and felt guilt stab.

"I'll come back with you at twelve," I said.

"Sure?"

I nodded. He raised a hand in parting, walked off and ducked into a newsagent.

On the corner stood a quaint place with a cherry-red sign announcing Bilberry Tearoom.

I opened the door to the jingle of a seashell wind chime and had to use my body weight to force it shut.

Behind a small counter filled with pre-made sandwiches and home-baked treats stood a red-faced woman drying a cup with a tea towel, an apron tied around her substantial waist.

She laughed at me. "My, you poor love. Look at the state of you."

She chucked me a fresh tea towel and I caught it and used the towel to dry my face before shrugging off my coat. As luck would have it, the sleet stopped.

"There," she said indicating a hook on the wall by the wind chime. Another coat hung on it, a denim jacket.

"What can I get you for?" she said, "I'm Madge, by the way."

"Ivy. Black coffee, please," I said glad to meet someone who seemed normal.

"That all? Hope you don't mind my saying, but looks like you could do with a pie or three."

I smiled. "Just coffee."

I sat down at a table in the corner that overlooked the road, giving me a view of a pretty thatched cottage. I looked away and scanned the café. There were only four other tables, all covered with checked cloths. There was one other customer, a young man whose long legs splayed out astride the table, too long to bend underneath. He wore a blue denim shirt and jeans and black-rimmed glasses. I watched him, bemused by the way he slouched way back in his seat, his chin level with the table top, fingers bashing away at the keys of his laptop with ferocious speed.

"That's Ralph. He won't hear you even if you shout down his bleedin' earhole," said Madge handing me my coffee. "He's writing a book. Next Stephen King by all accounts."

I wrapped my hands around the mug, savouring the heat

on my fingers, and watched Ralph. I wanted to know what his book was about. Guessed it would be science-fiction. I thought about asking him but he was so focused I didn't want to interrupt. With a start, I remembered I was supposed to be ringing Grandma. I whipped my phone out of my bag. She answered on the second ring.

"Ivy? Thank God."

"Sorry. I know, it's so weird not being able to text or ring, but you got my letter?"

"Oh yes," she said, "and what a relief it was when I did. No reception, what a shame. So, everyone's lovely and the little boy – Wren, is it?"

"Yeah. He's great."

"Good. And you're telling me the honest truth? Not trying to pull the wool over my eyes so I don't worry? This Mrs Waters is treating you well, yes?"

"Yeah. She's really nice. Eccentric, but -"

"Promise? Cross your heart and hope to die -"

"Stick a needle in my eye – yes."

"Good, good. Promise me you haven't started getting any fanciful ideas?"

I tensed. "No, Grandma. Everything's fine."

"But you said she's eccentric?"

"Only in terms of her dress sense, really." *And bizarre fear of technology.*

"Oh? Do tell."

"She likes to make and wear her own clothes. Victorian dresses."

"Really? Tickle my pickle. Well, as I always say, each to their own. If that's what shines your berry."

I laughed. "That's a new one."

She giggled and her giggle turned into the chesty cough that had been pestering her for a while.

I frowned. "How're you feeling?"

"Fine and dandy," she said, voice firm.

I sensed she didn't want to talk about it but pushed on. "Honestly? Have you made an appointment yet?"

"No, not yet. I'll make it tomorrow."

"Good," I said, unconvinced. "What else have you got planned for the week?"

"Scrabble with the girls. Shopping. Chores. Watching rubbish telly while eating stuff that's no good for me. Nothing exciting. You? Any fun outings planned with the little bird?"

"Not yet," I said feeling uncomfortable.

I had a horrible feeling that if I broached the subject of taking Wren out, I'd get shot down and discover a new level of weirdness, but I didn't want to tell Grandma that. Wren hadn't known what an aeroplane was, which suggested a lot of things, one being the fact that the poor boy had never left Fairwood House.

Chapter Fifteen

I ended the call as quickly as possible. I hated lying to Grandma, but if she knew what I knew, she might tell me to quit and come home straight away. That, or she'd worry I was turning paranoid again and tell me to try therapy. Therapy hadn't worked for my mum and besides, neither scenario worked for me. I couldn't leave Wren and there was no way I was dredging up the past to a stranger who charged fifty quid an hour. Plus I was responsible for Wren now. I needed to make sure he was safe, which meant finding out the truth about Lucinda Hastings.

I sensed eyes and looked up to see Ralph the writer watching me. I smiled and looked away, peeking up to see cute dimples in his cheeks.

"You're new," he said.

"I am."

"What lunacy brought you here?"

"Work. I'm a nanny."

"Who for?"

"Mrs Waters at Fair -"

"Fairwood House? Jeez. You're brave."

I laughed. "Why?"

He sat up a bit, took off his glasses and rubbed them on his shirt. "Haunted house on the hill one-oh-one. What's she like?"

"Mrs Waters?"

"Yeah."

I thought for a moment. Chose my words carefully. "Nice, but different."

"I heard she never leaves the house. Folks say she's an agoraphobe."

"I don't think so," I paused. I didn't want to be disloyal and gossipmonger but couldn't help myself. I lowered my voice, aware that Madge was pottering about behind the counter trying to eavesdrop. "She hates technology. Won't let anyone use their phones on the grounds."

"Really? Actually, I doubt you'd get service up there anyway."

"You don't, which makes it easier to accept, but I only get one day off a week so I can only use my phone then."

"Hence the long-awaited call to Grandma."

"Hey."

He grinned. "A writer's gotta steal from the real."

"I'm dying to know," I said, gesturing to his laptop, "what's it about?"

"Weirdly, it's about a fit nanny who goes to work for a crazy old dame in a haunted house."

"Ha, ha," I grinned, "so you think I'm fit?"

"I knew you wouldn't miss that -?"

"Ivy. Ivy Smith. Nice to meet you, Ralph."

He leaned over and we shook hands. His grip was warm and firm, and he smelt good.

My tummy went all fluttery. Ralph might have been more Stephen King than Tom Cruise from *Top Gun*, but I could probably live with that.

Chapter Sixteen

I was buzzing when I met Maddock. Ralph had asked me to meet him at the tearoom the same time next week and I'd said yes. Excitement made me forget about tact. As soon as the taxi dropped us off at the iron gate, I asked Maddock about his face.

"How did you get that cut? Really?"

About to unlock the first padlock, his hands stilled. Wind whipped our clothes, my hair and the heather. The air was loud and frenzied with hollow wails. Maddock leaned over bringing his face close to mine. Up close, I could see grey hairs protruding from his nostrils, smell beer on his breath. His skin was mottled and grey and I realised how unwell he looked.

"This," he said, stabbing a finger at his cheek, "is none of your concern. You'd do best to keep your eyes on the task and stop nosin' in on everyone and everythin'. Mrs Waters is a private lady. She won't take kindly to nosy little girls."

I wanted to poke him in his condescending eye, but resisted the urge. Fighting with an ex-con wasn't a good idea, especially when Mrs Waters was so fond of him.

He turned back to the padlock.

"Weren't you young and curious once?" I said.

He snorted and glanced over his shoulder, "I knew when to back off. You'd do well to learn that."

He locked the gate and I hurried along by his side. "You were good with Wren. He likes you."

Maddock grunted. "He's not as bad as people think."

"Why do they think he's bad? Did he do something?"

Maddock spoke through gritted teeth. "Just leave it.

Leave it or you'll get hurt, you hear?" There was a note of desperation in his voice.

He unlocked the second padlock and ushered me through. I waited for him to lock it then said, "Fine. I'll leave it. Just tell me one thing. What happened to Lucinda?"

He stared straight ahead and hurried forward. "What d'you mean? She left. Family emergency."

"And it didn't strike you as strange that she left without saying goodbye?"

He shrugged, opened the front door. I walked through and turned, catching a worried expression on his face which he disguised with a scowl.

"She didn't even say goodbye to Wren. Did you know that?"

He hacked out a cough and shrugged again. "She was a strange one. Never knew which way she'd turn. Happy as Larry one minute, mopey as sin the next."

He coughed again and left me standing in the entrance hall staring after him. I waited a few moments then followed him into the dining hall. He wasn't there but the kitchen door was open a few inches. I snuck across the room and peeped in. He and Ping were talking in hushed voices. Ping threw a tea towel on the floor, put her hands on her hips and snapped at him in Thai.

"Anything wrong?" Mrs Waters said.

I whirled around. She stood in the dining hall beside the table staring at me.

"No," I said.

The kitchen door slammed shut.

"Did you have a nice time in the village?" she said, stroking the back of a chair.

"Yes, thank you," I paused, needing to fill the silence, create distance from the fact she'd caught me spying on Ping and Maddock, "I met someone."

"Oh? Do tell."

I blushed. "It's not a big deal or anything. We chatted for a while. He's writing a book. It was fun."

"How exciting for you. What's his name? Is he handsome? Come, I'll have Ping fetch us a pot of tea and you can tell me all about him. Odette's having a nap so this is the perfect opportunity for us to have a natter."

I followed her into the living room and she rang the china bell. Ping appeared, cheeks pink, hands balled at her sides. I tried to make eye contact with her but she seemed determined to act like I didn't exist. I could feel the venom radiating from her pores.

Oops. If she hated me before, it was nothing compared to how she felt about me now.

Chapter Seventeen

The wind was wild but the sky had cleared and the sun hovered high above the house, yellow as a daffodil.

After quizzing me for an hour about Ralph, Mrs Waters told me that she and Ping were taking Odette for a walk on the moor. As it was my day off, she said I needn't watch Wren and that I could do whatever I pleased. He'd been instructed to stay in his room for the entire afternoon. I found out that Maddock was out chopping firewood, meaning that for a short time at least, Wren and I would have the house to ourselves, which was exactly what I needed.

As soon as they left the house, I took the stairs two at a time and found Wren in his room kneeling on the floor adding pieces of snail shell to the demonic creatures on top of his model house. He held a pot of glue and a brush and was so focussed he didn't hear me enter the room. I watched him, heart melting at the sight of his tongue pinched between his teeth, his brow knitted together in concentration. He selected a piece of shell and carefully placed it on one creature's neck. I shifted my weight and the floorboard creaked. He whipped his head around and smiled when he saw me.

"Ivy. You're back. Look. I'm adding to my Stone Demons."

"They look brilliant. So realistic. It looks like you're having a great time, but I was wondering if you wanted to play a game?"

He pushed himself to his feet, eyes bright. "What game?"

"We've got the house to ourselves, so I thought we could

play hide and seek."

He grinned. "I love hide and seek. Me and Lucinda used to play it in her bedroom."

"Great. I'll count to twenty. You hide."

"Where's allowed?"

I thought for a moment. "Anywhere downstairs. Not up here because we can't go in other people's bedrooms." Even though I wanted to.

"Yes!"

I smiled. "Quick - you'd better go. One, two -"

He ran out of his bedroom. It was a joy to hear him run. He was behaving like every six-year-old should.

I finished counting and headed down the corridor, stopping outside what I assumed were Ping's and Maddock's rooms. The urge to go in and have a look around was strong, but I couldn't do that – Ping had a terrible past. It wasn't surprising she found it hard to trust people and was intent on treating me like a criminal – though I found that ironic, given the fact Maddock was an ex-con. I wondered what he'd done. Nothing violent, surely. Mrs Waters wouldn't give a second chance to someone like that, not when Odette was in the house. Poor Odette. The scars on her back were ghastly. I'd seen at least six, each a long slash like someone had taken a knife to her skin.

I shivered. I needed to know what had happened to Odette but couldn't ask anyone. Asking about something like that wasn't just nosiness, it was morbid curiosity.

I headed downstairs, savouring the thrill of breaking one of Mrs Waters' rules. As long as Wren was back in his room before they returned from their walk, everything would be fine. Odette was out of the house so there wasn't any chance of Wren and her crossing paths and besides, what Mrs Waters didn't know wouldn't hurt her.

The maggots whined but I ignored them. Excitement whooshed through me and I hurried through the dining hall into the kitchen, guessing that the door in the floor I'd spotted when Ping had been arguing with Maddock would lead me to the rooms below. Slipping into the kitchen, I glanced around half-expecting Ping to pop out from under the table and screech at me, but the room was empty, surfaces spotless, pans hanging from metal hooks on the walls, a fire burning in the stove. I noticed a pink cloth and a bottle of Flash on the side next to the sink and smiled. Certain modern-day products were clearly acceptable in Mrs Waters' books. I was beginning to think she was like a vegan who ate dairy when push came to shove. I frowned, feeling bad. Each to their own, each to their own. That's what Grandma would say.

But you're not her, the grubs whispered, making me jump.

To my surprise the trapdoor wasn't locked. I knelt down and heaved up the oak door, which groaned emphasising its age. Wren probably wasn't down there, but I didn't care. Curiosity and excitement drove me. As a child, I'd loved exploring nooks and crannies in people's houses and I hadn't changed. Not only that, I needed to find out what had happened to Lucinda and the answer could be down there, waiting for me to set my beady eyes on it.

I could see the start of some steep steps but beyond the first couple, darkness reigned. Knowing I didn't have much time, I scanned the kitchen and spotted a pack of matches on a shelf beside an iron lantern. I lit the lantern and, feeling naughty and medieval, descended the stone steps, trailing the wall with my free hand to make sure I didn't fall.

The further down I went, the colder and danker the air became. A musty odour pervaded and I wrinkled my nose. I kept going.

At last, I saw ground. I turned and looked up at the hole, chilled by the idea of Ping shutting the trapdoor and locking me down here forever, but of course no-one appeared and I decided it was safe for me to continue with my search.

It seemed these rooms were still in use. Beside the wall stood a shelving unit that held numerous jars of food. I swiped a finger across a shelf to confirm these weren't long-forgotten things and found the shelves dust-free. I turned left and moved deeper. The lantern gave little light but enough for me to see a rabbit dangling from the ceiling just before I walked into it. I grimaced at the sight of the poor thing hanging by its legs, already skinned, its flesh bright pink. Its leg appeared torn as though it had been snared by a trap.

I hurried away from the carcass and moved toward a filthy mattress covered by a brown blanket. Mrs Waters had said no-one used the rooms down here anymore but this told a different story. I moved closer, grimacing at the stench of stale urine. Something moved under the blanket and I jumped back as a rat poked its head out and sniffed the air. It saw me and we locked eyes. I stamped my feet and said, "Bah" and it shot away and disappeared into a crack in the wall.

Luckily it hadn't been a spider. I looked up and held the lantern aloft, confirming my worst fears. Cobwebs smothered the low ceiling. My heart raced and I considered turning back. Wren would be waiting for me to find him, and I didn't know how long it would be until the others came back. I looked at the bed again, tried to make myself go back, but the need to know what they were hiding compelled me closer.

I knelt beside the mattress and lifted it up. Nothing lay underneath except for stone and dirt. I dropped the mattress and dust sprayed into the air making me sneeze. I made to stand up then froze. Just beyond the glow of the lantern was a white Nike trainer and a backpack.

I stepped over the mattress and placed the lantern on the ground. With eager fingers, I picked up the bag and turned it over. It was a black Nike bag and it wasn't empty. I unzipped the main section and tipped out the contents. In the shallow pool of light lay a pair of Ray Ban aviators, three Peppermint Cream sweet wrappers, a book called, 'Shooter's Bible' and a black leather wallet. I checked the other pockets but found nothing more than a piece of chewing gum wrapped in silver foil. Trembling with anticipation, I grabbed the wallet.

A scraping sound came from behind me. I shoved the wallet down the front of my dress, turned around and stared into the darkness.

"Ivy?"

I breathed. It was Wren. I picked up the lantern and made my way back to the steps. Wren stood halfway down, face pale, fingers on his pendant.

"Ivy. Did you think I was here?" he said, eyes darting toward the dangling rabbit.

"Yeah - I thought it would be a brilliant hiding place."

"They're on their way back. I was hiding in the library and I looked out of the window and saw them."

Oh God. Shit.

"Quick," I said giving him a small push up the stairs.

He ran up and I followed. When we reached the kitchen, I told him to run back to his bedroom. He left immediately, no questions. I closed the trapdoor as quietly as I could then blew out the lantern and put it back where I'd found it. Heart crashing, I dashed out of the kitchen and ran across the dining room into the entrance hall.

The door opened and Mrs Waters appeared, followed by Ping and the girl from the paintings. The naked girl from the landing.

Odette.

Ping glared at me and put her hands on her hips. It would have been comical if not for the fact that she obviously knew I'd been up to no good.

Mrs Waters smiled and said, "Ivy. It's about time I

introduced you to my beautiful daughter. Odette, darling, this is Ivy, our new nanny."

Odette stared at the floor, showing no sign she'd heard her mother. Mrs Waters gave me an apologetic look then turned and undid the buttons on Odette's coat.

The girl raised her head slowly as if in a hypnotic trance and rested her green eyes on mine. A small frown pinched her brow and she stared at me like a baby would, curious and unblinking, her hands rotating in slow circles at her sides. She began to murmur, her words indistinct, lips fast. I tried to work out what she saying.

"It's good to meet you, Odette," I said.

Instead of replying, she turned, lifted her skirt and skipped toward the stairs.

"Is the child in his room?" Mrs Waters said tracking her daughter's movements.

I nodded.

"Good, good. See you at seven for dinner?"

"Yes, that'd be lovely."

"Excellent. Ping and Mason shall be joining us tonight. Won't that be wonderful?"

"Great," I said with a fake smile, glancing at Ping who gave me a scathing look then headed for the kitchen.

I watched Mrs Waters follow Odette up the stairs, feeling like the worst person in the world for snooping. Even so, the second they disappeared I took the steps two at a time and hurried across the corridor back to my room, desperate to look inside the wallet.

Chapter Eighteen

I spread out the contents of the wallet on my bed feeling like a detective. Its ingredients were generic but told me a lot about the man the bag belonged to. There were a few cards and some coppers in the zip compartment. Totally absorbed, I grabbed the driving license and stared at the picture. The name on the card was Carl Maddock and it wasn't the Maddock I knew. According to the birthdate, this man was thirty years old with muscular shoulders and fiery red hair. The Maddock I knew was in his late forties and bald. But there was something similar about this man's face to Maddock's. Were they father and son? They seemed a bit too close in age for that. Cousins? Brothers, perhaps? Another piece of evidence supported this hypothesis: Carl Maddock had a tattoo of a scorpion on his neck identical to Maddock's.

The grubs cackled. I cringed and shoved the card back in the wallet.

The other cards weren't as useful – a Costa Coffee Club card and a Morrisons More card - though the third offered a clue about where he might be from: a business card for Protyre Garage and Tyre Centre in Westbury, Wiltshire.

A knock on the bedroom door made me gather up the cards and wallet and shove them under a blanket.

"Come in," I said in a voice higher than normal.

Wren opened the door. He held a book in his hand, eyes hopeful.

"I'd love to read you a bedtime story. Hang on. I got you this."

From my handbag I withdrew the tiny model aeroplane I'd bought in Weirlock. I handed it to Wren and he stared at it with wonder, eyes big as cherries. He whispered thank you and threw his arms around my waist, burying his cheek into my stomach.

"I love you, Ivy," he whispered.

I stroked his downy hair and said nothing, too choked up to speak.

We went into his room and snuggled up on the bed together to read *Charlotte's Web*, a story I'd loved as a child. I read to him for longer than I planned to. Once I'd tucked him in and kissed his cheek, I went back to my room to get ready for dinner, but couldn't resist having another look at the clues I'd found.

Excited to view my findings again, I lifted the blanket and gaped in horror at the bed. The cards and wallet were gone.

The maggots whined. Frantic, I whipped off all the blankets, pillows too, but there was no sign of the wallet or cards. I stared at the door, hoping in a strange way that Ping had come in and taken them, because if she hadn't, the crawlers had been right all along and I was slowly but surely losing my mind, just like my mum.

Chapter Nineteen

To my surprise, Mrs Waters brought out two large pizzas for dinner. She sat down in her usual place at the table with me to her left, Ping to her right and Maddock beside Ping. The cut on Maddock's face still looked raw. Maybe he'd been telling the truth and really had had a nasty encounter with a tree, but I doubted it. He saw me staring and frowned.

For a while, we ate in uncomfortable silence while Mrs Waters watched us, a glass of wine resting against her mouth, her little finger poking up.

"To new friends and new beginnings," she said lifting her glass.

We raised our glasses and clinked. Ping didn't clink mine, even though I held it out for her; Mrs Waters noticed and rolled her eyes when Ping looked down.

"Tell me Maddock, how's your writing going?" Mrs Waters said.

He slugged back some wine, burped and apologised before saying, "Not bad. Wrote a new one last night."

"It nice," Ping said, "Poem about rose. Very pretty."

Maddock's chest puffed out at the compliment and I realised this was my chance.

"You write poetry?" I said.

He nodded, eyes averted from mine.

"I love poetry," I said, "Shakespeare's sonnets are my favourite. Who're you a fan of?"

He hacked out a cough, thumped his chest. "I don't read it. Just write it."

"Yes," Mrs Waters said looking fondly at him, "It's been so cathartic for him. Helped him work through his troubled youth."

"If it hadn't been for writin', I reckon I'd still be a good-for-nothin' bottom dweller," he said jerking his head at Mrs Waters, "and if it hadn't been for this lovely lady here, writin' stuff down would never've crossed my mind."

"How did you meet?" I said.

Ping gave me a sly glance but said nothing.

"I lived with my aunt in London for a fair few years," Mrs Waters said, "We used to frequent the local fishmongers where Maddock worked."

"Proper nasty work, it was," Maddock said, "only place I could get work after the slammer. Used to sleep in the shed out back."

Mrs Waters shook her head and patted her hair. "I still find it hard to believe a man of your integrity ended up in such a place, but there you go – this is the way society functions nowadays."

"So, you met at the fishmongers where Maddock worked," I said, "but how did you end up working here?"

Mrs Waters leaned across Ping and rested her hand on Maddock's arm. "This incredible man saved my life, that's how."

"What? How?" I said leaning forward and ignoring Ping's scowl.

Maddock flushed purple and studied his plate. Mrs Waters removed her hand from his arm and said, "That day I'd gone on my own to the shop and purchased a gorgeous pair of lobsters for our evening meal. I was making my way through the shortcut behind Barrow Lane when out of nowhere appeared this odious brute with a knife. Fortunately for me, I'd been stupid enough to drop my glove in the fishmongers and Maddock had picked it up and followed me to give it back and what should he see as he walked around the corner but this savage beast trying to mug me. Well, I can tell you Maddock did not hesitate. He beat the beast to a bloody pulp." She grinned and bowed her head in his direction.

"Wow. What a story. And you offered him a job?"

"Yes. My father was killed in a car accident – which is part of the reason I abhor such odious machinery and have sworn never to own one – and I inherited the house. Of course, I grew up here so I knew how large it was. I'd been thinking about hiring a groundsman but when Maddock saved me, I knew I had to have him. I owe him my life, you see."

"No," Maddock said, "I owe you mine."

Mrs Waters smiled. "That's really very sweet of you to say that but -"

"Me too," Ping said smiling at Mrs Waters. In that moment I thought I glimpsed a nice part of Ping, but the second Mrs Waters looked away, Ping glanced at me sideways as if to say *You're not part of this. You don't belong here, with us. Piss off.*

I ignored her and seized my chance while the conversation wasn't too far off point. "It seems like you're almost family to each other. That must be really comforting. I only have my Grandma left. Have you got any relatives close by, Maddock?"

I felt the atmosphere change; it was in everyone's body language – Ping's chin lifted and Maddock's shoulders tensed. It was weird, but the tension in the room was palpable, like everyone's heartbeat had sped up making the air vibrate in a way that wasn't visible or audible but somehow strong enough for me to feel it. I swallowed a lump of pizza that had got stuck on the back of my tongue and tried to act like I hadn't noticed the change in the air, but chills skittered up my spine.

Maddock shook his head, eyes not on me but on his knife. Ping and Mrs Waters exchanged such a quick glance that I almost missed it. I'd hit a nerve. There was something they weren't telling me. Now I was absolutely sure of it, and it was linked to Maddock's relative: Carl Maddock.

I should have left it there, but the curious cat in my heart was scratching at the window desperate to be let out.

"Was Lucinda a good nanny?" I said.

"Yes," Ping snapped. "Very good. Nice girl."

"Wren misses her so much," I said looking at Mrs Waters' face, which was pained.

She patted her hair, raised her glass and looked at Ping and Maddock, "To a dear friend who we wish was still around to warm our hearts."

"A dear friend," they said.

I raised my glass. This time there was no happy clinking and I thought I saw Maddock's eyes moisten, but the moment was too brief to be sure and he pushed himself away from the table, making the feet of the chair squeal.

"I'm turning in. Night," he said glancing at Ping who nodded and stood up.

"Yes, that's probably a sensible decision." Mrs Waters yawned and smiled at me. "I think I'll turn in as well."

I was surprised. Earlier I'd got the impression I was in for another evening of chatting in the living room with Mrs Waters, but she yawned again and pushed back her chair.

"Good night, dear Ivy."

I thought about offering to help tidy away, but she was already walking toward the kitchen, her shoulders rolled forward in an uncharacteristic manner, which could have suggested fatigue or defeat. Or both. Or – my temples began to pound - maybe she was worried that I was going to discover what they were trying to hide.

The maggots started to sing, louder and louder, faster and faster. *One, two, three, four, five, once I caught a fish alive, six, seven, eight, nine, ten, I never let it go again.*

*

In my bedroom I went to the window and looked out at the starry night. Beneath the silver moon stood the wood. Was I paranoid or was I onto something?

I turned away from the window, but not before movement caught my eye. I stared as Mrs Waters walked across the moor toward the wood carrying a lantern. She paused to unlock the first padlock, hurried across the enclosure then unlocked the second.

As if sensing prying eyes, she turned and looked back at the house.

I yanked my head back, waited a few seconds then peeked past the curtain again as she disappeared into the trees. She had no crate or axe which meant she wasn't going out there to chop wood. What was she going there for?

I rubbed my eyes and sat on the bed. *She's a liar liar, tongue on fire* the maggots sang, their voices shriller than ever, their words burning my mind just like the flames that burned the wallet and cards in the fireplace – *what?*

I jumped up and darted to the hearth. There, blackened and burning on the logs, lay Carl Maddock's things.

Someone knows what I've done. What I've found.

My heart beat hard. Whoever had done this wanted me to understand that they knew I'd been snooping. They were sending me a warning, a silent message to stop. I'd have put money on it that the message was from Ping.

But I couldn't stop, not when there was a chance that Wren was in danger.

Chapter Twenty

Morning came. The sky was grubby, air dank. I pulled on another Victorian-style dress, this one the colour of a bluebell, and curtsied in front of the mirror. In my eyes there was fear but also determination. Beneath them hung shadows from a tortured night.

I turned from the mirror and paced the room, trying to clear my head. Images of Mrs Turner's face bombarded me – screaming at me to get out of the house - Liam cowering behind his father's legs - Mr Turner spitting threats and hurling my bags onto the street with such force my hairdryer smashed.

When I'd started there, everything had been so perfect but I'd ruined it.

I turned back to the mirror, reached out and pressed my hand flat against the glass to hide my face. I knew why I'd thought what I'd thought, but I'd been wrong. Telling Mrs Turner was the worst thing I could have done. I'd never forget the way she'd looked at me or the things she'd said. Her words cut deep, mostly because they were true.

And what have you learnt? Nothing nothing nothing the crawlers hissed.

Reaching for Wren's door I stopped as the sound of a piano flowed up the stairs and along the corridor, its music instantly recognisable: Tchaikovsky's Dance of the Little Swans. Once upon a time I had dreamt of becoming a ballerina, but terror had slain that dream when I was eight years old.

I walked along the corridor and looked over the banister. There, dressed in a white leotard, tutu and pointe shoes, moving so beautifully I couldn't take my eyes off her, was Odette. Across the entrance hall and around the staircase she danced, a dreamy expression on her face, her movements effortless. She performed a triple pirouette and applause rose above the music. I looked down. Mrs Waters sat on the stairs watching her daughter. I hesitated then joined her on the step. She smiled at me with trembling lips and grasped my hand. Tears smeared the powder on her cheeks.

"This is the first time she's danced in years," she said.

"She's incredible. Where did she learn?"

"I started taking her to Exmoor Dance Academy when she was three years old. She fell in love with ballet that very first day. Her teacher – a terrific dancer herself - said she was star in the making."

"How long did she dance for?"

"Only until she was fourteen."

"Really? Why did she stop?"

"She was in an accident. You see that scar on her back?"

"Yes."

Only one scar was visible. It protruded from the top of her leotard. When she'd danced on the landing, I'd seen six scars. I remembered the way they criss-crossed her back, one under the other, laddering her spine like three large kisses. The marks were precise, not random. There was no way they'd got there by accident, as Mrs Waters suggested. No. Someone had put them there. Someone had sliced them into her skin.

Mrs Waters' gaze remained on Odette. She sighed and nibbled her thumbnail. "It took her a long time to recover. She wasn't always like this."

I wanted to prod at her lie, press her for the truth. The maggots urged me to do it. I opened my mouth, clamped it shut. She wanted me to think Odette had been hurt in an accident but *why*? Did it have something to do with the wood? Was that why I was forbidden to enter? What was so dangerous about that pack of trees?

My mind formed a question. I opened my mouth to voice it, but couldn't get the words out. I glanced at the tears on her cheeks. At her hand in mine. At the way she watched her daughter with a mixture of pride and sadness pulling her up and pushing her down.

The maggots hissed. I pushed them away. Lying or not, something horrific had happened to her daughter. Something she didn't want to talk about or didn't want me to know about. Asking would make me seem insensitive. It would imply that I thought she was lying. I couldn't afford either result, so I stayed quiet and watched Odette dance.

"Isn't Ping incredible too?" she said turning her head toward the library.

Ping? So that was who was playing the music.

"Yes," I said, "she's amazing." *But weird.*

We watched the rest of Odette's dance in silence. When the music ended, we both stood up and applauded. Odette stared at us blankly then took her mother's hand and pulled her upstairs.

I went downstairs into the library. Ping was sitting at an ivory piano in the front left corner of the room staring into space. Her hands rested on the piano. With a squirm of disgust, I noticed that her pinkie fingernails were longer than the white keys. I cleared my throat and she glanced over her shoulder with a smile. Her smile dropped when she saw me.

"That was awesome," I said, hoping the compliment didn't sound fake.

Ping looked back at the piano. "Thank you, Ivy."

I considered trying to talk to her about the wallet and cards, but she closed the lid and hurried out of the room.

Chapter Twenty-One

Days passed and there was still no letter for Wren from Lucinda. He grew more upset and fretful each time Maddock said there was nothing. I grew increasingly frustrated and, though I hated to admit it, scared. I wanted to trust Mrs Waters but no matter which way I turned it, Maddock's relative's belongings had been hidden in the basement and Lucinda's departure didn't make sense. If she'd left due to a family emergency, she'd have written to Wren to explain by now. Who wouldn't? According to Wren they'd been really close. She'd told him she loved him every night for *six years*. She'd looked after him when he was a baby.

I brushed my hair and frowned at my reflection, hesitated for a moment then chose the bluebell dress.

There were three possible reasons a person like Lucinda - after leaving without saying goodbye - wouldn't contact a child they'd looked after for six years: one, she was seriously ill, two, she was locked up, or three, she was dead. I wasn't sure what to think but the more I thought about it, the more my tummy hurt and the louder the maggots sang.

I had to know and I'd finally decided how to find out.

*

I met Ralph at Bilberry Tearoom. He was wearing a white shirt and black jeans, smarter than last week. Sexier too. Not quite good enough to eat, but good enough to make my insides do belly flops. He looked me up and down, stood up and bowed like he was something out of *Pride and Prejudice*.

"My lady. Such a pleasure to make your acquaintance on

this fine winter's morn."

"You like?" I said raising the skirt of my bluebell dress and curtsying.

"Not like. *Love.* Coffee? Tea? Opium?"

"Black coffee's fine. I prefer coke, to tell you the truth."

Ralph's smile froze then he smacked the table and said, "Finally, someone I see eye to eye with."

I crossed my eyes at him, stopping when I noticed Madge standing next to me.

"Everything okay, me dears?" she said with a knowing smile.

"Everything's perfect," Ralph said. "This is our first date. We're breaking the ice."

"Like you do," Madge said.

She took our order and walked back to the counter, giving me an eyebrow wiggle when Ralph wasn't looking.

I looked at Ralph's laptop. "Thought you'd bring your book along in case I was boring?"

"I got some writing in before you arrived. Reached the final ten thou. If I don't write every few hours, it runs away from me."

"Tell me about your story," I said.

He cleaned his glasses on his shirt. "I'm not sure I should…"

"Pleeease."

"What the hell. Alright," he said clearly pleased, "I'll tell you – but only because you were brave enough to turn up dressed like that. Okay, so it's based on this folk tale that originated right here in Weirlock some two hundred years ago."

"Ooh. Go on."

He grinned. "One winter, when a blizzard hit Weirlock, the devil rose from hell in the form of a beast and roamed the hills searching for the perfect victim, who happened to be a young man by the name of John Thornby -"

"Not Ralph?"

"No," he grinned. "Now this John Thornby guy was the only son of the local Priest and was out chopping wood in the forest behind the church. On finding Thornby, the devil ripped out the poor man's still-beating heart, ate it and *became* the heart thereby giving himself the power to manipulate Thornby to do his bidding - an act of unspeakable evil on an innocent virgin by the name of Olive Wicke who went mad and danced to her death into Weirlock Bay, never to be seen again in daylight."

"Sorry to be such a dunce, but how do you *become* a heart?" I said.

He shrugged. "I don't know. You just do. Call it the uncanny."

"Ah ha. And this Olive girl - she's a ghost?"

"Yup. As recently as five years ago – and I tell you no lie - there was an eyewitness account by a local farmer who claimed he saw a phantom woman dancing on the bay just after sunset. Crazy or what? Anyway, folks still believe in it. Think she'll haunt the bay until she gets her revenge."

I hugged myself. "Creepy. It's a ghost story then?"

"Kind of - I don't know how to pitch it yet."

"It sounds awesome. Gripping and different. No really, I mean it. Have you written anything before?"

"Nah. I'm job hunting. Making the most of my free time."

"What sort of work are you looking for?"

"Anything related to writing, but it's so hard to get anything. Everyone says you need experience."

"I know. I did English Literature at Coventry but when it came to trying to get work it was impossible. I've always loved being around little kids – my Grandma was a teacher and I used to help out at school fairs and stuff when I was a teenager – so I thought I'd be a nanny."

"Why not teach, if you don't mind me asking?"

"I'm a wimp. I was scared of being responsible for so many kids. A couple I could cope with, but thirty, not a chance."

"You're not underestimating yourself?"

I shrugged, sipped coffee. "Grandma thinks I am, but I like being a nanny. I even like it at Fairwood House, though it creeps the hell out of me."

"Really? Why?"

"It's hard to explain."

"Tell me." He pulled on his ear lobe. "I'm all ears."

I inhaled, told myself to trust him. "Okay. It's going to sound like I'm nuts but I think something happened to the nanny before me."

"What, like she was murdered or something?" He grinned.

I didn't say anything.

Ralph leaned forward and lowered his voice. "Seriously?"

"I don't know. It's just…something feels off. It's weird. Wren said she didn't say goodbye. She'd been looking after him for *six years*. When you've been caring for someone that long you don't leave without saying goodbye."

"Yeah. Weird," he scratched his chin, "but murder? Don't you think that's a bit overkill – excuse the pun."

"I don't know. I found something. A bag under her old bed."

"Anything in it?"

"Just a Boots card with her name on. Nothing useful."

"Alright. Let's turn it on ourselves. Is there any reason at all you can think of that would make you leave a kid you'd been looking after for yonks without saying goodbye?"

"No. I can't think of anything that'd make me do that."

"Not even an emergency? Like, say, your Grandma dying?"

I shook my head. "I still think I'd find a second to say

bye. But maybe that's just me."

"I dunno. I'd do the same. Think how attached you'd get to someone after basically being their parent for so long. You're totally right. It doesn't make sense, but murder?"

"I know." I paused, slugged coffee. "I've got her address. Mrs Waters gave it to me. Her name's Lucinda Hastings. I was wondering if, maybe, given how I can't travel easily at the moment you could do me a huge favour and -"

"Where's she live?"

I pulled the slip of paper out of my bag and handed it to him. With an apologetic look, I said, "It's quite a long drive, so don't worry if -"

He held up his hand. "No worries. Gives me another excuse to avoid job-hunting. And I've always fancied being a detective."

"Okay - thanks. You're amazing. I can't believe you're actually going to do this for me given it's only our first proper date."

"What can I say? A man's gotta do what a man's gotta do to impress the woman he likes."

I felt myself blushing and quickly said, "I need to know she's alive and well. Once I know that, I can -"

"Stop being shit-scared half the time and terrified you're a paranoid nutjob the next?"

I smiled. "Exactly."

Chapter Twenty-Two

That night, Mrs Waters went to the woods again.

I'd taken to looking out of the window every evening in case she ventured out and exactly a week after the first time I saw her, she did it a second time, lantern in hand, steps fast - so fast they verged on psychotic. I knew it was crazy but I yanked on my coat over my pyjamas and left the bedroom clutching a lantern. The corridor was so dark I was rendered half-blind. I wanted to turn back, but the crawlers were getting louder every day. I had to make them stop. I had to know what Mrs Waters was hiding or I'd go mad.

We all have a touch of madness. It's what makes us human, silly they taunted.

I batted them away and moved faster.

Halfway along the corridor I heard the sound of mattress springs, rhythmic, repetitive. I grimaced; it was obvious what Ping and Maddock were up to. Sickened by the images that zipped through my mind I dashed past their room and ran down the stairs.

I hesitated at the silver bucket. My skin prickled and the memory attacked...

He's home early.

I think about going back into my room. Memories of them arguing, of the sound of him punching the wall, kicking holes in the doors, turning his violence on Mummy all explode in my mind one after the other like fireworks on Bonfire Night, making my head hurt so badly I worry I'm going to scream.

I look at the certificate in my hand and my heart sinks to my toes.

I turn to take it back to my bedroom, thinking I can show her tomorrow morning, and that's when the arguing starts -

Hurling the memory aside, I grabbed the spare set of keys from under the bucket, unlocked the front door and slipped outside into the crisp night. The moon gleamed pale gold giving me an ounce of light, but the house loomed darkly at my back and the wood loomed darkly ahead. Something like ninety-five percent of the world's oceans remained unexplored. I wondered how much of that army of ancient oak trees was the same. Wondered what it was about those trees that lured Mrs Waters away from the warmth of the house into their cold embrace a second time.

With Ralph's story about the devil in my ears, I unlocked the first padlock and ran to the next gate hugging the lantern to my chest even though the hot glass burned my skin. I froze at a sound coming from the woods. It was an agonized howl, more wolf-like than man-like. The crazy idea that Mrs Waters was a werewolf entered my mind and I rolled my eyes and opened the fence. It was probably a fox. Foxes made creepy sounds in the night. Sometimes they sounded like screaming babies.

Telling myself the sound had come from an injured animal, I hurried toward the wood.

I reached the kissing gate and hesitated. Nailed to the post was a sign. The writing was hard to read because it was so dark, but the words were just about legible. *Private land. Enter at your own peril.* It sounded like something from a horror story, but there it was printed in capital letters, black on white. I darted through the kissing gate, shivering at the memory of the dead rabbit in the basement and its crushed leg. I would need to be careful. Keep checking the ground for traps.

A dirt path appeared and I followed it, thinking about what I'd say if Mrs Waters saw me. I could say Wren was sick so I went to find her. The question was, would she buy it? I was a crap liar. But if she saw me, I'd have to lie. I couldn't exactly say I was worried she was hiding something in the wood so I'd followed her to find out what it was.

I focused on looking for the slightest glimmer of light, hoping I'd spot her lantern before she spotted mine, but the stars and moon were masked by the canopy above, and darkness enveloped the wood like the devil's cape, limiting my vision. Amid the gloom reared moss-smothered trees as gnarled and bent as arthritic hands. Unnaturally thick tree roots eaten with moss and fungi crawled across the woodland floor and wrapped themselves around the trees suffocating the earth.

With no warning, the path stopped. Roots and trees swarmed the space ahead. The stench of swamp rose and an owl whit-to-whooed, its voice very close. I looked up and saw a pair of yellow eyes glinting at me.

I darted forward and tripped. My knees hit the ground hard. Pain exploded in my kneecaps and nausea washed over me. I waited for the feeling to subside then pushed myself up and proceeded more carefully, picking my way through the root-smothered ground with timid steps.

Leaving the path was a stupid thing to do, but I couldn't stop and go back now. Another agonised howl broke the hush sending icy trickles down my spine yet pulling me toward the sound.

Deeper and deeper into the wood I went, palms sweaty in spite of the chill. Again, that sound, but this time it felt far more human than animal. I froze and listened. The scream came again then cut off abruptly. The wood went silent, but then I heard a sound I recognised: a slam; a door. A clanking of metal, a rattle, crunching, snapping.

I seized the lid of the lantern, whipped it off, blew out the light, groped for the closest tree and crouched behind it.

In utter darkness facing the direction of the sound, I

listened. The crunching grew louder, closer. Footsteps. Human. Whistling joined the crunch. It was Mrs Waters, whistling Twinkle Twinkle Little Star. I crouched lower as a soft glow came through the trees, bringing with it the ghostly figure of my employer, her silver hair billowing about her shoulders like a pair of net curtains.

Terrified she'd see me I pressed my face against the mossy bark, closed my eyes and held my breath, aware of my breathing being too loud. Her footsteps grew louder and louder, so loud it felt like she was an inch away - and then they began to fade.

I peeked out and saw the light from her lantern fading fast. Knowing I had no other light to guide me, I crept out from behind the tree and followed her, darting from oak to oak, stumbling and tripping but somehow staying on my feet.

She reached the kissing gate and I froze as she turned and looked back. For a terrifying second, I thought she'd seen me, but she carried on, still whistling, her footsteps springy, free arm swinging by her side.

I hurried to the kissing gate and watched her unlock the padlock, her figure barely visible now; so indistinct I had to concentrate to see her.

Like a car disappearing into fog, the light retreated as she headed to the next gate, and ebbed until I could no longer make it out.

The moon, however, was my friend. I waited another few minutes then ran to the iron gate. Using my stolen key, I unlocked it, stepped through, locked it, ran to the second gate and paused, listening and staring through the gloom to make sure Mrs Waters wasn't still outside. I looked at the house which loomed ahead, dark and silent. Hearing and seeing nothing, I unlocked the padlock, entered, locked it and sprinted across the enclosure. I hesitated at the front door then unlocked it and stepped into the pitch-black entrance hall. As quietly as I could, I closed the front door and twisted the key in the lock, cringing as it clicked. Turning to face the darkness, I shuffled forward aiming for the staircase, my hands outstretched in the hope I'd feel the banister. This was what it felt like to be blind. It was terrifying.

Shivering all over, my hand touched wood and I gripped the banister and tiptoed up the stairs, every part of me rigid with fear, every muscle spasming when a floorboard announced my presence.

After a few steps, I froze and strained my ears for the tiniest sound of movement within the house, but all remained deadly still and quiet.

Finally, reaching the landing, I paused and listened again. Again, all remained so quiet it was as if everyone in the house was dead.

I waited a beat longer then, unable to stop myself, dashed down the corridor back to my room, opened the door, darted inside, walked forward and groped for the edge of the bed.

Relief like I'd never known flooded my nerves and I shrugged off my coat and boots, and crawled onto the blankets and up the bed toward my pillow.

My hand touched something warm and soft. Something human. Skin.

Someone was in my bed.

I gasped and snatched back my hand.

In the darkness someone whispered, "He's mine, not yours."

Chapter Twenty-Three

It was a woman's voice, one I didn't recognise, which meant it had to belong to Odette. I held back the urge to scream at her to get. My eyes were still adjusting to the dark but I could make out her slender silhouette amidst the gloom.

"Odette, what are you doing here?"

She didn't respond. Though I couldn't see her eyes, I could feel them on me. I clambered off the bed and faced her.

"You should go back to bed," I said.

"You should go back to bed," she repeated.

I stepped back, unsure what to say or do. I didn't want to upset or alarm her but I was unnerved. It was impossible to predict what she'd say or do next, and I didn't want her to tell Mrs Waters that I hadn't been in my room. I racked my brain. She behaved more like a child than an adult, so I decided to talk to her like I would to Wren.

"What's your favourite colour, Odette? Mine's red."

She didn't say anything. Didn't move. She was so still she could have been dead.

I was about to try another question when she said, "I like silver like Mummy's hair."

"That's nice. I like silver too. It's a very pretty colour and your mummy's hair is very beautiful. What's your favourite food?"

"I don't have one."

"Do you have a favourite storybook? I know your mummy reads to you at bedtime, doesn't she?"

"I like Little Red Riding Hood."

"That's a great story. It's one of my favourites too."

"I like the bit where the Little Red Riding Hood eats the hunter."

Huh. That was a new version for me.

"I love Hansel and Gretel too. Do you?" I said.

"No."

That closed that conversation. I sighed, dog-tired, aching to lie down. With the fire out, the room was an ice box and I was chilled to the core.

"Shall I go and get Mummy and she can take you back to bed?" I said.

Instead of answering, she lunged forward and hissed at me, making me recoil and smash my back into the mantlepiece. I raised my hands in defence, but she didn't attack; she leapt off the bed and ran out of the room.

I listened to her footsteps fade, listened as a door creaked down the hallway then clicked shut.

With a shuddery breath, I felt my way to the door and closed it. There was no way of locking the door. I moved to the dressing table and pulled it across the floor, wincing at the scraping sound. Satisfied the door was blocked, I climbed into bed and pulled the blankets over myself. Only then did I realise I was shaking. I closed my eyes. Visions of what Odette could have done to me, the worst being of her slashing my back with a knife tore at my nerves.

I tossed and turned, trying to make my mind blank, but the onslaught continued. The maggots found their voices and I lay awake the entire night, besieged and tormented by the agonised screams I'd heard in the wood. It was like they were on repeat in my head. Over and over they tolled. Nothing would make them stop. Nothing, that was, until I allowed an awful idea into my mind: the idea that Mrs Waters had caused those terrible screams.

The thought made me feel ill but I couldn't dismiss it; the idea beat its fists against my skull and the grubs nodded their heads eagerly, telling me I was right. Mrs Waters was not only hiding something in the wood, she was hiding something terrible. As much as I tried not to think it, I couldn't help but agree that Mrs Waters wasn't who she pretended to be.

Maybe Ralph would be able to tell me differently when we next saw each other. Maybe he'd tell me he'd found Lucinda Hastings alive and safe at the address she'd given me, but I doubted it. I doubted it very much.

Chapter Twenty-Four

The next day, ironically, given the fact I'd considered using it as a lie the previous night, I found Wren in the dining hall looking ill.

I hurried over to him and touched his shoulder. "Wren, you okay?"

His face was yellow and purple shadows haunted the space under his eyes. He opened his mouth and threw up into his bowl of porridge. Tears dribbled down his cheeks and he stared vacantly at his sick. I grabbed a napkin and dabbed his mouth then picked him up.

"I'm taking you back to bed," I said touching his forehead with the back of my fingers. He was boiling hot. Heat radiated through his clothes and his hair was sweaty.

Ping walked over and stared at him. "Boy sick?"

"Yes. I think he's got a high temperature. Have you got a thermometer and a bottle of Calpol?"

She glanced back at the kitchen, looked at me and shook her head. I was surprised to see her give Wren's head a gentle pat. "You be fine, boy. I run cold bath. Okay?"

Wren retched and threw up over my shoulder. Ping's eyes widened and she grimaced, grabbed a napkin and tried to clean off the vomit.

"It's okay," I said. "You grab some water and I'll get him undressed."

She nodded and dashed away. I hurried out of the room, jumping at the sight of Odette in her white ballet outfit, her waiflike body pressed to the floor in a box split. Mrs Waters was nowhere to be seen. Odette's eyes shifted from me to Wren, who was moaning into my collar bone. Her hands began to rotate by her thighs. She titled her head and her dark hair fell over her face like a pall.

In a flat voice she said, "He's mine, not yours."

"He's not well," I said.

She acted like I hadn't spoken. With her eyes on Wren, she rose to her feet and walked up the stairs, ascending with slow, pointed steps and stopping halfway. She turned and stared down at me, her message clear. She wasn't going to let me pass.

I moved Wren to my left hip and put an edge in my tone. "You need to let me take him upstairs, so I can get him out of these dirty clothes and tuck him up in bed. He's poorly. He needs looking after."

"I can look after him," she said.

I fought my temper, reminded myself she wasn't well.

Slowly, I approached the stairs. I avoided eye contact with her and began to climb. My skin felt like it had been pulled over my body like cling film over a chicken carcass. My muscles were coiled tight, stomach hard. At any second she might launch herself at me, hiss and claw at my face or push me over, wrench Wren out of my arms, but she didn't move. Instead, she widened her stance and crossed her arms across her flat chest.

I stopped two steps below her and said, "Where's Mummy, Odette? Do you think she'd be happy if she saw you doing this?"

Odette's eyes bored into my crown. She didn't reply. A moment passed. Then another. I waited, hoping she'd give in and get out of the way but she dropped into a box split, spreading her legs across the width of the step. If she leaned forward now and gave my calves a shove, I'd fall. The fall wasn't great but with Wren in my arms, I'd be powerless to help myself and it was likely we'd both be injured. Wren clung tighter to me and moaned. He retched. Nothing came up.

"Please move," I said looking down at her.

She stared up at me, lips pushed out in a sulky pout. "He's mine. I can look after him." She stood up and held out her arms. A pleading, wild look entered her eyes and she whined, "Please, Ivy. Please. He's my baby bird. Give him to me. Please."

I gaped at her, the realisation knocking the breath out of me like a punch to the gut. Wren wasn't Mrs Waters' son. He was *Odette's*. I recalled her age: twenty-one. She must have been just fourteen years old when she had him. *Fourteen* — what the hell?

Horrified, I said, "I'll let you carry him but he's heavy. Are you sure you can manage?"

Tears swam in her eyes. She nodded keenly, jumped down the stairs and held out her arms smiling so hard I thought her cheeks might split.

Gently and slowly, I prised Wren's little body from mine and placed him in her arms. She gave me an ecstatic smile and, holding him in a baby carry, turned and walked up the stairs. I followed, hands up in case she lost her balance, but despite her scrawniness she was strong. She carried him along the corridor into his bedroom, lowered him to the bed and began to sing Twinkle Twinkle Little Star while stroking his forehead with her index finger.

I started to get him undressed and she gave me a questioning look as if to say, *Can I do it?* I nodded and watched her remove his clothes with the tenderest touch. Tears came to my eyes and I realised I'd been wrong about her: there was no way she was capable of hurting anyone, unless they were trying to hurt Wren, or take him away from her.

Ping walked in with two buckets of water and froze, mouth open. She dropped the buckets and water sploshed onto the floorboards. I flinched and the memory flashed up —

He shouts so loudly the floor vibrates. His voice is slurred.
Alarm bells blare in my head.

I creep across the landing and peep down through the bars of the banister. They're in the kitchen. Mummy has her back to me. She's on her knees, begging.

He's on his feet standing over her, smiling -

Looking at me quizzically, Ping said, "I get Mrs Waters."

She left the room before I had the chance to tell her it was fine. Odette hadn't noticed Ping; she only had eyes for her son who, I feared with rising horror, had been kept from her for his whole life.

Footsteps thundered down the corridor and Mrs Waters appeared with Ping behind her. Both women looked alarmed. I studied the floor and bit back the harsh words that threatened to burst from my mouth. Mrs Waters dashed into the room and crouched down beside Odette. Odette's cheek twitched and she frowned as Mrs Waters spoke to her, her voice so quiet I couldn't make out what she was saying. Odette glanced at her mother, eyes dull once more. Mrs Waters took her hand and led her from the room, giving me a sorrowful look before she closed the door.

Wren moaned, twisted and vomited over the edge of the bed, and Ping darted forward and began mopping it up. I took the cloth from her and told her to get the bath ready. She gave me a grateful smile and hurried off to fetch the tub.

"Why did Odette say that stuff?" Wren said in voice weak from sickness.

"What stuff?" I said smoothing his damp hair away from his eyes.

"She called me her baby."

Shit. He'd heard all of it.

I tried to work out what to tell him. My eyes fell on the window and the grey moor beyond that ended in a misty blur. Heavy sadness dragged on my heart. I scooted closer to him.

"I don't know, sweetie. There's a lot going on around here that I don't understand, but trust me, I'm going to get to the bottom of it."

Before the shit hits the fan, the maggots whispered.

Chapter Twenty-Five

Maddock and Mrs Waters were struck down with the same illness as Wren, so I arranged to go into Weirlock to buy supplies. It seemed Mrs Waters wasn't against using painkillers, rehydration tablets or tummy-calming peppermint capsules when it suited her.

Wren was sound asleep in bed, but Ping was to watch over him while I was gone. She was also in charge of Odette. Before I left, she handed me my phone so I could call a taxi. I thanked her and she nodded. She still only talked to me to deal with practical matters but the poison I'd felt earlier seemed to dilute a little more every day. It might not have been her who'd burned Carl Maddock's cards. Maybe Maddock had done it.

As soon as I got in the taxi and my phone got a signal, I rang Ralph to arrange to meet him at Bilberry Tearoom. To my relief, he was up for meeting at such short notice. I warned him I couldn't stay long and told him why I was coming to Weirlock. He was sympathetic but excited, saying he had something important to tell me. Fear ricocheted around my belly; what had he found out? If he'd found out what I feared, I knew what I'd have to do next and it wasn't going to be easy.

The driver dropped me off at a Boots pharmacy and I hurried in and bought the medicine using the cash Mrs Waters had given me. Supplies acquired, I hurried through the village to the tearoom, zipping up my coat to ward off the chill.

Just as I reached Bilberry Tearoom, snowflakes fluttered down feathering the sky. It was the first snow of the season.

The flakes were the size of my thumbnail and descending in their droves. Beautiful but deadly. This snow would settle for sure; the ground was dry from three days of clear skies and a fine layer of powder already dusted people's cars and rooftops. Soon, if the flurry continued so thickly, the moor would become a white ocean with Fairwood House its hostage.

I darted inside and saw Ralph immediately, not slouched in his seat like normal, but upright and alert.

Madge gave me a wink and a wave. The cafe was bustling and warm, rich with the smell of just-baked cake.

"Thanks for meeting me," I said sitting down and unzipping my coat.

"No problem."

"So, what have you got for me?"

"You're not gonna like it."

"Just tell me."

"There's no Lucinda living at the address you gave me. Never has been. According to the people living there, no-one younger than fifty lives on the street. I spoke to a couple of their neighbours and they said the same."

"So Mrs Waters gave me some random address?"

"Looks like it."

"But why? Unless -"

"Unless she's hiding something," he said, lowering his voice.

"And they'd received Wren's letter?"

"Yeah. They were more bemused by it than anything. Hadn't got around to binning it so they gave it to me. Here." He handed me Wren's letter. A chill trickled across my neck. I glanced at the letter then slid it into my handbag.

"You know what this means?" I said.

He nodded, face grim. "What're you gonna do?"

"Get my hands dirty. Dig around. Snoop some more."

"You don't really think they've done something to her?"

he said watching me closely.

"I don't know but I have to be sure." I thought about telling him about the weird screams in the wood but decided against it. "Look, I need another favour. I found this guy's stuff in the cellar. His name's Carl Maddock and I think he might have lived in or near Westbury in Wiltshire. I found a business card for Protyre Garage. Do you think you could go there and snoop around a bit? Try and find out if and when he last went there? He has a scorpion tattooed on his neck. I know it's a long shot but if he was a regular someone might know him and be able to tell us how long he's been missing. If he has been missing at all."

Ralph nodded. "Course. I'll go this afternoon – weather permitting. You think something's happened to this guy too?"

I shrugged and rubbed my eyes, hoping he didn't think I was nuts but pleased he liked me enough to help again. "I hope not, but finding his stuff with him nowhere around makes me think something might be up and with Lucinda Hastings missing too…"

He placed his hand on mine and gave it a gentle squeeze. Despite everything, butterflies came to life in my tummy.

"Meet me here on Sunday at eleven?"

"Love to." I drained my coffee. "Look, I'd better go. Wren needs medicine ASAP."

"Promise me one thing before you go?" he said.

I raised an eyebrow and yanked up my hood. I smiled. "That depends."

He didn't smile. "Promise me you'll watch your back?"

I hesitated then leaned down and kissed his cheek. "Cross my heart."

*

On the way to the taxi I rang Grandma. She answered on the first ring.

"You'll never believe it," she said breathlessly.

"Believe what?"

"You were right. About everything. About Mr Turner."

"*What?*"

"I am so sorry, my darling. I should have believed you. That poor girl -"

"Has he been arrested?"

"Yes. Word has it he's already confessed. The whole town's in uproar. Parents are withdrawing their children from the school. Headteacher's got some serious explaining to do."

"Why?"

"Rumour has it, Mr Turner had been giving her *private lessons* after school for months."

"Oh God. It's been going on longer than I thought."

"It's hideous. That poor girl and her poor, poor family. I dread to think what they're going through."

"And Mrs Turner."

"Well, yes, there's that poor woman too. Totally fooled, like everyone. Apart from you. You ought to be a private eye."

I rolled my eyes. "I told you what I saw. It didn't take much to put two and two together."

"Yes, you did tell me. You did and I didn't listen. I'm as bad as that wretched wife of his. I keep picturing her throwing you out and calling you all those names. Much as I feel sorry for her, when I think about how she treated you when you tried to tell her the truth, I feel like writing her a letter saying *Ivy told you so*. She owes you one hell of an apology."

"That's probably the last thing on her mind right now. Poor Liam. At least he's too young to understand what's going on."

"Yes, at least there's that." Grandma blew out a sigh. "You know what? I'll never second-guess you again, you hear? I'm such a dappy old bat."

I managed a laugh. "No, you're not. You're only dappy when you refuse to go to the doctor."

She snorted. "Tell me what you've been up to."

To cheer her up, I told her about Ralph. I tried to sound upbeat, but my cheeriness was forced. Thoughts of returning to Fairwood House lingered in my mind like ghosts with unfinished business. If I'd been right about Mr Turner, did it mean I was right about Mrs Waters?

Yes.

No.

Yes.

The time to doubt myself was over. I wasn't paranoid. I was onto something and I wouldn't let up until I found out the truth.

In my mind's eye I saw Mr Turner being arrested, saw myself giving him a triumphant smile, saw Mrs Turner apologising to me, Liam giving me a hug, myself crying and nodding and accepting her apology. The poor woman must be going through hell. I couldn't even imagine how it would feel to find out your husband and the father of your child was sleeping with another woman, let alone his seventeen-year-old student. I'd tried to help Mrs Turner recognise the signs, follow the clues and find out for herself. I ought to feel happy about being right but I didn't. Happiness didn't make your insides feel like they were curdling - fear did. The kind of creeping fear that came when you knew you'd been right all along about someone you thought you could trust. Someone like Mrs Waters.

Unlike my old employer, Mrs Waters obviously wasn't sleeping with a seventeen-year-old, but she was up to something bad - something to do with the wood - and if my suspicions were correct, something to do with Lucinda

Hastings and Carl Maddock.

I thought about confiding in Grandma, but knew what she'd tell me to do. I could hear her words almost as if she was saying them to me out loud.

And I couldn't go to the police because I didn't have any proof of any wrongdoing.

What I could do was follow my nose. I had to know the truth, for Wren's sake more than anything else.

Chapter Twenty-Six

The snow was already an inch deep when I tramped across the moor back to the house. To make matters worse the wind had picked up, forcing the flakes into a near-horizontal stream.

My eyelashes were dripping when I entered the house, which struck me as too quiet and still. Silence hugged the walls. I shrugged off my coat and hung it on the stand.

The silence was short-lived. Noise in the form of Ping screaming my name cut it off like a tambourine clash. I looked up to see her panic-stricken face floating moonlike in the half-light of the landing.

She raced down the stairs. Sweat pasted her hair to the cheeks. She seized my arms in a pincer-grip and panted, "Have you seen them?"

"Who?"

"Odette and Wren."

"No. Why?"

"They gone. I go bathroom. Come back and -"

"Where've you looked?" I said scanning the hall and seeing all three doors closed.

"Everywhere. They not here."

"Have you looked down there?" I said pointing at the floor.

"Yes. Down, up. Whole house."

I could smell the sourness of fear on her breath. I grabbed my coat, a shrug and a scarf off the coat stand and hauled them on. "That means they're outside. Get your coat."

She ran upstairs and returned a few seconds later in her

coat and hat. I already had the door open. Snow blew inside and settled on the door mat. Wind whooshed into the room chilling the air, warning us to stay where it was warm and dry. Ping grabbed the umbrella from under the bucket. Forcing back the memory, I bit my lip and shook my head. "Too windy."

She dropped it and we hurried outside into the whirling snow.

Shielding my eyes, I scanned the enclosure. It was empty. I searched the snowy ground. No prints. I looked at the white moorland beyond. That also lay bare; a flawless white sheet, untouched by woman or boy. Both gates were topped with snow and swung wildly on their rusted hinges. Past the second fence raved the wood where the oak trees lurched into each other as if possessed by demonic spirits.

The arctic air seeped through my clothes into my flesh, telling me to move.

I pointed to the moorland behind the house and said, "You look over there. I'll look in the wood."

"You get lost."

"I won't." I whipped the scarf off my neck, ripped it and pulled on a blue thread. It unravelled. I looked at Ping, saw she understood and said, "If you find them, get two pans and smash them together. Hopefully I'll hear you."

"Be careful, Ivy. You not so bad."

She stomped around the back of the house with her head down, hand on her hat to stop it flying off. I carried on unravelling the scarf and crunched across the enclosure as fast as I could. Snow buffeted my body, pushing me to the left. I pushed back and ploughed on, knowing there wasn't much time. Wren had a fever and I doubted Odette had taken the time to wrap him up. If he was outside in this weather for too long he might catch pneumonia. A host of other terrible things could happen before that. He could be snared by one of Maddock's traps; fall and break his ankle;

or try to run away from Odette and get lost. If Odette wasn't familiar with the wood, the chances were high that she'd get them lost and they'd freeze or starve to death.

I set my eyes on the snow-flecked path. Fortunately, up to this point, the branches above had caught much of the snow, so the ground was patchy. I doubted Maddock would set a rabbit trap here, but the path broke off soon and then there would be a free-for-all. I'd need to be careful and keep checking the ground. Abruptly, I realised that when Mrs Waters had told me that the wood was dangerous, she must have been referring to the animal traps. Why she hadn't just explained that was another question.

I stopped just beyond the gate and shouted Odette's and Wren's names. Whistling wind tore at the trees and billowed through the gaps but no voices made it back to me. The light in the wood was the colour of sour milk and the trees drooped, heavy with snow. I turned, tied the end of the thread around the wooden post, and gave it a tug to make sure it was secure.

I entered the wood, eyes roving down, around, down, around, down, around. I hollered their names into the trees every few seconds. I knew in my heart that my voice was being swallowed by the wind, but carried on calling, repeating their names as loudly as I could until my voice broke. I looked back the way I'd come to check the blue thread. It ran like a vein through the wood from the gate to my hand. Once I left the path, this would get me back to safety.

Follow the blue cotton thread, follow the blue cotton thread, follow, follow, follow, follow, follow the blue cotton thread!

It was the maggots come to taunt me. Grandma would tell me I was crazy for doing this and she'd be right. But I had to help them. Mrs Waters and Maddock were too ill to come out in this weather. It was up to me and Ping to bring them home safely.

The path ended and the ground began to crawl with snowy roots and rocks. I screamed their names again and icy air tore at my throat. I listened to the wind, desperate to hear Wren's voice, but there was nothing human about the noise raging through the trees.

I picked up my pace, glancing down and around, down and around. Thought about the terrible howls I'd heard when I followed Mrs Waters in here. Since then, I'd tried to block them out and now, as I wandered further into the wood, they haunted my ears. It hadn't sounded human initially but the final scream had and now that I was here, I felt pain riding the wind.

Some sixth sense pulled my eyes through the snow and trees to a dark object some distance away partly obscured by an uprooted tree. I hurried toward it, forgetting to look down. The closer I got, the more distinct it became and I realised it was a building made of a similar stone to Fairwood House. The structure was the size of a small garage. In front of the building sat a tree stump speared by an axe. Scattered around the stump were splinters of wood. A pile of logs covered with snow. A rusty wheelbarrow. A metal bucket filled with half-frozen water.

I winced. It came again and I held my hand to my chest as stabbing pains attacked my breastbone…

I see the metal bucket, smell the sweet rot of fish. I feel like I can hear them - hundreds and hundreds of them, squirming and writhing and slithering against each other; talking to each other in their hideous, slippery voices.

I see him place the bucket on the ground in front of her knees. See him walk round to stand behind her. See his fingers grip her long blonde hair.

I hear the breath shudder out of her and I want to go to her. I want to save my mummy. Make him stop. But I can't. I never can.

He looks up and sees me. Smiles. Gives me a little wave.

I turn to run back into my bedroom but not before he does it -

"Fuck off!" I screamed to no-one.

I cringed and massaged my temples, knowing I couldn't afford to lose it. Wren's life was at risk. If I wasted time, he could die.

The maggots jeered and told me to *get a friggin' jiggy on*, which didn't make one bit of sense, but helped push me into action.

Flexing and unflexing my fingers, I took a deep, steadying breath and approached the building. There was one window on the left wall, its panes green with mould and mildew. Bars covered the window, reminding me of a prison cell. I walked closer to the cabin and peered inside. Behind the grimy glass hung blinds. The slats were drawn almost flat. It was too gloomy inside to make anything out. I walked back to the door, hopeful Wren and Odette were in there taking refuge from the snow. I tried the door handle but a padlock on rusty chains prevented entry. There was no way they could be in there.

I turned to leave the building, but a sound made me stop. An urgent tapping. It was close. I scanned the surrounding trees, saw no-one. The tapping continued accompanied by a muffled moan.

I listened harder and realised with prickling skin that the tapping and moaning were coming from the building.

Heart beating hard, I picked my way around the side of the cabin and walked right up to the window. Pressing my forehead to the grime-smeared glass, I peeked through the narrow gaps between the slats. An eye stared back at me. I pulled my face back and allowed my vision to adjust to the interior gloom. I could just about make out a man's face, eyes wide and urgent, a dark strip of something covering his mouth. The man's head began to jerk up and down and he moaned and moaned, eyes so wide they looked like they were going to pop out of his head.

"Don't worry," I said, somehow managing to sound

calm. Terror consumed me but my focus was needle-sharp. I ran over to the tree stump, shoved my boot on top and grabbed the handle of the axe. I pulled and it came out with surprising ease and I carried it across to the door.

The chain and padlock were crusty with rust. Aiming for the most rusted part, I smashed the axe down on the chain again and again and again. On the fourth strike, the chain broke and rattled to the ground. I dropped the axe, seized the door handle and yanked open the door, retching at the foul stench that wafted out. Sewers and rancid chicken. Human filth.

I tried not to think about what was causing the smell and stepped into the cabin.

The man appeared in front of me in the centre of what was clearly a containment cell. The room contained a single mattress, a bucket, two toilet rolls, a plastic bowl with an inch of brown water in it and a heap of dirty blankets and clothes. That was all. I looked at the man. Tear trails ran through the muck on his face and his eyes ran wild. Even through the grime I recognised him from his driving licence: Carl Maddock. Living and breathing, but only just, by the look of his gaunt face and concave stomach.

He shuffled toward me. His clothes were filthy, knees torn through. His hands and ankles were tied together and a terrible smell emanated from his body. He held out his wrists and jerked his head at the axe. I turned and picked it up. I placed the axe on the black cord that bound his wrists and gasped - two fingernails on his right hand had been pulled out.

He jerked his head as if to tell me to hurry. I began to saw through the cord with the axe, but he shook his head and motioned up and down, eyes fixed on the lethal edge. I didn't trust myself, but he nodded, telling me to do it. I took aim, held my breath and brought it down, whip-fast. The cord broke and he grabbed the axe off me and used it to cut the cord around his ankles before ripping the black belt down over his bottom lip to hoop his neck with such force I thought he was going to tear off his ears.

Without a word, he stumbled past me out of the cabin.

"Hey - wait!" I said. He couldn't just run off. He needed help. *I* needed to help him. I needed to find out why he'd been locked in there and who was responsible, but despite his fraught appearance his stumble grew to a run and he disappeared into the trees.

I grappled in my pocket for my phone, pulled it out with trembling fingers and checked for service. There wasn't any. Of course there wasn't.

I looked back the way I'd come, tracking the blue thread to where I'd dropped the scarf at the chopping block. I wanted desperately to follow that thread back to the kissing gate, sprint past the house and run out to just past the outer fence, where I'd get reception, call a taxi and be driven to safety, far away from here and the madness of this place. But there was Wren to think of. He was out here somewhere with Odette whose mind was little more than a child's.

No. I couldn't leave without Wren. I wouldn't. I had to be sure he was safe and I had to get him away from this place.

I turned to leave then stopped and turned back. I stared at the axe. Mrs Waters or Ping or Mason or maybe all three of them were guilty of locking up a human being and torturing him. There was no way I was wandering around without a weapon.

Snow already dusted the axe head. I bent over and seized the wooden handle. The axe felt good in my hand, its weight reassuring. I caught sight of my twisted face in its metal wedge and looked away, repelled by what I knew I'd do if forced. I'd done it before to protect my mum. I'd do it again to protect Wren if I had to.

I strode back to the scarf and headed deeper into the woods to find them.

Chapter Twenty-Seven

Snow slashed across my vision and the wind continued its bitter onslaught. Looking down, I saw that my fingernails were blue. But at least I had a full set of ten. Eight more than Carl Maddock. Still, I wouldn't be able to stay outside much longer if the wind kept up. But I had to keep going or Wren might die. There was no greater motivation than that. Though the grubs needled, I knew I wouldn't stop until I found him.

The wood became denser the further I trekked, the snow sparser on the ground, and the wind less vicious due to the closely packed trees which became both a blessing and curse; though they blocked the piercing wind, they also slowed me down. I weaved between them, steps careful and too slow, toes frozen beneath the thin leather of the boots Mrs Waters made me wear.

I approached another fallen oak. Something small and sharp had slipped inside my boot and it was beginning to hurt. Placing the rapidly shrinking scarf on my lap, I sat down on the fallen trunk and hooked my foot onto my left knee. I unlaced and yanked off the boot, tipped it upside down and watched a stone hit the mossy ground. Movement caught my eye and I looked past the stone. Beside a rock, lay a dead pheasant freckled with snow. Maggots writhed around in the beautiful bird's open belly.

A cold sweat broke out on my body and I stared at the throng of white worms, unable to move. My vision blurred black and I dug my nails into my palms as the memories thrust themselves forward. I closed my eyes against the squirming beasts but it was too late. The blacks of my eyelids weren't enough and I saw it happen all over again…

Mummy's on her knees in front of the bucket. She's crying. He's gripping the back of her head, laughing. He leans forward and whispers something in her ear that makes her eyes go wide.

She starts begging and saying she's sorry, but he's shouting over her, calling her horrible things, using words I know are wrong even though I've never heard them before.

I grip the banister and will her to fight back. And she does. She grabs at his arms and tries to pull them off her hair, but he's too strong. He laughs and smashes her cheek into the cabinet. She screams and her body goes floppy.

I open my mouth to yell at him to leave her alone, but fear has taken my voice. I feel warm liquid running down my legs and know I've wet myself. I begin to cry.

He releases her hair and grabs her chin, twists her head and kisses her on the mouth. She lets him, like she always does.

I feel like I can breathe again because it's all over now.

But it isn't.

With a cruel laugh, he grabs the back of her head again and pushes her face down into the bucket of maggots.

I begin to count, sure he'll let her go very quickly, sure no-one can be this cruel, but the seconds go on and on and on and on.

Mummy holds the sides of the bucket and struggles with all her might. But not for very long. Suddenly, her movements slow down and then her body stops moving altogether.

I stare at her body and pray for her to move. Silent tears stream down my cheeks. Mummy's dead. Mummy's dead. Mummy's dead. The words go around and around my head like horses on a zombie carousel.

He yanks her head out of the maggots and…

She's alive! She's dragging in huge gulps of air. Two white worms are stuck to her face and she tears at her cheeks, ripping them open to get the maggots off. And he's laughing at her. And then he's grabbing handfuls of the squirming mass and pinching her nose and shoving them down her throat, and she's choking.

Again, I think this is it. She's going to die. He's going to kill her.

But then he stops, kicks her to the ground. He stamps his foot into the bucket, crushing the slimy grubs to a paste. He seizes Mummy's hair, yanks back and smears the half-dead goo onto her cheeks. She's sobbing.

I am too. I look down. My certificate is scrunched up in my fist, the beautiful black writing smudged beyond recognition. I realise that things will never be the same again.

He lets her face flop to the floor. With a wink at me, he leaves.

As I watch Mummy suck air into her lungs, I think I'm lucky. He let her breathe again – he let my mummy live.

But deep down I know living isn't the right word for it. Mummy's eyes might open and shut, and her body might still work, but nothing will work properly on the inside, not after this.

*

The snow had stopped and the wind had died.

Shivering all over, I avoided looking in the direction of the dead pheasant, gathered the remains of the blue scarf and tugged on my boot. With numb fingers, I picked up the axe.

The wood lay still, the quiet unbroken by man or beast. I called Wren's name several times but there was no response. With a heavy sigh, I got up and moved on, threading the cotton through the trees. I looked left and right, horrified to note the daylight souring, unable to believe dusk had come so soon. How long had I been out? It couldn't have been that long, could it?

My bones felt brittle beneath my skin as if they were about to snap. My mind fought to return to the past, but this time self-control triumphed and turned my inner eye to Wren and pictured him working on his models; Wren foraging; Wren running and smiling; Wren and I escaping this place together.

I reached a swamp and halted. A keening whimper made

me look to the right. I followed the sound and saw a red deer lying on its side with its eyes closed. It sensed me – I could tell because its nostrils began to flare and its chest rose and fell faster, but it didn't try to get up. It was in too much pain. I looked at its hind legs and saw the cause: a steel trap clamped down on the poor creature's bone. Blood matted its fur and turned the underlying moss brown. Froth webbed the animal's lips. It tried to raise its head then slumped back. Its keening intensified and blood trickled out of its mouth. It was dying, suffering. I knew it wouldn't survive.

I looked at the axe.

The deer opened its eyes and stared at me. It whimpered and pawed the ground.

I looked at the axe again. Thought about Wren and Odette. There was no time.

The deer coughed and more blood trickled past its lips.

I looked away from its pained face. Didn't give myself time to think. Heart tearing in my chest, I took aim then swung. Up, down. Alive, dead.

I checked it was dead. It was.

Breath rushed out of me and I stumbled forward and threw up in the swamp, the surface of which was edged with a grey film. I sucked in sharp breaths to fight the nausea, but it was no good. Another wave came and I vomited again and again until there was nothing left to bring up. Wiping my mouth with the back of my hand, I slumped back onto my bum and blinked out tears. My sick floated on top of the foul water adding to its stench. If only Ralph could see me now…

Tummy calmer, I made to push myself up, but something in the murky liquid caught my eye. Something solid and large beneath the sludge and grime. On my hands and knees, I reached for a stick and picked it up then stretched out my arm and prodded the object. It was heavy. It barely moved. I prodded again with more force, making it dunk lower into the foul water then bob up to the surface.

Something rose out of the swamp. The toe of a boot - a brown boot just like mine.

My heart pounded. I crawled alongside the swamp and positioned myself opposite the shoe. If I lay on my chest and stretched forward, I could grab the boot. Compelled by some morbid desire, I reached out. I had to stretch so much that I felt the skin and muscle under my arm burn, but I managed to hook my fingers around the toe end. Gripping tightly, I dragged the boot to the edge of the swamp then, using my remaining strength, heaved it up and onto the bank.

The boot was attached to a leg. A leg that was purple, swollen and covered by a ripped stocking. Its partner, also attached to a leg, surfaced as well. Both shoes were brown ankle boots. Victorian style. *Just like mine.*

The rest of the body remained under the scummy water – I could see it bulging there, an inch beneath the foam, bloated and rubbery as a dead seal.

I pushed myself to my feet and stared down at the legs, reminded weirdly of the wicked witch crushed by the house in *The Wizard of Oz.* The maggots' voices drifted upward. For once, they were melancholy, as if sharing my distress.

Someday I'll wish upon a star
And wake up where the clouds are far behind me
Where troubles melt like lemon drops...

I choked back a sob. This person's *dreams* had melted like lemon drops. There wasn't any rainbow left for this person, just the harsh finality of death and a pair of black horses braying the way to doom.

My stomach clenched. I knew what I had to do and the maggots murmured their agreement. They needed to know who it was as much as I did.

My heart seemed to stop as I leaned over, seized both boots and dragged the body out of the swamp. Unable to look directly at it, I kept dragging until my peripheral vision told me the whole corpse was on the bank. I allowed myself a split-second glance up. The body was bloated and grey and definitely female.

There was no doubt in my mind now as to who it was. It was the old nanny; my predecessor, Lucinda Hastings. It had to be.

I doubled over as all of my suspicions and fears collided.

Lucinda was dead, Ping and Maddock knew about it and Mrs Waters was a lying, scheming psychopath. If I didn't get Wren out of here, we were both going to be in big trouble.

Chapter Twenty-Eight

Night wrapped itself around the woods. Bats twitched and darted in the gloom above my head, flying so low I had to duck. My fingers shook and my heart slammed; the scarf was almost at its end and the weather was vicious again, blustering with such force that the trees folded and thrashed against the wind. Branches creaked and shook. Any moment one might fall and crush me and then what good would I be to Wren?

I stopped. I couldn't see further than a yard ahead. Thoughts of turning back leaked into my mind. I could go and get help. I had my phone. All I had to do was retrace my footsteps, sneak past the house and make it to where I'd get reception. I could call the police and they'd be here in moments. They'd hunt for Wren and Odette, find them and arrest Mrs Waters, Maddock and Ping. It seemed crazy that I hadn't thought of this before.

I turned around and blundered back the way I'd come, struggling to feel the fine thread with frozen fingers. At the swamp, I began to count so I could tell the police roughly how many steps it was to the body. It was slow progress. I made it to the stone cabin and carried on. At the kissing gate, I saw the house aglow with lanternlight and heard the smash of pans.

Ping had found them.

Shit. Mrs Waters had Wren.

It would be hard to sneak past the house without Ping seeing me, unless I waited in the wood for ages and then risked it, but…what if something happened to Wren in the meantime? What if Mrs Waters was angry at him for leaving the house and decided to act on her rage?

There was only one option: pretend. Put on a show. Lie. I had to get Wren out of the house without them seeing us. I couldn't leave him. Which meant I had to go back inside, with them, and wait for the right time to act.

Leaving the scarf on the ground, I hurried across the moor to the house where Ping continued to create an awful cacophony in her effort to tell me she'd found them. I wondered again how involved she and Maddock were. It seemed crazy that Maddock would know about his own flesh and blood being locked inside the cabin and let it carry on, but he had to know, didn't he? It didn't seem possible to hide something like that for long. Had Lucinda found out and tried to run? Was that why they'd killed her? What if Wren knew as well? What if he and Odette had stumbled across the cabin too? Was Mrs Waters evil enough to kill a child?

Visions played havoc with my mind and the maggots piped up telling me to run, leave Wren, save myself. But they were brutal beasts. They came from cruelty. I wasn't cruel and I wasn't a coward.

I froze.

The axe. I'd left it in the wood. I should have brought it with me, just in case.

I looked back toward the black trees.

"IVY! THEY OKAY!" It was Ping. I glanced over; she'd seen me.

"That's great. What a relief," I said, closing the distance between us, stomach tight.

"You lip blue. You okay?" she said ushering me inside. She closed and locked the front door, pocketing the key in her apron.

"I'm fine. Where's Wren?"

"Bedroom."

"I'll go check on him," I said dashing past her.

I took the stairs two at a time and hurried along the

corridor. If I could get Wren and sneak him out of the house before Mrs W –

Mrs Waters was pacing the floor in Wren's room with hands on her hips dressed in a red dressing gown. Wren was curled up in bed fast asleep. She rushed across the room and drew me into her. I hoped she couldn't feel the urgent hammering of my heart through my coat.

"Thank goodness you're back," she said.

A faint smell of vomit wafted around her. I let her hold me for a second then pulled away and glanced at Wren.

"What happened?"

Mrs Waters looked exhausted. It was hard to picture her hurting anyone, let alone torturing an innocent man. She slumped down on the bed, stared at her knees and began to weep. I stared down at her, repelled mostly, but feeling something else as well. Her tears seemed genuine, her feelings real.

She peered up at me. In my adult life, I'd never seen a person look so drained and hopeless. It was like she'd transformed from a beautiful rose to a dead leaf in the space of a day. In that instant, she reminded me of my mum. She looked broken. And utterly helpless.

She looked at me imploringly and said, "All I want is for her to get better. For her to be well. Happy and well and at peace. Stress makes it worse. That's why I decided to keep the child from her. But I'm beginning to think I've made a dreadful mistake. What if I've made her worse? They – Ping and Maddock - tried to tell me, but I wouldn't listen."

"And what about Wren? What do you want for him?" I said, unable to stifle my anger at her total lack of consideration for Wren and what her actions had done to him.

She frowned up at me. "What about him? He's not Odette."

She looked at the window.

I followed her gaze, saw my reflection in the black glass.

Our eyes met and she looked away first, bent her head and began to pick at her thumbnail. Her hair was greasy and lank. It fell forward hiding her eyes. She said, "I'm afraid you wouldn't understand. It's better this way, trust me."

I rolled my tongue around my mouth. *Trust her? I'd rather trust a cobra.* I tried to think of a way to make her leave the room.

She groaned and dragged her hands down her cheeks pulling at her eyes and skin.

In my ears, the crawlers began to wail. Dizziness swept behind my eyes. I leaned my shoulder against the wall and watched her. She didn't seem to want to leave the room. Somehow, some way, I had to make her leave.

"Are you worried about him?" I said glancing at Wren.

"No. I just don't trust him. I'm worried he might run away. Odette said things to him – things she shouldn't have said."

"What sorts of things?"

She looked at the window again, but this time I didn't follow her gaze. She seemed to be trying to work out how to answer me. She tore off a cuticle, drawing blood. She didn't seem to notice what she'd done.

"Odette's very confused and she likes to play make believe. Sometimes she lies." She snapped her head around. "She hasn't said anything strange to you has she?"

I felt her eyes boring into mine and looked at my boots, unable to hold her gaze. "No. Nothing."

"Really, Ivy?"

"Yes. I mean, no. She hasn't said a word to me. I've barely seen her."

"That's strange," Mrs Waters said, wiping her eyes. "Because Odette told me she went into your room one night."

There was a subtle edge in her voice. It was the first time

she'd looked dangerous. She slipped her thumbnail into her mouth and began to suck the blood. With her skin so pale she made me think of vampires and blood and guts. I imagined poor Lucinda in the room, her ghost hovering beside me, lips mouthing something I needed to know. I blinked and she was gone. The maggots caterwauled and danced like loons, drumming their fists against my skull in a hellish beat, desperate to be heard, to be released.

"Actually, she did come to my room. I didn't say anything because I didn't want to get her in trouble."

"Don't you think you should tell me something like that?"

"I'm sorry. I thought -"

"Don't be sorry. Just tell me next time, okay?"

"I will."

"She also told me she spoke to you in the hall. Is that so?"

"Yes. She wanted Wren."

"And you let her carry him up the stairs?"

I nodded.

"Why did you do that when I've explicitly told you to keep the child away from her?" Her voice was pure ice.

The maggots screeched so shrilly I winced. "Something she said made me realise he was her son, and there was this need in her eyes. This desperation to hold him. I know it was wrong but I couldn't stop myself. And she was so happy when I gave him to her – you should've seen her."

Mrs Waters looked down at her lap and yanked a loose thread off the cord of her dressing gown. She raised the thread to her mouth and angled her head as if contemplating the mysteries of loose threads. She stood up, drifted over to the fire, knelt in front of the grate and stared into the flames.

I glanced at Wren. He was still asleep, lying unbelievably still.

She sighed. "I know you felt you were doing the right

thing by letting her hold him, but that was the catalyst that set her off."

I didn't say anything. I wiped my palms on my coat. I was too hot but I needed to keep it on for the moment we made our escape.

"I thought you were perfect," she said, "I still think you're wonderful, but you must, must, *must* obey the rules."

"I'm sorry. I won't do it again."

She turned and smiled at me. "It's fine, dear. I'm just relieved you're okay. And Odette will get over this stumbling block. It'll take time, but time, I have."

"And Wren?" I said, "He must know now that Odette's his mother."

She yawned so hard her jaw cracked. Strangely, on the crack of her jaw, the maggots silenced. She rose to her feet and walked over to the bed. Perching halfway up, she reached out for Wren's face. I tensed and stepped forward, terrified she was going to hurt him. Her fingers hovered above his hair, quivering and white. After a moment, she stood and headed for the door.

"Do you mind staying with him?" she said placing a hot hand on my shoulder, "I think I need to go back to bed."

I forced myself not to flinch at her touch. My heart skipped at her words. This was it. She was leaving me alone with him.

"Of course," I said.

"And Ivy," she said, pausing at the door.

"Yes?"

"Thank you for being so kind to Odette."

Chapter Twenty-Nine

I hurried over to the bed and smoothed Wren's hair back from his forehead. He was burning up. I wondered if Ping had given him any medicine yet. Probably not.

"Ivy?" Wren's eyes were wide open. "I wasn't asleep. I was pretending."

I smiled to hide my shock.

"How're you feeling?" I said helping him sit up.

He shrugged. "Weird."

"It's okay. You need to do exactly what I tell you -"

"I need to tell you now," he said, brow furrowed, eyes moist.

"Tell me what?"

"I lied before. I lied to the police officer."

I helped him stand and hurried to the wardrobe. "That's okay. It doesn't matter. You can tell me all about that later, but we need to -"

"But it was about Lucinda," he whispered.

I looked back at him, hands frozen on his coat, "What about her?"

"I should've told him, but I didn't want to get her in trouble."

"Told him what?"

Wren's eyes filled. "Told him that it was her. The lady in the picture. Her hair was a different colour and it was really long, but it was her."

"What?" I said taking a moment to process what he was saying, "Are you saying that Beatrice Giles is Lucinda?"

They all knew. Maddock, Ping, Mrs Waters. They'd all lied to Sergeant Zachery. All of them knew Lucinda/Beatrice was dead. The horror of it sent another lash of dizziness whipping behind my eyes. I steadied myself against the wall as image after image bombarded me and the reality hit: I'd been living with a pack of murderers. Why hadn't they killed me yet? Was it because they still thought I didn't know about Carl?

With quivering hands, I grabbed his coat and hurried over to him. "Hey. It's okay. You wanted to protect her. We can tell the policeman when we get out of here."

He looked up, puzzled.

"We need to leave. Now," I said helping him into his coat.

"We do?"

"Yes. I'll explain everything later. But right now, I need you to let me carry you downstairs and out of the house. Okay?"

He glanced around the room. His eyes landed on his house model. "Can I bring my models?"

I shook my head. "I can't carry them too and we need to be quick."

I picked him up, bent over, grabbed the cuddly bee from the bed and tucked it between our chests. He wrapped his arms around my neck and buried his face in my shoulder.

"I'm scared," he said.

"Don't be scared. Everything'll be fine. Trust me."

I opened the door and peered out. The corridor was dimly lit by candles and as silent as the grave. I inched out of the room, pulling the door but not shutting it, then crept along the corridor. There was no time to grab any of my stuff and besides, carrying Wren across the snowy moor to the outer fence was going to be hard-going as it was. I was exhausted from searching the wood. Hungry too. And I wasn't very strong. I knew I could carry Wren to the outer fence though. I had to. He was in no fit state to walk let alone run. And as soon as we left the house, running would be essential.

Though I tried to place my feet gingerly, the floorboards creaked. I didn't pause, didn't slow. At the top of the stairs, I looked down into the gloomy valley below, half-expecting Mrs Waters to charge out of her room and grab my neck or Maddock to come out and see me, lunge forward and knock Wren and me down the stairs in his effort to stop us. I saw myself at the bottom, body twisted, Wren crushed beneath my cracked ribs. I blinked and the vision cleared but not before the maggots began to sing, their voices shrill and taunting. *Run, run as fast as you can, you can't beat me, I'm the maggot-pie man!*

Head clanging, I grabbed the banister with one hand and wrapped my free arm around Wren's back.

"Hold tight," I said.

He shivered against me.

I rushed down the steps, wincing with every sound. At the bottom of the stairs, I grabbed the lantern off the round table then dashed to the bucket. By now, I was sure Ping would've gone outside and locked the fences. I bent over, back straining with the effort, lifted and slid the bucket backward. The spare keys were there. Sighing with relief, I grabbed them and fumbled to find the front door key. The keys slipped out of my hand and hit the floor with a clatter.

"What you doing?" Ping said.

I looked around to see her standing in the dining hall doorway.

I glanced down at the keys then up at her face. She took several steps toward me, eyes on Wren. Wren's body hardened against mine. I could feel the pacing of his heart on my breast. I held him tighter.

"He's really sick," I said, "I need to get him to the hospital."

"You ask Mrs Water?" she said taking another step.

I nodded, forcing myself to meet her eyes. Her face

relaxed and she patted Wren's head, bent over and plucked the keys off the ground. She unlocked the door and handed me the ring of keys. She passed me the lantern.

"I already lock fence. Snow stop but take careful. You good lady, Ivy."

"Thanks Ping." She was horribly close to me, so close I could feel her lies vibrating in the air around us.

I darted past her into the cold night, relieved she hadn't offered to walk with me. As soon as I got to the outer fence, I could call the police.

Crunching across the snow-frosted heather, I framed what I was going to say to the person who answered my call. Address: Fairwood House, Weirlock, top of the hill; reason: found a body and a man locked up in the wood; Ivy Smith and Wren Waters. Was that the best order to tell things in? Address then reason then names? Or should it be reason, address, names? Did I need to start by stressing how urgent the situation was – would the person on the other end of the line sit up and listen and react more quickly if I mentioned the dead girl in the woods first?

I looked down. Wren was asleep. I felt his saliva on my neck. He was a hot water bottle covering my torso so I barely felt the cold, but icy sweat licked my armpits. I glanced back. The house stood there, windows glowing like cats' eyes, smoke curling out of the chimneys like breath, its inhabitants too close.

I reached the first gate and unlocked it with a shaking hand. This time I managed not to drop the keys. The iron gateway squealed like a stuck pig. I didn't bother locking it. Speed was more important than pretense, and I wasn't going back. I hurried across the moor straining to see the outer fence, but the lanternlight didn't carry far.

Wren became heavier and heavier and my lower back whined at the weight pressing on my spine. I wanted to shift him to my right hip, but didn't want to wake him. The less he knew about all of this the better. If he was asleep his fear would retract and he'd recover more quickly from this trauma in the years to come. I wondered what they'd do with him. He'd probably be put into the adoption system and end up being fostered with different families throughout his childhood. The thought was horrible. An idea came to me, warm and comforting as buttered toast; I could try to adopt him and become his guardian. It would be a lengthy, difficult process, but maybe, just maybe, I could make it happen. No. I *would* make it happen. In the short time we'd known each other, we'd formed a bond. Wren trusted me and though it was too soon to say I loved him, I definitely felt the stirrings of a strong attachment and a horrid, sinking feeling when I thought about abandoning him to a bunch of strangers.

Thoughts of taking Wren into my care and giving him a loving, safe home buoyed me above my fear and I walked with more energy, the lantern swinging at my side spilling light into the darkness. In a matter of minutes, the police would be here and we'd be home-free, away from these atrocious people.

I could see the iron gate. I ran the last few steps. Placing the lantern on the ground, I swapped the keys into my free hand and jammed the key in the padlock.

I felt a presence behind me and glanced back.

Maddock ran toward us swinging a lantern. "Don't fuckin' move!"

Breath frantic, I turned the key in the padlock. Wren clung to me, pulling on my neck. The padlock clicked and I shoved open the metal gate, but Maddock grabbed my hood before I could take a step. He yanked me back and Wren gasped and fell to the ground.

Maddock seized my arm. I tried to twist out of his grasp, but his fingers hooked into my flesh like one of his snares. He gave my arm a hard yank and I nearly threw up from the pain.

"Wren. Get here," he said, "Nanny's doin' a bad thing. You need to come back to the house with me right now."

Wren glanced at me then up at Maddock. He looked terrified. I stopped struggling, haunted by Wren's expression, knowing there was no way I could get out of Maddock's grip without losing an arm.

"Good girl," Maddock wheezed. "Now, we're going to walk back to the house in a calm, orderly fashion." He tugged me close and said in my ear, "Be a good girl and we won't hurt you."

Chapter Thirty

The maggots went to town; taunting, teasing, stabbing, gnawing, dragging their greasy, white bodies down the sides of my brain like nails down a blackboard.

Every step closer to the house, my feet grew heavier, my heart harder. I knew that if Wren and I were going to survive I couldn't surrender to the beasts savaging my mind.

Maddock locked the inner gate and shoved the key in his pocket then pulled me roughly across the enclosure. Wren walked a couple of paces behind. When Maddock paused at the front door, I gave Wren what I hoped was a reassuring smile.

"In," Maddock said gesturing for Wren to enter first.

He dragged me into the house and locked the door, never loosening his grip on my arm, which I knew would be purple when I got the chance to look. *If I got the chance.*

Ping stood at the foot of the stairs staring at the floor.

"Take the boy to his room and stay with him," Maddock said.

Ping nodded, marched forward, grabbed Wren's wrist and tugged him up the stairs. Wren looked back at me, eyes wide, face white.

"He needs medicine," I called.

Ping slowed for a split second but didn't look back. She ran up the stairs, forcing Wren to run too. When the sound of their steps faded, Maddock locked the front door and pocketed the key. The keys I'd used were still in the padlock of the outer gate. I wondered how many sets of keys were in the house.

Maddock jerked me toward the living room.

"What are you going to do to me?" I said trying to make my voice strong.

"That's up to Mrs Waters, not me."

"Please help me, Maddock. You're not a bad guy. I know you don't want any of this."

Maddock stopped and snapped, "This is all your own doin'. If you'd just kept well away, you'd have been fine. Instead you had to go sneakin' round, stickin' your nose in like Nancy Drew."

He opened the living room door and shoved me inside. The fire was dwindling, shrouding the room in shadow and casting the ballerinas' silhouettes as black bodies on the cream walls.

"Get as many cushions and blankets as you can carry," he said letting go of my arm.

I scowled at him but began collecting. I grabbed the plum blanket off the chaise longue, another two off Mrs Waters' armchair and three cushions. There were more cushions to be had but I couldn't carry anything else. I turned to face him, arms wide with the load. "What are these for?"

He seized my arm and led me out of the room across the hall where the shadows piled on top of each other, reminding me of the pile of dead sheep I'd seen at a knacker's yard as a child. Mum's boyfriend had worked there for a short stint before getting fired for apparently 'having too much fun on the job'. Was Maddock having too much fun too? I looked up at his face. His chin was set. The vein in his temple pulsed.

He led me into the dining hall where flames licked the flute like serpents' tongues. I felt my own tongue loosen. Unable to stop myself I said, "Imagine if I was Ping. Imagine someone doing this to her. I'm a person too. I've got feelings. Impulses. I'm sorry I stuck my nose in where it didn't belong, but -"

"Be quiet."

"Please. This isn't right. You know it isn't. But if you own up now, tell the police she forced you -"

"Shut it or I'll make you." He yanked my arm so roughly I gasped but, despite the pain, I kicked his ankle as hard as I could. He started as if bitten by a snake, whirled round and pulled me onto my tiptoes so that our noses were only inches apart. "Do that again and you'll give me no choice."

He dragged me across the dining hall and I stumbled along beside him, dread rising like water in a cave as he pushed me into the kitchen.

He headed for the trapdoor and my stomach turned to lead.

"No. Please don't."

"Sorry, but you haven't given us much choice."

He wouldn't meet my eyes. I stared at the trapdoor, maggots keening.

"Maddock, you don't have to do this. Look, I won't say a word to anyone. I like all of you. I'm sure you're only doing what you think's best. Hey – you could let me go? Tell Mrs Waters I escaped? I promise I won't say a word."

He snorted and shoved me closer to the trapdoor.

"On your bike," he said, pulling a lantern off the shelf. He pushed me against the table then stood an inch away while he lit the lantern. I could feel his body heat radiating from his damp shirt. Sweat dripped down his cheeks and his chest heaved up and down as he tried to breathe. He hacked out a wheezy cough and, though it hit the air above my head, I smelt the sour stink of his breath as it floated down. I found myself wishing he'd have an asthma attack; and pictured myself giving him a swift kick in his gut before running away.

"Please -" I said.

"Drop that stuff."

Obediently, I let the blankets and cushions fall from my arms. He handed me the lantern, gave me a stern look then turned to the sink and grabbed a glass from the cupboard. He filled it with water and handed that to me as well. I thought about smashing him in the jaw with the lantern and chucking water in his eyes, but before I could make up my mind to do it, he grabbed the back of my neck and dug his fingertips in so hard that shocks of pain shot into the base of my skull.

"Open it," he said, pushing me to my knees.

Unable to balance properly or ease my fall, I dropped heavily onto the stone floor and winced at the pain. Glaring up at him, I placed the glass on the ground and stared at the bronze handle.

"Maddock, please don't do this. There are rats down there and -"

"And how d'you know that I wonder?" he said raising an eyebrow. "Do it."

His fingers dug in further. The pain was unbearable. I turned the handle and raised the heavy door, letting it slam against the ground.

"Go," he barked.

I gave him one more pleading glance but he shook his head and pressed his boot into my spine. Trying not to cry, I moved onto my bottom, picked up the glass of water and shuffled toward the hole. Water slopped onto the floor but at that moment I didn't care; all I cared about was how long they were going to keep me down there. Giving me water suggested they didn't want me to die - not yet, anyway.

Inhaling a final breath of clean air, I descended the steps on my bottom, using my heels against the next step to drive me forward and down as my hands weren't free.

Darkness below swallowed the light from above. The blankets and cushions tumbled onto my head and I jumped, spilling more water. The trapdoor slammed, sending a wave of cold air onto my neck. I heard the key crunch, click, scrape as Maddock withdrew it from its chamber. I visualised him shoving the key in his pocket with his thick fingers. Pictured him blowing out the candles on the shelves then leaving the kitchen to go upstairs and lie down in his nice warm bed. Pictured the two of them – Ping and Maddock – discussing me in low voices, and Mrs Waters sitting on Odette's bed, stroking her hair.

Lastly, I pictured Wren all alone in his bedroom without anyone to hug him and tell him everything was going to be okay.

It was then and only then that I allowed tears to fall.

Chapter Thirty-One

The only thought that pulled me out of immobilising hopelessness was the realisation that they wouldn't kill Wren. Mrs Waters had let him live this long. She might not have given him a loving environment, but she'd made sure he was fed and clothed. She'd let him build his models and insisted he have an hour outside every day. She'd talked about sending him to school, so she clearly wanted him to have a future. And unlike me, Wren didn't know what they'd done to Lucinda and it was clear he had no idea about the man I'd let out of the cabin. Mrs Waters might begin to worry I'd told Wren about Lucinda, but I could tell her otherwise - if she ever let me out of here.

I wondered if I should've told Maddock that I'd let his relative out. He might have been so grateful to me for doing what he couldn't – for whatever reason that was – that he'd have let me go. But I had this odd feeling that he knew and he didn't want him let out. How could he live here for so long and not know? And why would a man his size and strength not take action? The only plausible explanation was that Mrs Waters had some kind of hold over him, but that didn't ring true either – Maddock had praised her to the skies. Unless he'd been acting. If so, he was a bloody good actor. I didn't know him well enough to know if he was bright enough to pull off such a convincing show. I was inclined to think he wasn't. Ping seemed the sharper of the two.

Remembering how she'd averted her gaze from mine when Maddock had dragged me into the house gave me a spark of hope. Maybe she was another victim in all of this. Maybe she was here against her own will. But she seemed genuinely fond of Mrs Waters too – intimidated yes, but according to her past she owed Mrs Waters a huge amount for saving her from a life of enforced prostitution.

Whichever way I looked at it, I couldn't convince myself Maddock or Ping were swayable. Their loyalties lay with Mrs Waters through and through, so any attempt to persuade them to help me would be futile.

But that didn't mean I wouldn't give it a go. If I got the chance to talk to Ping alone, I'd try. The worst she could do was tell Mrs Waters, and Mrs Waters probably already knew what she was going to do to me.

They hadn't killed me yet though, which meant there was still a chance I could survive this, and in order to survive I had to cling on to the little things, like the fact Maddock had given me water, light and blankets. That had to mean something good, didn't it?

The maggots didn't seem to think so.

One, two, three, four, five,
Once I caught a fish alive,
Six, seven, eight, nine, ten,
Then I stabbed it with my pen.
Why did you stab it so?
Because it saw the body, oh!

Chapter Thirty-Two

Like fear, the cold worked its way into my veins and settled. I shuffled down to the final step and placed the lantern on the ground. I sipped a little water, placed the glass beside the lamp then made my way back up the stone steps for the cushions and blankets. I carried them down, dropped the cushions on the floor then wrapped the blankets around my shoulders, picked up the lantern and glass and inched my way past the food shelves toward the dirty mattress I'd seen before. I wasn't tired but the time would come when I needed some shuteye and, disgusting though it was, I'd have to use the mattress as a bed.

For now, I placed the lantern and glass beside the thin pillow then walked back to get the cushions. I carried them back to the mattress, took one blanket off my shoulders and covered the bed with it before arranging the three cushions on top so that they stood up against the stone wall providing me with a clean, soft backrest. Positioning myself on the bed, I leaned into the cushions and exhaled one long shivery breath into the rank air. It wouldn't take long for me to get used to the smell; soon it would sink into my skin and hair and I'd hardly notice it at all, but for now, the smell was enough to make me retch. I yanked my coat over my nose and mouth, which helped a bit. My eyes began to adjust to the gloom and I strained to see what lay beyond Carl Maddock's backpack. Last time I'd been here, I hadn't searched the whole space. There was no need to now, but curiosity and the need for distraction made me push myself to my feet.

Wary of spiders and rats, I held the lantern low to the ground and scanned every inch of floor before I stepped on it. I didn't look up and kept my head bowed, fearful of the nasty creatures that hovered in the ceiling.

Shuffling past Maddock's bag, I remembered how I'd felt before when I'd found his stuff. The sunglasses, book and sweet wrappers lay where I'd left them. I picked up the book; if I was here for a while, something to read might be the only thing that kept me sane. I had little interest in guns but reading something was better than sitting alone for hours and hours with nothing to do but think about what was going to happen to me. I tossed the book onto the mattress and carried on walking.

After another few steps, the orb of lanternlight revealed I'd reached the end of the room. I approached the stone wall, neck tingling. A black canister of spray paint with a red band beneath the muzzle lay on the ground. I picked it up and shook it, found it empty. I replaced the can on the flagstones and lifted the lantern to head height, shocked to find the wall smothered with graffiti.

The left side of the wall was painted with an enormous comic strip composed of six squares.

Square one showed a man buying a gun from another man. The caption under the picture said *Once upon a time, there was a man who bought a gun.*

Square two showed the same man standing in front of a police station.

Square three had the man climbing a tree with the gun slung over his back.

Square four had him lying on his front on a branch, gun aimed down at a group of police officers heading toward the station.

Square five was a close up of the gun in a pair of hands, a bullet exploding from it with a BANG! bubble beside.

Square six showed five figures lying in puddles of blood,

each wearing a police uniform. To the right of the dead police officers was written: *They all lived happily ever after. The End.*

I looked away, sickened by the twisted mind that had imagined this death mural.

On the other side of the wall, I saw another ghastly image: a drawing of a gnarly tree with a woman hanging by a rope. Under the picture in capital letters were the words DING DONG THE WICKED WITCH IS DEAD. I moved closer to the woman's face. The likeness was unquestionable. It was Mrs Waters.

Underneath her hanging corpse, the artist – if you could call him that – had signed his name. *Carl Maddock.*

I didn't know how to feel about the picture, especially now I knew Maddock's relative was a sadistic bastard who fantasized about killing police officers – if indeed, it was a fantasy. Please, I begged to no-one in particular - *please* let it be a hideous desire he'd never acted on and never would.

I'd let him out. I'd set that monster free.

I thought back to his face, his eyes. He hadn't seemed evil at all, just desperate and scared. But you could never truly tell what was going on in someone else's mind.

Was that why they'd locked him up? Because they knew what he was planning? Maybe he'd gotten drunk and confessed or maybe he'd kept a notebook and they'd found his plans - but why, if that was the case, hadn't they turned him in? Why take justice into their own hands and lock him up rather than call the police and let them deal with him? It didn't make sense. Unless he had some kind of hold over them...

I turned my back on the wall and paced the length of it with my lip snagged between my teeth. They'd killed Lucinda. She can't have been evil too. The only thing that made any sense was that Lucinda found out about the man locked up in the cabin and tried to go to the police; what he'd possibly been planning to do was one of the most depraved acts imaginable, but that didn't mean Mrs Waters could deal out her own form of punishment. I expected Lucinda was just like me; she'd found out and tried to run, and just like me, they'd caught her. Then they'd killed her. So why hadn't they killed me?

Just because they haven't yet, doesn't mean they won't.

"Shut up!" I screeched.

I stilled, heart pounding. I'd spoken back to the maggots again.

Afraid of what that might mean, I grabbed the lantern and hurried back to the mattress and pulled the blankets up over my head as if that would stop their chant, but it only made them worse. I tossed and turned and pressed my hands to my temples, grinding my teeth and willing them to stop but their voices grew louder and louder.

Twinkle, twinkle little star
You have come so very far
Up above the world so high
Like a lamb you're gonna die.

Chapter Thirty-Three

I had no watch to tell me the time and no window to indicate sunset or sunrise. The glass of water was empty and I was thirsty and unable to sleep, so my perception of time was probably off but it felt like I'd been down here for days.

I emptied my bladder in the glass then moved the container to the other end of the room.

For who knows how long, I lay on the stinking mattress with my eyes wide open, terrified that if I did sleep, a rat would scuttle over and eat my tongue. I told myself it could be worse; I could be hypothermic, but the blankets and cushions - which I'd stuffed inside my coat – maintained my core temperature.

Hunger eventually drove me to the shelves at the bottom of the stairs. Every jar was clearly labelled in small, neat handwriting. Ping's no doubt. There were various types of pickle, from beetroot to pig's trotters – the latter of which looked like something you might pull out of an alien's brain. I dropped the jar of trotters back on the shelf. In my hurry I didn't put the jar down properly and it rolled onto the floor and smashed. Brine leaked, salting the air. The trotters lay there like limbs in the aftermath of a massacre.

I turned from the spilled trotters and grabbed a jar of pickled eggs. Grandma's favourite. I ate three and a half, cheered a little by how good they tasted, then shuffled back to the mattress. A second later, the trapdoor creaked and light spilled down the stairs. I gaped, dazzled by the light. Every muscle in my body tensed.

Maddock charged down the steps. "Come."

Guided by his lantern, I hurried to the foot of the stairs

and scrambled up the cold stones into the kitchen. Sunlight streamed in through the latticed windows. I winced and shielded my eyes.

Maddock grabbed my collar and shook me, making the cushions fall to the floor.

"Come on. She's waitin'," he barked.

Blinking tears from my eyes, I frowned up at Maddock, who released my coat and took hold of my arm more gently than before. He steered me out of the kitchen through the dining hall across the entrance hall. Pausing outside the living room, he said in a low voice, "Do what she wants and you'll be okay."

I glanced up, surprised by his warning. Questions teetered on my lips, but he opened the door and ushered me into the room.

Sunlight blasted in through the windows and the fire danced. Mrs Waters sat in her usual chair sipping tea, finger raised, ankles crossed. Her dress bagged around her chest and her cheekbones stuck out like razors. When she looked up at me, her expression was pained.

"Please leave us," she said.

Maddock nodded, rushing out of the room as if he couldn't leave quick enough.

She gestured for me to sit. I perched on the chair, folded my arms and stole a glance at the iron poker lying on the hearth. It was only four or five strides away.

"Would you like some tea?" she said.

I nodded. She shook the china bell and after a minute or so, Ping scurried in, picked up the teapot and filled a cup. Elderflower, just like before. Only this time, the air was stiff with the unsaid.

Ping walked over and handed me the cup. To my surprise, her eyes flicked up to mine. In their darkness, I saw concern. Concern for me or concern for herself, I didn't know. I took the cup and she hurried out of the room, closing the door with a long creak. Before she closed it, I glimpsed Maddock's broad back and realised that he was guarding the door. I glanced once more at the iron poker then pushed the idea to the back of my mind to join the maggots, who had begun to murmur.

I blew on the tea then sipped it. In spite of everything, my tongue tingled with pleasure.

"Good?" she said.

"Why did you lock me up?" I said.

"I'm sorry for doing that. You must understand it was a very last resort. Maddock didn't want to disturb me because I was so unwell so he made the call himself. While you were safely secured below, I had Maddock install a lock on your bedroom door, so you'll be able to return to your rooms once we're done here."

"Why lock me up at all? I don't get it."

She sipped her tea then replaced it on the tray. Patting her hair, she leaned forward. "How was your Grandma when you last spoke to her? Healthy, I hope?"

The conversation shift took me by surprise and I frowned at her. "Why are you changing the subject?"

"I expect she misses you a great deal. Who wouldn't miss such a sweet girl as yourself?" She nodded to herself, relaxed back into the armchair and said, "Yes, and I imagine you'd like to see her again?"

I stared, stomach hard. "What do you mean by that?"

She sipped her tea and stared at the space above my head. "I'm merely establishing a mutual desire. We both want you to see your grandma again."

"That's not exactly going to happen if you keep me locked up though, is it?"

"Keeping you locked up is the last thing I want to do, Ivy, believe me, but I have to take necessary precautions to protect everyone."

"Protect them from what?"

She ignored my question and said, "I simply need you to be patient and try your very hardest to trust me."

I bit back a cutting reply.

"It's very important you're honest with me now, okay?" she said.

I swallowed more tea, noticed the cup trembling and put it down.

"I need you to tell me why you lied to Ping. Why you told her I'd given you permission to take Wren to the hospital."

"He had a raging fever and I was really worried about him. I should've spoken to you first and got your permission but I didn't want to waste any time…or take the risk that you'd say no. How is he?"

Her eyes narrowed. "Fine. The medicine you bought worked wonders. He's in his room playing with his models as we speak."

"Can I see him?"

"Not yet, no." She eyeballed me. "If you tell me the truth this time, I'll let you see him."

She knew. She knew why I'd taken Wren and tried to run. The maggots began to wail.

"Tell you *what?*" I said, "There's nothing more to tell. He was really sick, so I took matters into my own hands. That's it."

She sighed and rearranged her skirt. The room fell silent. The air grew dense and unbreathable. Coal smoke drifted up the chimney. I shifted my weight, tried to believe I could talk myself out of this. There was no way she could know for sure that I'd seen the body.

Unable to bear the silence, I said, "There was no need to lock me up. I was only trying to help. I wasn't taking Wren away for good. Why would I? You've been so good to me. Wren's happy here. I don't understand why you think I was taking him away."

She shot to her feet and lunged forward. Grabbing my shoulders, she screamed, "You saw her - I know you did because Maddock followed you!"

I shook my head and tried to protest, but she grabbed my face and said in an achingly tired voice, "Ivy, listen, you have to trust me. I know you saw her, but it's not at all what you think. It was an accident."

Eyes stinging, I said, "I don't know what you're talking about." But my words were hollow. At least, I thought, she didn't know I'd freed that man from the cabin.

She let go of my face and turned her back on me. "It's alright, Ivy. I know why you took Wren and left, but it's not as straightforward as it seems."

"Tell me how it is then."

She sighed and turned away. I tensed as she walked over to my chair. She sat down and lay her fingers on my wrist. I wanted to whip my hand away but she removed hers before I could, slipped her thumbnail into her mouth and bit off a piece of skin.

"I thought you were so nice," I said, unable to steady my voice, "but you're a murderer. You're all murderers."

"You're quite mistaken," she said pulling me round to face her and wiping a tear from my cheek. "I'd *never* have hurt Lucinda. I loved her. She lived here with us for eight years. She was family, just like you."

"You mean *Beatrice*?" I said standing up and moving away to stand in front of the fireplace.

"Well yes, that was what she used to call herself before - "

"Before what? Before you took her hostage?

Mrs Waters shook her head and stared up at me. She looked vulnerable and small.

I noticed her eyes were wet and rolled my eyes. "I suppose you're going to tell me she was another one of your so-called rescue projects?"

"I wouldn't put it like that, but yes, in a way she was. She was homeless and when she asked for help, I took her in."

She said it so matter-of-factly it was hard to work out if she was lying. Ping opened the door and stepped into the room. "It true," she said looking at me.

Mrs Waters smiled at her. "Thank you, Ping."

Ping nodded. She gathered the tea things and hurried out of the room. Maddock pulled the door shut.

"We didn't kill her," Mrs Waters said.

"Then why's her bloated corpse out there floating in a swamp?"

"It was an accident. A terrible, terrible accident."

"If it was an accident, why didn't you report it to the police?"

Mrs Waters sat down in her chair and put her head in her hands. Abruptly, she looked up. "Maddock," she said, making me jump.

Maddock opened the door and lumbered into the room.

"Take Ivy to her room, please, and have Ping draw her a bath. She may see the child for five minutes before you lock her in."

"Yes, Mrs Waters."

I opened my mouth to speak but she left the room covering her face with one hand.

Maddock jerked his head for me to follow. I hesitated. I was close enough to grab the iron poker. I could plunge it into Maddock's gut then run upstairs, grab Wren and -

Maddock strode across the room and loomed over me, eyes driving into mine as if he could read my thoughts.

Obediently, I turned and left the room. In the hall I stopped at the foot of the stairs. Chills unfurled down my spine. Maddock pushed me forward.

Chapter Thirty-Four

Maddock stood in the doorway of Wren's bedroom staring at his shoes and whistling a jaunty tune. It was obvious he felt uncomfortable but was trying to pretend he didn't.

I wrapped my arms around Wren and felt his head, relieved to find his temperature normal. He pressed himself into me like a bear cub and I stroked his hair and inhaled the baby smell that still clung to his head. His fingertips dug into my back as if to say *don't go*.

Maddock cleared his throat to signal impatience. I longed to whip my head round and tell him to eff off, but didn't, knowing my loss of control would affect Wren. As it was, I knew he could sense the tension in the air. The entire house was thick with it. Tension radiated from our skin and slithered through the spaces between rooms. It stiffened our spines and clipped our tongues. There was no hiding the friction between us, and children were shockingly perceptive. They weren't versed in society's art of deception. They were primal little beings capable of sensing the truth behind adults' lies. In this case, the truth was so horrific that I hoped Wren never read between the lines and worked it out. Death had taken place in this house and I was under house-arrest.

No matter how Mrs Waters twisted it, Lucinda Hastings/Beatrice Giles was dead and they'd covered it up.

"Don't go," Wren said looking up at me with misty eyes.

I hesitated, turned to Maddock. "Can I stay here with Wren?"

Maddock shook his head and shifted his weight.

I blew out an angry breath and crouched in front of Wren. Holding him gently by the shoulders, I looked into his eyes and said, "I won't leave you."

"Promise?"

"Promise. Cross my heart and hope to fly. Stick a pickle in the sky."

He smiled as I crossed my heart. I made to stand but he tugged me back down. He glanced up at Maddock – who was pointedly looking at his watch - then snatched something out of his pocket and thrust it into my hand. He turned and walked over to his models. Shocked, I bit my lip and casually slipped the long, metallic object into my coat.

Maddock already had the door open. I noticed with rising fear that he seemed intent on not looking at me. I wondered if it was because he knew what was going to happen to me in the end.

He locked the door, trapping me in my bedroom. I swivelled, stared at the solid board of oak and listened to his footsteps carry him away with creaks and thuds. When I was sure was gone, I slipped my hand into my pocket and withdrew the object Wren had given me. It was a pair of metal scissors soiled with brown rust. I slid my thumb and middle finger through the holes and prised the blades apart then snapped them shut with a small smile.

*

Lying there, I thought back to when I first went to live with Grandma, how there was nothing to me. I never smiled, never laughed, never went to other kids' houses for dinner, parties or sleepovers. Truth was, I was never invited. I was so quiet at school that a particularly nasty group of girls gave me the nickname Shy-vee and made it their mission to torment me.

On the last day of Year Eight the leader of the group, Tanya Grimes, followed me into the girls' toilets joined by her three cronies Gemma, Faye and Kitty who reminded me of Siamese cats. I heard them giggling, talking about me in bitchy stage whispers. I knew what they were doing and tried to ignore them but their words dug deep and tore out chunks of my heart.

"Shy-vee's such a chav, isn't she?"

"Shit, yeah!"

"God – did you see those shoes she was wearing today?"

"Reckon she got them in Poundland?"

Laughter reverberated around the room. It seemed to slither under the door into my cubicle.

"You know she lives with her grandma?"

"Really? How sad."

"Apparently, her mum's bat-shit crazy. Beat her and locked her in the attic like every day."

"That must be why she's so weird."

"Just 'cos your mum's crazy, don't mean you have to be such a snob."

"Or such a slag. Did you see the way she was lookin' at Ben in P.E.?"

"What a loser."

"Yeah, as if he'd ever look twice at her."

"Shows she's as mental as her mum."

They giggled again and one of them kicked the cubicle door. The lock was broken and the door swung in, revealing me sitting on the toilet hugging my knees, tears soaking my cheeks. They ran out of the room laughing hysterically.

I waited for half an hour before leaving the toilets. Grandma was frantic by the time I slunk into the car park, but the moment she saw my face, she knew something had happened. I'd told her about them before and she'd told me to rise above it, not to lower myself to their level, not to let the words of a pack of stupid, insecure girls hurt me. I didn't want to talk about it but she made me tell her.

As we drove out of the car park, her jaw set in a way I'd not seen before and I felt slightly scared by the look in her eyes. I expected her to drive us straight home or to Macdonalds to cheer me up like she'd done before. Instead, she drove to the Mount, the notorious hang out spot for teenagers in our town.

It was a sultry Friday afternoon. She parked on the lane that led to the hill and told me to stay in the car.

I waited a few minutes then got out and followed.

It only took me seconds to spot them. They were sitting on the grass smoking and chatting to the popular boys in the year above. And there was Grandma dressed in one of her flowery dresses striding up to them.

I don't know how she knew but she honed in on Tanya. She didn't even say anything – just gestured for Tanya to come. Tanya giggled nervously and looked at her cronies for support, but they were all suddenly extremely interested in stubbing out their fags and checking their phones.

"What you want?" she said.

"Come here," Grandma said softly.

They knew who Grandma was. They'd all seen her pick me up from school.

Tanya giggled again and tried to catch her friends' eyes. One of the boys jerked his head at his mates and they loped off. Faye muttered something to Gemma and Kitty and they grabbed their bags and left too.

"Hey, guys - wait for me," Tanya said standing up, but they didn't glance back.

Tanya swore and put her hands on her hips. Sticking up her chin, she said, "What?"

Grandma leaned in close to Tanya. I couldn't see her face or hear what she said, but I saw the fear in Tanya Grimes' eyes and the way her chin trembled. All of a sudden, she didn't look like an evil, scary girl; she looked young and vulnerable just like me. She nodded, turned and picked up her bag then walked away as quickly as possible without breaking into a run.

Grandma never told me what she said to Tanya but they never bothered me again. After that Grandma was my hero and I learnt to stand up to bullies, which was exactly what I was about to do.

Chapter Thirty-Five

Huddled in bed under the blankets, I lay as still as the dead.

The door creaked. Footsteps on floorboards.

I waited. The pocket of air in front of my mouth was warm and wet. My teeth no longer chattered, but the maggots did. I willed them to shut up, but their voices rose in a shrill cackle.

The floor creaked as Ping took a tentative step toward the bed. "Ivy? You okay?"

Water sploshed onto the floor. Thuds sounded as she placed the buckets down. I felt pressure on my shoulder. Gentle pressure.

"I know this lot take in," she said in a shaky whisper, "But you got trust Mrs Water. She good lady. She make mistake, yeah, but don't everyone sometime?"

She shook my shoulder gently. "Ivy? You come now? I do bath."

I sniffed. "Okay. You go start it and I'll be there in a second."

The maggots hissed. Told me she didn't deserve what I was about to do.

I ignored them and waited for the bed to shift, for her to stand up, move away, pick up the buckets. She was so trusting. Too trusting.

Guilt slammed into my ribs as I threw back the blankets, leapt off the bed and wrapped my arms around her throat. Her body jolted and she gasped and dropped the buckets with a clang. One fell over. Hot water pooled around us. Steam drifted between our legs like mist.

I held the rusty scissors to her neck. "Don't make a sound. If you do, I'll stab. Keys. Now." My voice shook, but I tightened my fingers on the scissors, pushed her forward and manoeuvred her through the lounge into the bathroom.

She shook her head. I felt her tears on my hands. "No. I can't. No Ivy. No. I sorry. We all sorry. We not bad people. We only want help."

"You dumped a girl's body in a swamp," I said, "It's too late for sorry. *Keys.*"

"We had to. We -"

"Shut up."

I swapped the scissors into my left hand and kept my arm around her neck while I searched her pockets. I found the keys in her apron and snatched them out.

Pushing her to her knees I used the belt of my coat to tie her wrists together then tied the end around one of the bath tub's feet. The tub weighed a ton so there was no way she could move it. There was still the problem of her screaming. I scanned the room and saw nothing, then remembered my dressing gown cord. I grabbed the gown off the hook on the bathroom door, yanked out the cord and tied it around Ping's head, making sure it covered her mouth. Tears streamed down her cheeks and snot bubbled onto the cord.

Guilt stabbed and I said, "I'm sorry. They'll find you soon."

She shook her head frantically and moaned. I froze and pointed the scissors at her eye. "Don't make a sound. If anyone comes and tries to stop me because they heard you, it'll be your fault when I stab them in the gut."

Her eyes widened but she went quiet and bowed her head. I watched her for a moment, horrified but wanting to be sure she'd got the message. She didn't move. The maggots cackled and I flinched, desperate for all of this to be over.

"I'm sorry," I said again before closing the bathroom door and hurrying back to the bedroom.

I slid the scissors into my pocket and slotted the key into its chamber. Chest thrumming, I stepped out of the room and peered up the corridor.

It wasn't empty.

Chapter Thirty-Six

Odette stood a few doors down staring straight at me. She was dressed in her swan costume again, hair in a bun, skin impossibly pale. From this distance I couldn't see if her arms and legs ran with goose bumps, but imagined they must; the landing was freezing and an icy breeze made the skirt of her tutu flutter moth wings. It was hard to tell where the breeze was coming from. All the doors on my side of the corridor were shut. I wondered fearfully where Mrs Waters was. If she was in one of the rooms, she might hear us.

"Hello, Ivy," Odette said dreamily.

Her hands were cupped in front of her as though she held something. She smiled at me. The whites of her eyes glinted below the lantern to her left turning them into pearls.

I raised my hand and put my finger to my lips. She grinned and skipped toward me with her hands cupped in front of her. The floorboards uttered brief creaks that made my shoulder blades crunch together and I shook my head and mouthed 'no' then put my finger to my lips again. To my relief, she stopped skipping and tiptoed closer smiling like a toddler with a chocolate biscuit.

When she was a couple of steps away, I walked back into my bedroom. On the threshold, I turned and smiled, gestured for her to come in.

"Why don't you sit on the bed then you can show me what you've got there?" I said glancing around the room. I needed something to silence her with. *Think, think, think...*

She clambered onto the bed, crossed her legs and looked up expectantly.

"I found him in my apple," she said.

"Found what?" I said, rummaging around in the chest of drawers.

"Come see."

"Wait a second," I said. My hand landed on a pair of tights.

But Odette was off the bed at my side thrusting her hands in my face. She uncurled her fingers and I stared at the centipede on her palm. It lay on its back, numerous black feet quivering in the air.

I grimaced. "That's nice. What're you going to do with him? Shall we set him free?"

She wrinkled her nose and hid the centipede from view, pulling her hands to her chest and looking away. "I like him. I want to keep him."

"Okay. Odette, where's Mummy?"

"I don't know. Sometimes she goes off and doesn't tell me where she's going."

"She's not in your room? Or her room?"

"I already told you, I don't know."

She knelt on the floor and let the centipede go. With her arms she created a barrier so the insect couldn't escape. I watched her for a moment, wondering if she could tell me anything useful, aware that I needed to hurry.

"Do you know where Maddock is?" I said kneeling on the floor beside her and slipping my hand into my pocket to touch the scissors.

Odette tickled the centipede's back and it froze. She frowned. "Yes. He's gone to check on the man in the woods."

"Who?" I said, stomach dropping.

"The man Mummy keeps in the woods. He's a bad man. He did a really bad thing. She keeps him there to keep everyone safe."

"What did he do?"

Odette raised her hand then lay her arm back down on

the floor. The centipede scuttled across the circle and bumped into her wrist. It turned left and followed the path of her arm heading back around to her face, where it stopped as if confused. She began to hum Twinkle Twinkle Little Star. Abruptly, she pushed herself into a cross-legged position. The centipede sensed its chance and scurried away.

"What did he do, Odette?" I said shuffling closer to her.

She began to crawl after the centipede, still humming.

"Odette?"

She stopped humming and glanced over her shoulder at me. From this angle I could see the top of one of the slash-shaped scars poking out of her leotard. The centipede hit the wall under the window and turned right then scurried alongside it. Even though I hated the thing, I felt sorry for it.

I crawled after Odette and touched her shoulder. "You can tell me, Odette. I won't tell anyone. I promise."

She looked away and focused on the centipede again.

"The man in the woods is a bad, bad, bad man. The baddest man in the world's what Mummy says. She says the devil's inside him."

I didn't say anything. The centipede headed back toward her.

"He needs to be in a cage, Mummy says."

"Why? What did he do?"

Odette raised her hand and said, "This."

I flinched as she slammed her hand down on the centipede five times. After the fifth strike, she turned her palm over and stared at the gooey mess on her pale skin. She looked up at me. Tears slid down her cheeks.

She looked at her hand and whispered, "Oh no."

With a little gasp, she smeared the blood over her tutu. Her eyes rested on the purple stain. Her hands rotated in slow circles.

"Mummy will be mad," she said.

I looked down at the tights in my hand. I couldn't do it.

She was just a child. A traumatised, confused child.

Trying to sound excited I said, "Why don't we play a little game of hide and seek? You hide in this room or in there – in the lounge area - and I'll count, then come and find you. Okay?"

Odette's eyes lit up exactly like Wren's had. She jumped to her feet, "Yes please!"

"Great. I'm going to count down from one hundred to give you plenty of time to find a good place to hide, so it'll be quite a while before I come looking for you. Ready?"

She nodded.

"On your marks, get set, go. One hundred, ninety-nine…"

She squealed and whipped her head from side to side looking for a hiding place. I ran to the bedroom door, covered my face with my hands and watched her through the gaps between my fingers. She squealed again then ran into the lounge. Seizing my chance, I slipped out of the room and locked the door then darted across the corridor to Wren's bedroom.

Déjà vu swooped over me as I opened Wren's door and scanned the room, but the sensation cut off the instant I realised he wasn't there. The room lay empty, curtains billowing wildly around the open window.

I ran to the window and stuck my head out possessed by the awful idea that Wren might have jumped, but there was nothing on the ground except for purple heather swaying in the wind. An object to the left caught my eye and I almost screamed. Wren was balanced on the window ledge of the next room along. His hair blew around his face whipping in his eyes. His back was pressed into the wall but his legs wobbled. He'd made wings out of leaves and cardboard and tied them to his arms with string, which were held out at horizontal angles to his body.

"Wren," I said, "Come back over here. Come inside."

He looked at me out of the corner of his eye but didn't move his head. I leaned out as far as I could and reached for him. The wind buffeted my body and I wondered how on earth he was still standing on the ledge.

"I'm going to fly away like an aeroplane and get help," he shouted over the wind.

"You can't fly, Wren. Humans can't fly. Only machines can fly."

"Birds can fly. I'll fly like a bird. See my wings? Do you like them?"

"They're good, yes, but you need to listen to me. Reach out really slowly and give me your hand. I'll pull you in."

"No. I want to get us far away from here. You and me. I want to see an aeroplane. I don't want to stay here. I don't like it here anymore."

"I know, sweetie, but we'll get out another way. This way's not safe."

"But I can do it. I know I can. I tested my wings by jumping off the bed. They work."

I looked down. Wished I hadn't. "They won't work for a drop this steep. Trust me, Wren. If you try to fly from up high, you'll hit the ground very, very hard and hurt yourself."

His whole body wobbled. With tears in his eyes, he said, "But my name's Wren and a wren is a type of bird and birds can fly. That's what Lucinda said."

"Come on," I said, making myself sound stern, "Give me your hand. I'll pull you in."

"I can do it," he shouted, "I can get you and me away."

"Wren. Give me your hand."

I leaned out further and reached for him but my fingers were still a foot from his. I saw him suck in a deep breath as if readying himself to jump.

"No. Don't. Please don't. Your wings might snap when you jump and you could break your legs." I pulled myself up onto the ledge and turned to face the wall then shuffled to the very end. Gripping the window frame with one hand, I leaned out as far as I could and reached for him. I could almost reach him. Almost, but not quite. My fingers were still a few centimetres away from his arm.

He looked at me and smiled. "Don't worry, Ivy. I just remembered. Birds flap when they fly so if I flap my wings, I'll be okay." He jumped.

I screamed and stretched out – got nothing but thin air. My fingers slipped and I fell, but managed to grab on to the ledge. I swung my other arm back and dangled from both hands, glancing down to see Wren plummeting to the ground at break-neck speed and a dark figure running toward the house, lurching forward and catching him before he hit the ground.

The impact of Wren landing in his arms made Maddock fall to his knees.

Wren got to his feet and pointed up at me. Maddock looked up and shouted, "Hang on!"

I would have rolled my eyes if the pain hadn't been so bad and the fear of falling so real.

My fingers were sweaty and beginning to slip. The maggots wailed and I went dizzy from the strain on my arms. I wasn't strong enough to hold on any longer. I was going to have to let go. Any second now. I told myself to count to ten. Make it to ten and I'd be okay. I heard steps pounding the stairs. One, two, three, four – I couldn't do it – I couldn't hold on any longer – steps pounded the corridor – five, six, seven – *oh god, oh god, oh god, shit, shit, shit.*

I was letting go…

Chapter Thirty-Seven

Mrs Waters appeared above me, hair wild. She hesitated a split second then grabbed my forearms and hauled me up through the window. I landed on my knees at her feet and massaged my arms.

"My, that was a close call, wasn't it?" she panted.

I stood up and stared at her. "Get out of my way. I'm leaving."

"I'm afraid I can't let you do that."

I pulled the scissors out of my pocket and pointed them at her.

Her face blanched and she took a step back. "Ivy. This is panic talking. This isn't you. You wouldn't hurt a fly, let alone me."

"You're keeping me here against my will. I want to go. Now." I stabbed the scissors at her to punctuate the message.

This time she stayed put and folded her arms. "You go then. If that's what you want, but Wren stays here."

Her unspoken words lingered between us like spoilt milk.

"You wouldn't hurt Wren," I said trying to convince myself more than anything.

She raised an eyebrow but didn't respond.

I gnawed the inside of my cheek, trying to work her out.

"If you let me leave with Wren, I won't tell anyone about what you did."

"We both know that's a lie," she said. "You're too good. You'd drive yourself insane wondering about her family. But I can tell you one thing: Beatrice only had one person looking for her and that was her husband, a man who used to beat her to within an inch of her life."

"I'm not listening to any of this crap. It's probably all lies. Get out of my way."

She shook her head. "I don't want to keep you here against your will. I really don't. I don't want to hurt you either – that's the very last thing I want."

"Then let me and Wren go."

She looked over my shoulder at the open window. "You just need time. Given time, you'll come to understand that my actions aren't motivated by wickedness. Once you understand that, once you grow to love us, you won't ever consider telling the police."

"Move."

"No. You're a good person, Ivy. You won't hurt me."

"I will if you don't get out of my way. I've done it before."

"If you hurt me, you'll hurt Odette too and she doesn't deserve it."

"Get out of my way," I said but my tone lacked conviction.

I looked at the scissors. Imagined using them on her. Pictured the blood. The colour draining from her face…and then I pictured Odette's reaction to her mummy's pain, and I remembered my reaction to seeing my mummy suffer all those years ago.

She reached out and wrapped her fingers around the scissors. Tightening her grip, she pulled the scissors into her stomach making them pierce the fabric of her dress. She tugged the scissors in harder but didn't wince. Blood beaded on the metal tips.

Her lower lip trembled as she said, "I deserve this. I know. Some days I think about ending it all, but then I think about Odette. I can't leave her alone in this sick, frightening world. You see that don't you?"

"I'll do it," I said, but my hand trembled on the scissors.

She pulled the tip further into her stomach. This time, she flinched. Blood trickled down the metal blades and the trail reached my finger, smearing my skin. A droplet gathered, grew to the size of a pea then fell. It dropped to the oak floorboard without a sound. Footsteps pounded the corridor. Mrs Waters and I stared at each other.

Gently, she pushed the scissors back. Space opened up in my mind. The maggots strode into the opening and whispered *There's always a little reason in madness.* Their words pierced my certainty. I let her turn away from me, let her stride across the room, let her go. To my surprise, the maggots applauded. With the sound of clapping in my ears, I slipped the scissors back into my coat pocket.

Mrs Waters opened the bedroom door as if nothing had happened and Maddock walked in carrying Wren like a baby.

"Silly little mite thought he'd do a Superman," Maddock said lightly, taking in the atmosphere between us. He placed a shaky Wren on the bed. Wren darted a frightened glance at Mrs Waters before picking up his book.

"Everythin' alright here?" Maddock said looking at her.

"I think an escort might be in order," she said. "Come, let us reconvene in the living room. The boy will stay here."

She closed Wren's window and placed a gentle hand on my arm. I flinched but didn't back away, conscious of Wren who perched on the edge of the bed pretending to read. I walked over to the bed and ruffled his hair. His eyes remained fixed on his book, but his shoulders dropped.

"No more trying to fly, okay?" I said kissing his forehead.

He glanced up at me with worry in his eyes then at Mrs Waters who strode away without another word. Wren looked at Maddock, who was waiting for me to leave the room.

"I'll see you soon, sweetie," I said.

"Promise?"

"Promise."

The moment Wren looked down at his book Maddock

jerked his head toward the door. Not wanting to upset Wren, I left the room without a fuss. After a few steps, I slipped my hand into my pocket and grasped the scissors, trying to work out what to do. I didn't want to hurt anyone, but I couldn't stay here. I couldn't pretend everything was okay. Someone had died. An innocent woman had been killed and her death had been covered up. A man had been imprisoned for God knows how long. Wren wasn't safe here and neither was I.

Maddock paused at the top of the stairs and gestured for me to go down first. I obeyed and descended slowly, my hand sweating on the scissors in my pocket.

The entrance hall echoed with our steps and gloom encroached like storm clouds. Soft light emerged from the doorway of the living room and I imagined Mrs Waters sitting there beneath her ballerinas waiting for me. Her long legs would be crossed, hands clasped on her lap. I could picture her easily enough, but it was impossible to predict her words. Or her actions. She knew I wanted to grab Wren and go but she didn't want to hurt me. So how, exactly, was she going to keep me here against my will? And she knew I still had the scissors. Why hadn't she taken them away?

I paused on the slice of light outside the living room and listened to the flames crackle within. I squeezed my eyes shut and shook my head. I didn't want to hurt anyone. I really didn't.

Maddock nudged my leg with his foot and I pushed the door open. It creaked long and low like an old man's dying groan.

The maggots wailed. I tried to ignore their warning. I tried to tell myself they were wrong, but deep down I knew they were right.

Chapter Thirty-Eight

"Please, sit," Mrs Waters said.

I perched on the edge of the chair.

She nodded as if pleased by my lack of argument and went to speak but I got there first. "Take them, please." The maggots hurled themselves against the walls of my brain and shrieked like hags as I withdrew the scissors from my pocket and held them out to her.

She leaned forward, took them from me and placed them on the table. "Thank you. I know that must have been very hard."

"You've been good to me. You've never done me any harm. I'm willing to try to get my head around all of this."

My voice sounded robotic. I hoped it didn't to her, or to Maddock, who stood to my right with his hands behind his back. He shifted his weight and I caught a whiff of vinegary sweat. He was still wheezy from the stairs. To my surprise he strode over to Mrs Waters, bent down and whispered something in her ear. Her hand moved to her heart and all colour drained from her cheeks.

They exchanged panicked whispers and I caught fragments of what they were saying. They were talking about Carl Maddock. How he'd escaped.

Oh shit.

Mrs Waters stood abruptly and said, "Ivy, give me the key to your room. We need to act quickly or everyone in this house will be at risk."

I handed her the key. "What's wrong?"

They both ignored me. Mrs Waters passed the key to Maddock. He grabbed my arm and hauled me to my feet.

Digging his fingers into my skin, he pulled me from the room giving me no choice but to follow.

"Maddock, I know what you were talking about. I know about the man in the wood. Tell me what's going on."

He stopped halfway up the stairs and yanked me close. His breath reeked of stale beer. "How do you know?"

"He's your brother, isn't he? When I was down there, I found his stuff. What did he do? Why was he locked up? Was it Odette? Did he do something to her?"

His fingers tightened on my arm and I winced. He radiated rage but fear too.

"It was you, wasn't it?" he said.

I looked away.

His jaw clenched and the vein in his forehead throbbed. "You stupid, stupid girl. Always meddlin' in matters that don't concern you."

My heart skipped. He dragged me up the stairs so roughly I nearly fell. I struggled to stay upright as he pulled me down the corridor. He unlocked my bedroom door and shoved me inside.

Odette was curled up on the bed crying. She looked up and saw me, and her sweet face twisted. She scrambled off the bed. Stabbing her finger into my chest she said, "You lied. I'm telling Mummy."

"I'm sorry. I had no choice," I said.

She rolled her eyes and stuck out her tongue then stomped past Maddock out of the room, slamming the door.

A banging sound came from the bathroom and I cringed as Maddock locked the bedroom door then turned to glare at me. "Where is she?"

I didn't see the point in lying. "Bathroom. I'm so -"

He pushed past me and strode away. Frantically, I looked for something to protect myself. I didn't know if Maddock would hurt me for what I'd done to Ping, but I had to be prepared. I tore through the chest of drawers, my makeup bag, the wardrobe, but found nothing of any use. Shaking now, wishing I'd not handed over the scissors, I moved to stand on the other side of the room behind the bed. Backing into the corner I tried to think of the right thing to say to calm him down when he came back, but thinking was almost impossible because the grubs were shrieking *Told you so, told you so, now they'll never let you go. You're gonna die, you're gonna die, eaten in a maggot pie!*

Over and over and over they shrieked. It felt like someone was repeatedly smacking my head with a brick.

Blackness pulled at the corners of my eyes and I sank to my knees and covered my head with my arms, begging them to stop. Telling them I'd listen next time, that I'd be better, braver, stronger, smarter – and, to my surprise, they stopped.

*

Ping walked into the room and our eyes locked. Even from this distance, I could see that she'd been crying. As she stared at me, she massaged her wrists, which were purple.

I'd done that to her.

Guilt tightened its fist and I opened my mouth then closed it, unable to find the right words. I reminded myself that she was part of this. She knew what had happened to Beatrice and hadn't gone to the police. She'd done nothing when I'd been locked in the basement and had stood by when Mrs Waters had locked that man in the cabin in the wood - but if Odette was telling the truth and the graffiti on the basement walls was anything to go by…

No. I wouldn't let myself believe their actions were justified. They'd covered up a murder. Ping was just as bad as the rest of them.

I blinked. My mind had blinded me to the present. I stumbled back as Ping strode toward me. Maddock appeared in the lounge doorway holding the cord I'd used on Ping. I stood firm as she walked up to me. She stopped a yard away.

She dipped her head to the side and frowned. In a small voice she said, "You hurt me, you bitch."

She stepped forward and slapped my cheek hard then ran to the bedroom door, which Maddock was holding open for her. She left the room with a rasping sob.

I touched my cheek. Tears stung my eyes.

Maddock shut the door. He waved the dressing gown cord at me making it swing like a pendulum, back and forth, back and forth, back and forth, counting down the seconds. For some unknown reason, Grandma's weathered face appeared behind my eyes. The idea that I'd never see her again made my heart pound.

The maggots began to whisper, their voices dark and intimate. *He didn't lock the door. He didn't lock the door.* This time I didn't try to ignore them or push them out. I listened as they told me what to do.

I looked up at Maddock. Glanced at the cord dangling from his hand. "You're worried your brother's going to come back, aren't you?"

He grunted and walked toward me.

"What happened? Did he and Ping spend a little too much time together?"

He stopped. The look in his eyes sent chills down my back. Satisfied, I said, "He shagged her, didn't he?"

"Shut up."

"I bet she came on to him. I've seen his picture. He's good-looking."

"Shut *up*."

"Was it in your bed? It was, wasn't it? God, Mrs Waters told me what Ping used to do for a living, but I didn't think —"

"Shut the *fuck* up."

He stormed forward and slammed both hands onto the wall next to my face. I jerked my knee up into his groin as hard as possible, and he groaned and doubled over. Seizing the moment of weakness, I charged into him and he stumbled back. The maggots cheered as I swivelled away and threw myself onto the bed. Crawling across the blankets, I cried out as something grabbed hold of ankle and yanked me backward. Glancing around I saw Maddock on his knees, a meaty fist wrapped around my leg, reaching out with his free hand for my other calf. The maggots screamed and I smashed my foot into his nose. Blood spurted from his nostrils and he gasped, but didn't let go of my ankle, so I kicked out again catching him in the chest, but it wasn't enough to throw him off balance and he lunged forward and grabbed me round the waist. I thrashed and clawed at his arms and face, but he moved one huge hand to the space between my breasts and pinned me down before climbing onto the bed and straddling me. I screamed at him to get off and tore at his arm, but he managed to grab one of my flailing hands and then the other. Shuffling himself further up the bed, he straddled my ribs with his enormous thighs and used some of his weight to pin me to the bed. He began to bind my wrists together with the cord and I writhed beneath him, but he was too strong. Once my hands were tied, he shuffled backward to the edge of the bed and pulled the cord down toward my legs. I thrashed around and tried to kick him but he moved his bulk off my left leg and kept his weight pressing down on me then seized my free leg in his hand and wrapped the cord around my ankle.

"No, Maddock - please. Not my ankles too," I said.

He acted like he hadn't heard me and tied my ankles together so tightly that my ankle bones grated against each other.

"Don't," I said as he pushed himself off the bed and walked toward the door.

"Don't bother screamin' or shoutin'. Won't do any good."

"Mrs Waters didn't tell you to tie me up," I shouted after him, "when she finds out, you'll be in deep shit."

He turned at the door and gave me a grim smile. "Because of you, she's got much bigger things to worry about now."

"Why on earth would he come back? Anyone in their right mind would run and never stop running if they'd been locked up like that."

Fear clouded Maddock's eyes. "He's not right in the head. He was ruined years ago."

"How? What do you mean?"

"Let's just say his old man wasn't right in the head either."

"Why? What did he do? Did he beat him or something?"

"Or something."

He opened the door to go.

"Wait. If he's coming here to hurt us you can't leave me tied up like this. Please untie me. Just lock me in. I promise I'll be good. I won't try to get out."

"You hurt Ping. I don't give a shit about you anymore."

"I'm sorry. I really am. I was just scared."

"It's too late for that. Stay quiet. Mrs Waters'll send me to untie you soon as it's safe. For now, keep quiet."

"No. Please -"

He shut the door. I heard the key jam into the lock and crunch. Shit. The maggots began to whine. I stared at the locked door then down at my ankles. I brought my wrists up to my teeth and began to tear at the cord like a hyena ripping into a carcass. The material frayed and threads of cotton came away in my teeth. The grubs' whine transformed into an urgent murmur and I threw myself into the task of shredding the cord, hoping Mrs Waters and Maddock were wrong.

Only a psychopath would risk coming back to his or her captors. Then again, only a psychopath would cover a wall with the kind of graffiti I'd found in the basement.

Chapter Thirty-Nine

I tore away another thread and spat it onto the bed. My jaw felt like it had been corkscrewed open. I massaged the aching muscles and gave myself a break. The cord was frayed but my effort and resultant agony had achieved little impact. I was tempted to shout for help and nearly did a few times, only to swallow the impulse for fear of Wren trying to come to my rescue or Maddock's brother hearing me – if he was even around, that was.

It was so unlikely Carl Maddock would return. Under normal circumstances, the idea would have made me laugh. And yet, worry niggled away at me like an itch I couldn't scratch.

Maddock's certainty had been impossible to deny. His eyes and voice and body language – everything about him – had screamed conviction. And fear. He was convinced he'd come back to the house, but was he right?

When I'd freed the man from his prison, he'd looked terrible. Gaunt, drawn face. Shadowed eyes. But when he'd moved, he'd moved with surprising speed. And instead of seeking my help, he'd fled. He'd not even asked me if I'd called the police.

At the time I'd assumed panic and fear directed his actions, but now…

I licked my lips. Tried to crush the dread swirling in my stomach.

Maddock had said his brother wasn't right in the head.

Words sprang to my mind. Deranged. Demented. Dangerous.

No. He won't come back. That's crazy talk.

I bit into the cord and tore. Bit and tore. Bit and tore. Bit and tore.

*

My jaw had been put through a meat grinder. I stopped gnawing at the cord and took another break. According to the clock, I'd been lying on the bed for two hours. In that two hours nothing had broken the quiet.

I surveyed the damage I'd done. I wasn't even halfway through. Dressing gown cords were bloody tough to saw through – who knew? This one had been a gift from Grandma two Christmases ago. I remembered the pleasure in her face when I'd held it up and admired it. There was something so comforting about a dressing gown. Something homely and warming. Grandma's dressing gown was lilac with white spots. When she wore it, she gave the best hugs – snuggly, I-love-you-to-bits hugs I never wanted to end. She also had a black silk Kimono that she wore in warmer weather. Red, pink and white flowers were embroidered on it. It was so low cut that it revealed the tiny tattoo of a swan that graced the top of her right breast. Swans made Grandma feel peaceful.

I thought about what made me feel peaceful and an image of Grandma and I sipping English Breakfast tea together in the lounge of her terraced cottage sprang to mind. I clung on to the picture and tried to remember our last conversation over tea, but the image blurred and instead I saw myself and Mrs Waters sipping elderflower tea the day I arrived at Fairwood House. How naïve I'd been to think she was such an innocent woman, but she'd fooled Sergeant Zachary too. I wasn't the only one duped by her charm.

I looked back down at the cord around my wrists and stretched my jaw, bit down on the material and began to tear again, stopping at the sound of the key crunching in the door.

Ping walked into the room carrying a tray. She walked with her chin raised. A heavenly aroma of Thai broth wafted into the air making me salivate. She placed the tray on the dressing table, turned and walked up to the bed. Without looking at my face, she helped me to sit up and shuffle back up the bed so that I could lean against the wall.

I murmured, "Thank you."

She picked up the bowl and sat on the edge of the bed.

"Open mouth," she said.

Surprised by the gentleness of her voice, I allowed her to spoon broth into my mouth. It was a fraction too hot but deliciously spicy. My nose began to sweat and I looked up into her eyes to find hers glistening with tears. I wanted to speak to her, but after what I'd done, I couldn't find the right words. Anger rose up at the memory of her hitting me and tussled with confusion and guilt. Was she as guilty as Mrs Waters in all of this? Maybe. Maybe not. I recalled what Mrs Waters said Ping had been through and my guilt spiked.

"I'm sorry," I said.

She acted like I hadn't spoken and spooned more broth into my mouth. Raising her chin, she moved away from the bed. She replaced the bowl on the tray then knelt down in front of the grate and lit the fire. As soon as the flames began to rise, she picked up the tray, turned and left the room.

I flinched at the sound of the key twisting in the lock.

Chapter Forty

Despite the fact that my teeth were wrapped around the dressing gown cord, I found myself thinking about my first kiss.

In my late teens, having grown in self-confidence and happiness, I started chatting to a girl in my 'A' level English class. Like me, Annalise was obsessed with Harry Potter, boys and shopping, which meant we had plenty to talk about. She only lived a five-minute walk away from Grandma's house, so we hung out almost every weekend at hers or mine stuffing our faces with Ben and Jerry's and binging on Harry Potter and anything with Tom Cruise in.

On Annalise's seventeenth birthday, her mum said we could go to the local pub on our own for the night and Grandma – to my surprise – had agreed.

Excitement reached epic levels. We went shopping together and bought new outfits then spent three hours getting ready in her bedroom – which was, to my absolute envy, a blissful shrine to Harry.

When we were finally ready, Annalise's mum dropped us off in town a minute's walk from the pub so we wouldn't be seen getting dropped off. Bubbling with excitement and the bottle of red wine we'd shared getting ready, we tottered toward the pub feeling terribly grown up.

The Red Lion was the place everyone in our year went on a Friday and Saturday night because you didn't need ID to get in. Still, my belly went crazy with nerves as we said hi to the bouncer and hurried past him into the weird smell of stale beer and teenage boys. Music pounded the air and every heterosexual boy in the building checked us out in degrees of subtlety ranging from unsubtle to extremely unsubtle. Annalise and I turned to each other and giggled as we approached the bar, and my heart leapt into my throat as the most gorgeous-looking boy on earth took our order. Our eyes met and I smiled at him and held out my hand to shake his. He laughed and shook my hand. Annalise took the piss out of me for doing that for most of the night, but afterwards, when the bell rang for final orders and we waited outside the pub for the taxi to pick us up, the very same boy tapped me on the shoulder and asked if he could have a private word with me.

Drunk as a skunk, I followed him round the side of the pub. Without even saying anything, he leaned in and kissed me. It was, in my seventeen-year-old head, the best moment of my life.

We kissed again a couple of times when Annalise and I went back to the pub, but nothing more ever came of it because he confessed he had a girlfriend who was pregnant. So much for love at first sight.

Eight months later, Annalise moved to Australia and I never saw her again. Every now and then we texted each other, but these days she was a busy lawyer with little time for chitter-chatter.

I stopped tearing at the cord and tried to imagine kissing Ralph. My chest tightened at the thought of never getting the chance to make a go of things with him. There was something there between us. I'd felt it - I was sure he had too.

I refocused on ripping through the binds and plunged myself into a daydream where all of this was over and I was taking Ralph home to meet Grandma for the first time and, for a sweet, short while, was soothed by dreaming the impossible.

*

Ping arrived an hour later carrying two buckets of steaming water. Her blouse sleeves were pushed up to her elbows revealing the bruises on her wrists. My handiwork. I fought the guilt pressing on my chest, and watched as she walked past the bed into the adjoining room.

The sound of water sloshing into the tub carried through the lounge area into the bedroom. I looked down at my bound ankles and wondered what she was going to do. There was no way she could carry me into the bathroom. Was Maddock going to do it? She'd have to untie my wrists to get my clothes off, which meant she'd see the damage I'd done to the cord. And if she didn't untie my ankles, how was I going to get in the bath?

She appeared in the doorway and stared at me. Her face was touched by shadows so it was hard to read her expression. Beyond the window, dusk was falling, growing greyer by the second.

"I'm sorry I hurt you," I said.

She ignored me and walked up to the bed. I tried to catch her eye as she withdrew a pair of kitchen scissors from her pocket.

"Still," she said, leaning down and cutting through the cord on my ankles.

Surprised, I thanked her. She ignored me.

"Go," she said gesturing with the scissors.

I shuffled off the bed and walked across the room. On passing the mirror I caught a glimpse of myself. I looked dirty and pale. The thought of a bath was appealing. I hadn't bathed for days. My teeth felt furry, my hair greasy, skin full of grime. As if reading my thoughts, she told me to sit on the toilet seat then squeezed toothpaste onto my toothbrush for me.

"I cut cord now. Be stupid, I call Maddock. He outside

room."

I nodded and held out my wrists. Her eyes widened at the damage I'd done to the cord, but she said nothing and snipped through the bind. Relief was immediate. I glanced at the bruises on Ping's wrists knowing I'd got off easy in comparison.

"Thank you," I said taking the toothbrush from her.

She nodded and aimed the scissors at me as I brushed and spat in the sink. I turned away from her, undressed and slipped into the water savouring the feel of it on my skin. Sinking under, I allowed myself a few moments to disappear. Tears leaked out of my eyes. Ping's kindness was killing me. I rose out of the water and used the bar of soap to wash before climbing out of the bath and taking the towel from her.

"Thank you," I said.

She nodded again.

"Look, Ping, I'm sorry. I really am but you've got to understand why -"

"I understand," she said, meeting my eyes for the first time, "you scare. Make sense. But got trust Mrs Water. She good lady."

"I thought she was, but how can she be? I saw the body. I saw the man locked in the cabin. Did you know two of his nails had been torn out?"

"He deserve," she said in a hard voice.

"*Why?* What did he do? And what the hell happened to Lucinda, or Beatrice, or whatever her name was? If it really was an accident, why didn't one of you call the police?"

She sighed and gestured with the scissors for me to leave the room.

I stood my ground. "Please. Tell me. I need to know."

"He very bad man. Done very bad thing. He deserve everything she do."

"Okay, but what did he do? Did he do something to

Odette? I saw scars on her back -"

"Not for me tell. Sorry."

"What about the nanny? Please. I have to know. If you want me to believe Mrs Waters is a good person, tell me what happened."

Ping bit her lip. She glanced around as if someone might be listening. She sucked in a sharp breath and said, "Odette think Lucinda take Wren away. Odette go crazy. She push Lucinda down stair. Lucinda break neck."

I stared at her, unable to speak. She looked down at the scissors in her hand and flicked them toward the bathroom door. I pulled the towel tighter around my body. I wanted to know more but couldn't form the words. Ping gestured for me to move and I obeyed.

"Get dressed," she said.

Keeping the towel around myself, I got dressed then sat on the bed and held out my hands for her to tie them up. She bit her lip and stared at me as if trying to work out something.

I cleared my throat. "Do you really think he's going to come back?"

Her eyes flicked up to mine. Her fearful expression sent shivers down my arms.

"Surely he won't come back? Not after being kept in that cabin. Only a crazy person would do that," I said, letting my hands flop to my thighs.

"He crazy," she said, darting a glance at the door. "And evil."

"Have you seen the stuff he drew on the wall in the basement?"

She nodded.

A loud knocking on the bedroom door made us jump.

"Everythin' okay in there?" It was Maddock.

"Okay, yeah," Ping said quickly. She pulled a piece of rope out of her apron pocket and hesitated.

I held out my wrists again and said, "It's okay."

She stepped forward and placed a finger to her lips. "Shush now."

To my surprise she pocketed the rope, turned and scurried to the bedroom door. She gave me a smile and left the room. The lock crunched in the door and I looked down at my hands in disbelief. Ping was all right after all.

I shook my head, unable to wrap my head around the fact that Odette had accidentally killed Beatrice Giles, but knowing it was the only explanation that made sense.

I still didn't know why they had shut Carl Maddock in the cabin. What on earth had he done?

I walked over to the window and looked out at the wood. I jumped at the sound of the lock and whirled around to see Maddock storming in holding a piece of rope.

"Sit," he said, jerking his head at the bed.

"But -"

He stood over me. "Now."

I sighed and sat on the bed. Muttering darkly, he tied my wrists then trailed the rope down and tied my ankles together. Hog-tied once more, I rolled onto my side and tried to get comfortable. I didn't look at him.

He mumbled, "Sorry", left the roo,m and locked the door.

I stared down at the rope on my wrists. With a sigh, I began to gnaw through it. Would rope be easier to bite through than dressing gown cord?

I turned my head and spat out fibres, jolting as a gunshot split the air.

Chapter Forty-One

I lay on the bed, neck raised, head forward, teeth frozen on the rope. Straining my ears, I listened to the silence wondering if I'd imagined the sound of a bullet blasting from a gun. I listened and listened and the silence dragged on and on and I began to think I had imagined it. No gun had sounded. Fear had made me hear something that wasn't there.

I began to relax and the maggots screamed *BANG BANG, YOU'RE DEAD, FIFTY BULLETS IN YOUR HEAD!*

They were right: a gunshot *had* sounded. I hadn't imagined it. Someone had fired a gun in the house.

I didn't think Mrs Waters had any guns, but I hadn't explored every room. It was possible she'd weapons hidden away somewhere - it would be stupid to put anything past her. But who would she – or anyone else in the house - be shooting at? Either Mrs Waters had freaked out and imagined Carl Maddock had come back for revenge, or he actually had and one of them had fired a gun.

I pictured Mrs Waters holding a gun, pointing it at someone while dressed in one of her Victorian dresses and though the picture was weird, it didn't seem impossible. If anyone had the gumption to fire a gun at someone, it was her.

As far as I was concerned guns were like rare poisonous plants from the rainforest. I'd never held one – never even touched one. They were alien territory. I'd seen photos, but I'd never even imagined what it would be like to shoot a gun because I'd never thought I'd find myself in a situation where

I'd need to. And when I'd been in the basement, I hadn't opened the gun book because the mural had disturbed me so much.

When I was very little, for a brief time, I'd wanted to become a police officer, but when the police had shown no ability whatsoever to arrest *him* and help my mum, that dream had vanished and it wasn't long before I began to loathe the police for their weakness. But right now, tied up on the bed, I longed for the sweet sound of sirens to destroy the silence.

I strained my ears for voices – things smashing – people shouting. Nothing broke the quiet, so I turned my attention back to gnawing through the rope. The maggots battered me with snide comments one second and cajoling ones the next. They told me not to give up. Told me to stop being a weakling and get a grip. I saw Grandma again and Ralph and Wren's sad little face, and I ripped and tore at the rope like a rabid dog, but the twists wouldn't give. Beginning to panic, I stopped biting and scanned the room. When I'd looked for a weapon before, I hadn't found anything but I hadn't looked in the bathroom. I needed something to cut through the rope. Something sharp.

It was a lightbulb moment. The maggots cheered.

The mattress was quite a distance from the ground, so I swivelled around so that my body was parallel to the length of the bed, shuffled up to the edge and moved my legs over the side. Bracing myself for a painful fall, I let my legs lead me and rolled off the bed. My legs cushioned the fall but the impact bruised my side and my left leg took most of the hit. Wincing, I rolled onto my front and moved into a crawling position. The rope allowed me wiggle room but not enough to crawl quickly, so I started to half-crawl, half-commando drag my body around the end of the bed toward the lounge doorway.

My stomach muscles and arms burned as I struggled

across the bedroom. Gritting my teeth, I crawled into the lounge and dragged myself across the wooden floorboards. Sweat soaked my back and dribbled into my eyes, and a weird thought popped into my head: *If this isn't a workout, what is?* The maggots laughed and I uttered a half-laugh, half-groan as I pulled my body into the bathroom.

My eyes found my washbag. It was on the sink where I'd left it, open and enticing, but high up. There could be a pair of nail scissors in the bag. I couldn't remember if I'd packed them.

Praying I had, I dragged myself over to the base of the sink and pushed myself onto my knees. I tried to reach up for the washbag, but the rope went taut and I couldn't straighten my arms. I sank back and pulled my legs around so that I was sitting like a pixie then reached up again, but my hands were even further from the bag than before.

Sighing in frustration I scanned the room again and my gaze fell on a bucket sitting in the corner of the room. Cringing against the memories, I moved myself onto my front and commando-crawled over to the bucket. When I was close enough, I reached out with my bound hands and grabbed the rim of the bucket then turned and dragged it across the floor toward the sink. At the sink I turned the bucket upside down then somehow, hurting my knees in the effort, pulled myself onto the upturned bucket. Now, able to reach the washbag, I knocked it off the sink and lowered myself off the bucket onto the floor.

The grubs whooped. A small pair of nail scissors lay on the ground.

I snatched them up and attacked the rope, snipping and tearing at the thick material. It was taking ages but it was working. My hands protested against the awkward way I was bending them backward. The metal handles burned my skin. Ignoring the pain, I focused on the task and, after another fifteen minutes or so, ripped my wrists free.

A moment later, a second gunshot came, followed by a scream.

I heard Wren shouting. I shouted back, telling him to be quiet, but he carried on calling for me.

I untied the rope around my ankles, kicked it off and pushed myself to my feet. I raced out of the bathroom into the bedroom and tried the door, just in case, but it was locked.

Wren's voice came. "Ivy. What was that? I'm scared. Ivy."

"Shush. Be quiet. Go back to your room and hide. Stay in there and don't make a sound."

"Why? I don't understand."

"There's no time to explain. Just do as I'm telling you. I'll come and get you as soon as I can. Okay?"

He didn't say anything.

"Wren? Promise me you'll do as I said?"

"Yes. I promise."

"Good boy."

I heard him scamper across the corridor, heard his door shut.

I span around. The only exit available to me was the window. I tried it, found it unlocked. It opened out onto the enclosure where the wind had begun to howl beneath the pre-dusk sky. Cold air rushed into the room. Freedom was so close in one way, but also not close at all. I couldn't drop from the window for fear of breaking something, so I'd have to somehow lower myself to the ground, and do it without being seen.

An idea jumped into my head and I ran back into the bathroom, grabbed the nail scissors and carried them back to the bedroom where I yanked the bedsheet off the bed and cut it lengthways into two thick strips. I tied one strip around the top right bed post, which stood only a short distance from the open window. I gave the sheet a couple of hard yanks. It seemed secure. I began to twist the sheet as tightly as I could then tied the second strip to the first and twisted the second strip. I stretched out the length of twisted material, pleased to see I had about six feet to play with. Not content to leave it there, I did the same to one of the velvet blankets, tying one strip to the twisted sheet, then the next. Now I had a good ten feet of rope, which ought to be long enough to get me close to the ground. I could jump the last few feet.

Hoping I'd worked it out properly, I tested the strength of the knots again then lowered the makeshift rope down the side of the house. It may have been a ridiculous idea but I couldn't think of a better one.

I yanked on another jumper then pulled on my coat. Lastly, I tugged on a pair of gloves. I patted my pocket to check my phone was still there. It wasn't. Cursing under breath, I turned to face the open window. I wasn't athletic and my upper body was quite weak. I inhaled a gulp of air and told myself this was nothing. In the grand scheme of things, climbing down the side of a house was nothing compared to facing a person with a gun.

The sound of running met my ears. Someone was legging it down the corridor toward mine and Wren's rooms.

I grabbed the top of the makeshift rope and climbed out of the window. My arms ached as soon as they took my weight. I pressed my heels against the stone wall, and began to descend.

Someone was rattling the door, trying to get in. They started smashing the oak. Smashing and smashing. Smashing with something bigger and stronger than a fist.

The wind attacked me, flinging my hair across my face and buffeting my sides. My cheeks stung and my coat flapped around my body. I clung on more tightly and continued to crawl down the side of the building. Looking down I could see that my rope ended some distance from the ground. I'd misjudged it quite badly.

I looked up to see Carl Maddock leaning over the window ledge peering down at me. The wind whipped his hair back from his face revealing deathly pale skin above a black jumper. He grinned and shook his finger at me as if telling me not to be so naughty then raised his left hand. In it he held a gun.

"Climb back up or I'll shoot," he said.

Terror pulsed in my chest but I hesitated only an instant. In that instant, the maggots shrieked at me and I listened.

I let my feet drop from the wall so that I was dangling then let go of the rope and dropped. A moment later I grabbed the rope and hung from it, arms about to pop from their sockets. Now, only a few feet from the ground, I let go and landed on my hands and feet.

A bullet ripped through the air inches from my head and I sprinted across the enclosure as another sounded, blasting the earth to my left, spitting up soil and grit that stung my legs. I reached the stone bench and climbed onto it then stood on tiptoe and grabbed the horizontal rail between the lethal spears. Finding strength I never knew I had, I pulled myself up and locked out my arms like a gymnast then pulled my right leg up. Bending it awkwardly, I placed my foot in a gap between the spears. A shot hit the air and the bullet skimmed my left shoulder. I screamed and would have speared myself on the fence if I hadn't dived forward. The spears ripped through my coat as I fell over them. I landed hard on my back. Another bullet came but this one connected with a railing and sent a harsh clang ringing across the moor.

Expecting another bullet, I rolled onto my hands and knees and pushed myself up then ran for the second fence. When no bullet came, I glanced over my shoulder. Carl Maddock wasn't in the window anymore.

Shoulder screaming, I ran to the second fence and

stopped. It was too high. There was no stone bench to climb on this time.

I tried to haul myself up the railings but kept slipping down. Looking back, I saw him run out of the house loading bullets into his gun.

Chapter Forty-Two

I scanned the fence and looked for a way to scale it, but there was nothing to stand on.

I glanced back – Carl Maddock was at the first gate.

For a terrifying moment it was as if my legs had stopped working, like my brain had lost the ability to send a message to my limbs and tell my body what to do. I stood there like a broken robot staring at my pursuer, unable to move. A nerve under my eye twitched and sweat dribbled down my cheek. The gate clanged as he ran away from it toward me raising his gun, a smile contorting his face, his movements quick and confident.

I still couldn't move. Fear spasmed in my heart and brain. Carl Maddock ran fast, so horribly fast, and I couldn't make myself move. I thought about surrendering then, about sinking to my knees and putting my hands in the air and begging him to stop, but the maggots slashed at my head and screamed in my ears. I winced at a sudden explosion of pain in my temples. They shrieked their orders and I jerked into action and yanked off my coat and extra jumper. Dizziness misted my vision yet I remained on my feet, turned sideways, sucked in my tummy and tried to squeeze between the railings…I was wedged, trapped between the metal poles feeling stupid and terrified - and then a miracle happened and I was free and out the other side.

Unable to believe it, I hesitated a fraction too long and a bullet whizzed past my ear. Turning, I saw Maddock sprinting toward the fence, gun raised, eyes wild.

The maggots gave me a savage kick and I turned and ran for the wood. Another bullet skimmed my right ear. I stumbled and gasped at the pain. Blood dribbled down my neck. I stumbled forward, regained my footing at the kissing gate and weaved in and out of it as a bullet split the post behind me. As if externalising my terror, the wind wailed through the trees like a demented spirit. Icy drizzle fell and I welcomed it against my burning skin. Half-running, half-stumbling I followed the path as far as it went before heading in the direction of the cabin.

An idea pieced itself together in my mind and I clung to it, drove my arms and legs forward and wove in and out of the skeletal trees, eyes up then down, constantly checking the ground and route ahead for hazards that could bring me crashing down.

"STOP!"

I turned. He was sprinting through the trees raising his gun again. Whirling back around, I tripped and fell. My knees smashed onto a root. I pushed myself to my feet as another shot hit the tree to my left. Bark and moss exploded in my face, splinters dug into my skin. Blinking frantically, I threw myself forward.

The cabin was in sight. Not long and I'd find what I was looking for. I turned left and headed for the swamp. I hoped I was heading in the right direction. Prayed I hadn't got it wrong.

Looking back, I was shocked to find he'd vanished. I wondered if the thought of seeing his prison had been enough to deter him and hope filled my chest, but just as hope came, the maggots reared their heads and bared their teeth warning me not to stop, so I plunged on through the trees and kept going.

I almost missed the deer's body. If it hadn't been for the smell, I would have run straight past.

Fear overrode squeamishness and I strode up to the corpse and grabbed hold of the axe handle. Intentionally not looking at her face, I slammed my foot onto her shoulder and heaved the axe out of her bloodied hide. Then I made the mistake of glancing at the wound. Maggots already swarmed there, white and plump, wriggling and writhing as they gorged on her flesh. I turned and threw up. Panic clogged my airways and I gasped for oxygen, heart frantic. A crunch made me spin around but the wood lay empty. The feeling of being watched pricked my senses and I stared through the trees. It was hard to believe he'd give up so easily, not when he'd come back after being locked in that cabin.

Raising the axe to my right shoulder, I crept from tree to tree, heading back the way I'd come. Every muscle in my body was tense. Even my jaw felt wired. The axe felt good in my hands despite my palms being wet with sweat. I could feel eyes on me but nothing happened. No bullets, no shouts. The wood seemed dead apart from the wind, which wailed and howled as if it knew what was about to happen.

Swiping drizzle from my eyes, I sank to my heels behind a fallen tree and listened. Despite having walked for the last few minutes, my chest rose and fell like I'd just run a marathon, so I allowed my heart time to rest and strained my ears for the slightest sound. Dusk was falling to a sallow grey that drained the wood of colour. I licked my lips and touched my ear. The blood had congealed. I inspected my shoulder, unsurprised to find it shiny with fresh blood. I wasn't losing it by the gallon but I was still losing it.

Glancing around to make sure I was alone, I gritted my teeth and pulled off my jumper then tied it around my shoulder as tightly as possible. The pain was intense and my shoulder throbbed in response. Blinking out tears, I stood up. Having rested, the cold air had found its way through my T-shirt and the sweat on my skin made me shiver.

I couldn't stay still. I had to keep moving.

Looking right then left, I raised the axe and stepped out from behind the tree.

A bullet smacked the axe blade and the axe flew out of my hands. I staggered back and tripped, hit the ground hard and screamed as pain spliced my coccyx. I rolled onto my front, reached for the axe and dragged it toward me. The crashing of feet met my ears and I looked up to see Carl Maddock hurtling through the trees.

"Stay there." He stopped and aimed the gun at my face. Victory sparked in his eyes. He stood with his legs wide apart, an almost casual slant to his shoulder. His chest rose and fell and beads of sweat dotted his forehead and upper lips. Two dots of colour flushed his cheeks. He raised one eyebrow and took a step closer – a slow, cocky step that mirrored his smirk.

"Put it down and come with me," he said.

I stared at the gun and strained to hear the maggots but they'd lost their voices. Uncertainty paralysed me. My fingers slipped around the axe shaft.

"If you come quietly, I won't touch a hair on your pretty head."

There was no way I could trust this man. If I moved, he might shoot; if I stayed, he might shoot; if I stayed, he might not kill me but he certainly wasn't going to let me go. Either way my chance to help Wren would be gone.

I tightened my grip on the axe, began to lift. It was heavy. My hand shook. My palm was wet with sweat.

He shook his head and tutted like I was a naughty schoolgirl. "Don't."

With a guttural groan, I dragged the axe up, pushed myself to my feet and fled. He roared something I couldn't make out and lunged after me, but didn't shoot; I glanced behind and saw him trip and fall.

Facing front, I darted through the trees and hit the path at a sprint. My jumper slipped off my shoulder and sweat stung my eyes as I weaved in and out of the kissing gate. Glancing back, I saw him running up the path. He raised his arm, took aim and shot at me; I screamed and ducked as the bullet went wide.

I ran and ran and reached the outer gate, ran through it then turned and slammed it shut. It wouldn't lock automatically but it would slow him down. This time when he raised the gun no bullet sounded; only an empty click. I glanced back. He swore and shoved the gun down the back of his jeans. I turned and sprinted for the inner fence. He was without bullets now, which gave me a chance.

With a final surge of energy, I heaved open the gate, darted through and slammed it shut then headed for the front door.

My hand hit oak as he yanked open the gate. I couldn't breathe. I saw my face in the plaque. Saw myself twisted beyond recognition. Blood on my skin.

He was only metres away. I seized the door knob and pretended to struggle with the door. The grubs cheered as his feet pounded the ground behind me.

When he was almost on top of me, I whirled around and swung the axe at his face.

Chapter Forty-Three

The axe handle connected with his raised arm and he cried out but didn't back off. Lunging forward, he tried to grab the axe from me with one hand and seized my neck with his other. I lashed out with my foot and kicked his calf. While pain ricocheted through my toes, he barely reacted. His fingers squeezed my neck as I smashed the axe up into his chin. His head jerked back at the impact and he roared and let go of me. Clinging onto the axe for dear life, I whirled around and yanked open the front door then headed for the stairs - but he was too fast. Halfway up, he grabbed my T-shirt and yanked me back. I was lucky – he'd lunged too far. When I twisted away he let go and fell face-first onto the steps. I stamped on his hand and ran up the rest of the stairs. He screamed at me to stop, hoarse with rage.

Shoulder burning, I ran along the corridor, reached my bedroom and hesitated. I didn't know what the hell to do next. He was still coming for me; I could hear his feet thundering up the stairs.

I ran into my bedroom and closed the door then hid in the space where the door would open. My chest heaved and I frantically tried to control my breathing as the sound of his footsteps stopped.

My breathing was too loud, but I told myself he probably knew which room I was in anyway – he would have heard the door shut.

A floorboard creaked outside the room. Wren was probably still in his bedroom, across from mine. I hoped he'd stay quiet. A sharp pain speared my stomach at the thought of him doing anything to Wren and I squeezed the axe handle tighter.

Another creak came. And another. I raised the axe.

The door clicked and creaked inward. The maggots held their breath.

I stepped out and swung the axe into where I thought his head would be but he was on his hands and knees crawling into the room. With a roar, he dived forward and rugby-tackled me to the ground. I hit the floor hard and dropped the axe. Kicking up with my knees, I thumped my fists into his face but he pressed the length of his body on top of mine, pushed me down and pinned my hands to the floor by my head.

I stopping struggling and lay still.

He smiled and stared into my eyes, thinking he'd won. Sweat drifted off him in salt-sweet waves and beaded his forehead. A purple bruise bloomed under his chin from where I'd hit him.

He glanced at the axe. It lay on the ground a metre to his left. I glanced at it too and fought a burst of ice-cold fear. The maggots lay still, their voices cut off. I willed them to say something – anything – but my head was empty. I never thought I'd want them to stay but now they were gone, I felt blank and utterly helpless. Panic clogged my throat and I felt my eyes begin to water.

"Ah. Don't cry. I'm not that bad. Honest," he panted.

"What've you done to the others?" My voice shook and I flinched, desperate not to show him how scared I was.

His eyes glinted. He smirked and lowered his face to mine. In my ear he said, "Not dead yet, honey, if that's what you mean."

"Get off me," I said yanking my ear away from his mouth.

He jerked his head up and frowned at me as if offended. "Just another stupid bitch thick as shit, up herself."

Shocking myself, I snapped, "And you're just another

stupid bastard with a chip on his shoulder."

He shook his head and laughed, let go of my wrist and grabbed the axe. "Ooh, I love a feisty one. What's your name, honey?"

He hauled me to my feet and wrapped his free hand around the back of my neck. He held tightly but didn't hurt me, though I sensed he would if I tried to break free. Pulling me close, he raised the axe to my cheek. "Your name?"

"Ivy."

"Good girl. Try anything, I'll change my mind and use my friend here." He jerked his head at the axe.

He winked and pushed me out of the room. On the landing, he opened Wren's bedroom door. Horror seized me as the door creaked open to reveal Wren standing in the centre of his room, a chisel clutched in his left hand, eyes wide with fear. His whole body was trembling.

Carl pushed me to my knees, crouched down and placed the axe on the ground.

Ever-so-softly, he said, "Come here, Son."

Wren looked at me then back at Carl. In my heart, fear collided with shock. *Son?*

"It's Daddy," Carl said, "I'm taking you home."

"Ivy?" Wren said.

"It's okay. Put that down now and come with us, okay?"

He placed the chisel on his desk. I eyed the chisel, wishing there was some way I could grab it and plunge it into one of Carl's eyes, but he hauled me to my feet and gestured for Wren to leave the room. Wren walked up to me and slipped his hand into mine. A small act of defiance, but one that Carl decided to let go.

"One happy family," he said, pulling me out of the room.

Wren walked beside us as Carl manoeuvred me down the corridor. He held the axe in his free hand and I noticed Wren looking at it, eyes huge with terror. I gave his hand a squeeze and he squeezed back and looked up at me. I smiled and he

returned the smile, though his trembled. My heart cracked –
I needed to give him a cuddle and tell him everything was
going to be okay but the words would die on my tongue. It
wasn't going to be okay.

It was obvious now why Mrs Waters had locked Carl
Maddock in the cabin. Why she'd ripped out his nails.

He'd done something terrible to Odette. Exactly what
he'd done, I didn't know but..if Wren was *Odette's* son and
Carl was his father…

I tasted acid in the back of my throat as some of the
pieces slotted into place.

I looked down at Wren's auburn hair. He was, now that
I saw them side by side and awful though it was to admit, the
image of his father.

At the top of the staircase Carl paused. "Ladies first."

Though every bone and cell in my body protested, I
moved to pull Wren along with me, but Carl shook his head
and whispered, "He's holding *my* hand now. Try anything,
you know what'll happen."

He waved the axe next to my face. I let go of Wren's
hand and he gave a whine of protest.

"It's alright, Son," Carl said, "That's it. Hold my hand.
Good lad."

I felt the axe head nudge my spine and walked down the
stairs. Outwardly I looked meek; inwardly I tore out his eyes
with my nails and slashed his throat with an imaginary knife.

My childhood had taught me a lot about men like this
and I knew there was one good thing about them: let them
think they'd won and their arrogance made them let their
guard down.

Just like Mum's boyfriend.

If I could do it as a girl, I could do it again as a woman.

Chapter Forty-Four

Carl Maddock pushed me ahead and ordered me to turn left. I obeyed and drifted spirit-like over the floorboards toward the dining hall door. I could hear Carl's heavy footfalls and the pitter-patter of Wren's feet as he scurried to keep up. I wanted to look back and give Wren a reassuring smile but didn't, because the axe remained pressed into my spine. If I turned or slowed, Carl shoved me with the metal axe head. I could already feel a bruise forming.

In the dining hall the table lay bare. The room was cold and echoey. Carl prodded me toward the kitchen. Once inside, he steered me to the trapdoor and told me to open it. I knelt on the hard stone and did as I was told. He placed the axe on the kitchen counter and turned to Wren. I swivelled on my knees and watched as the bastard bent down to bring his face an inch from his son's.

In a gentle voice he said, "I'm going to ask you to stay in here for a bit now. It's for your own safety. I promise I'll come and get you soon, when it's safe. Stay in here like a good boy for me, okay?"

Wren's eyes flitted to mine. I gave him a small nod. He looked back at Carl and said, "Okay."

"Okay, *what?*" Carl said.

Wren hesitated, licked his lips. His chin trembled as he said, "Okay, Daddy."

I watched, helpless to do anything as he patted Wren's head and guided him through the trapdoor. Wren had only gone down five steps when Carl slammed the door shut.

"There's no light down there," I said, "He'll be terrified." Carl shrugged. "He won't be in there for long."

"Put me in there with him."

He grabbed the axe off the counter and yanked me to my feet. "You're coming to see the fun. You've got important lessons to learn, honey."

He pressed the axe into my back and steered me out of the kitchen. A memory came to me: the first time I saw Mrs Waters. Her statuesque figure appearing, her smile, laugh, weird clothes. The way she disarmed me with her charm, made me believe she was someone I could trust. I remembered the smoothness of her hand and her lavender scent. She'd seemed motherly and honest and warm. But she'd been harbouring terrible secrets. I'd been hiding mine too, but they weren't as bad. Neither of our secrets were as dark as the evil man she'd kept from civilisation. If Mrs Waters hadn't taken matters into her own hands and locked him up, would the legal system have found him guilty and imprisoned him? Or would a clever lawyer have got him off? Would he still be roaming the streets raping and torturing innocent girls?

Right now, it didn't matter. Mrs Waters had tried to exert her own justice, but I'd come along and sabotaged it. And now he was going to make everyone suffer.

Carl shoved me across the entrance hall. I tried to tell myself that regardless of my choices, this show would have played out anyway, but the harder I tried to convince myself, the more I realised that none of this would have happened if I'd kept my nose out of other people's business. If it wasn't for me, Carl would still be locked up in the cabin, Wren would be safe – miserable yes, but safe – and no-one would be in danger.

Carl paused outside the living room door. I listened and heard nothing coming from the room. His breathing hitched. I glanced up to see his cheeks flushed, a manic look in his eyes.

"Just you wait," he said.

He raised the axe to his shoulder and grabbed the back of my neck. Pulling my face close, he said, "Watch and learn, honey. Watch and learn."

Wind howled beyond the walls of the house like a pack of wolves. The howling got in my head and muffled the maggots panicky voices. I tried to hear them but the wind was too loud.

No. It was my time to take control.

I gave Carl a coy smile and his eyebrows shot up.

"Don't play," he said digging his nails into my neck.

"I'm not."

His eyes turned to slits. Bringing his mouth a centimetre from mine, he stared into my eyes. I held his gaze then let mine drop.

A smile tugged up the corner of his mouth and his gaze dropped to my lips. I dropped my chin and stared at the floor to give the impression of subservience, hoping he'd believe it. He sniggered, opened the living room door and pushed me into the room.

When I saw the bodies, I screamed.

Chapter Forty-Five

Carl smiled. He pushed me further into the room.

Blood. So much blood.

Chaise longue not cream. Red now. So much red.
Two bodies. One sprawled on top of the other.
Ping and Maddock.
Dead.

A strange feeling skittered behind my eyes. I leaned against the wall and sucked in sharp breaths. The grubs hid in the creases of my brain. I could feel them trembling. I looked away from the bodies. I didn't want to see them; didn't want to believe they were dead; couldn't accept that the man holding an axe to my back was capable of such atrocity. If he could murder his own blood, what could he do to Wren and me?

"This is what happens when you cross me," he said. He forced my chin up.

There was blood on the walls, on the tapestries, on the china ballerinas. I blinked rapidly.

Carl pushed me across the room. He paused beside Ping and Maddock's bodies and turned my face to look down at them. "This is what'll happen to you if you don't do exactly what I say."

I closed my eyes but blood blossomed in the blacks of my eyelids. I could smell the blood. See the blood without opening my eyes. I imagined myself lying there, my chest a caved-in, blood-soaked cavity, my eyes open but blank and unseeing like Maddock's. I imagined Ralph lying underneath me, his face pressed flat to the soiled ground like Ping's, his glasses cracked and broken at Carl's feet.

Carl stroked my neck. "Don't worry, honey. If you're a good girl you'll be fine."

I sucked in a breath.

He kicked open the door to the library and steered me into the room.

Odette and Mrs Waters were on the ground tied up, their wrists and ankles bound together by thick rope that trailed from their ankles to the piano. Black rags gagged their mouths. A knife protruded from Mrs Waters' side. Blood drenched her dress and soaked into the floorboards. Her chin rested on her chest, which rose and fell in little hitches. Damp bits of hair clung to her face.

She turned her head a fraction and tracked Carl's movements as he guided me onto a rocking chair in the corner of the room and forced me to sit down. I tried to catch her eye but her gaze was fixed on him. Odette glanced from Carl to me, her eyes slow, face death-white in the dreary light.

The room was cold. There was no fire, only stacks of books and the piano. Wind battered the windows and dusk dimmed the room to a dismal grey that made Mrs Waters look dead. I watched her for a few moments afraid she was dead, but her chest rose and fell again. A strange kind of relief overwhelmed me; she wasn't the monster in all this. He was.

He placed a hand on my shoulder and said, "Words, words, beautiful *fucking* words. Sometimes it's just justice. Simple, *fucking* justice. Justice and a *fucking* axe. Don't you just wish you'd done that now, Harriet?"

Mrs Waters' eyes met mine for a fleeting moment and I saw strength as well as pain. Her eyes darted to Carl. They narrowed. A smirk tugged at her mouth as she hissed, "You're a coward, Carl, and you've always talked too much. Get on with it, will you? I'm bored. Or are you too scared to finish what you've started? As I recall you always were rather premature."

She threw her head back and laughed, and I wondered how much the movement hurt her insides. I also wondered why she would taunt him. Aggravating him was the last thing she should be doing. I wanted to say something. Tell her to apologise and beg for his forgiveness, to say anything she could to appease him and persuade him to let us go, but the maggots hissed at me to be quiet. To wait. See what kind of game she was playing. She knew this man. Maybe that meant she knew how to get inside his head. How to play him.

She aimed a dark smile at him, raising one eyebrow in a taunting manner. Odette brought her hands up and covered her face. She tried to rock but being tied to her mother stifled her movement. Instead, she jerked her head back and forth and began to moan.

Mrs Waters acted like she was unaware of her daughter's distress. She leaned her head forward and said, "Do it. Finish me off. Put me out of my misery. I *dare* you."

I flinched. Carl tightened his grip on my neck.

"You'd like that, wouldn't you, bitch?"

She grinned. I tried to catch her eye but she would only look at Carl.

"You're a pathetic coward, just like your father," she said.

Carl let go of my neck and strode over to her. Crouching down, he grabbed her face and forced her chin up. "If you think talking about him'll get to me, you're wrong. I'm twice the man he was. He means nothing to me. But the kid – he's everything. I'm gonna show him how to be a man. Bring him up to know that bitches like you need to pay for what they've done."

He laughed and pushed her face away then hurled the axe into the bookshelf. It connected with a bang that made the books shudder and crash to the floorboards. Odette jumped.

I stared at the axe. It was over the other side of the room, closer to him than me. Adrenaline pumped around my body.

Mrs Waters whispered something.

He leaned in, eyes flinty, and said, "Speak up, Harriet. Parting words and all that."

"I said, I can't believe you killed your own brother."

He frowned. "*Half*-brother."

"Yes, but still your flesh and blood." She looked at him curiously.

"He knew what you'd done to me. He let it happen. He let me rot away in there for all that time. He deserved it," he said, a tremor in his voice.

"Maddock was practically a father to you growing up," she said, "He raised you. He got you the job here. He *loved* you, Carl. He loved you and you killed him."

"He deserved it. He knew I was locked up and did nothing to help me."

"And why do you think that was? You *raped* Odette. You cut her back, scarred her for life in more ways than one. You very nearly *killed* her when she was just fourteen years old. Maddock knew that was wrong, but he still loved you. He's always loved you. He's the one who stopped me from killing you. If it wasn't for Maddock, you'd be dead."

"Liar," Carl said.

She chuckled. "If I'm a liar, why do you look so forlorn all of a sudden?"

"Shut up," he said.

"Maddock was a good man who loved you. Took care of you when your mother died."

"Shut *up*."

"Did he apologise before you shot him in the face? I bet he did, didn't he? Despite what you did to Odette, he never stopped loving you. Knowing you were in there cut him up inside, but he knew I was right to punish you. What you did to Odette was pure evil."

He paced the room and dragged a hand over his eyes. "I

said, shut the fuck *up*."

"He loved you. He wanted you to make a go of it here. He spent weeks telling me all about you. About what you'd been through. At first, I didn't want to help. From what he'd told me, I thought you were beyond saving, but he never gave up. He worked on me until I finally gave in and do you know why he did that?"

Carl froze and stared at the floor. I could hear his teeth grinding.

I wanted to tell Mrs Waters to stop, to shut up. Winding him up wasn't working; it was only making him mad, but she ploughed on, a wicked light brightening her eyes.

"He did that because he had a heart. Something you've never had."

For a moment, he stood there, still as a stone. Slowly, he turned his face to hers. I stared at the back of his head then at the axe on the other side of room.

"Say that again," he said. His voice shook.

She grinned. "With pleasure. You're dead inside. And a coward. A pathetic, rotten, little coward."

He grabbed his crotch and thrust it in her face. "Dead? How dead d'you think I was when I used this? When I made a fucking kid."

"A child who's good and kind and absolutely nothing like you. A child who will *never* be like you. I should have realised that a long time ago."

He laughed and stabbed a finger at her eye. "That's where you're wrong, bitch. I'm taking him and there's shit you can do to stop me."

"He hates you," she said, "Wren *despises* you."

He lunged forward and backhanded her face. Mrs Waters cried out and Odette screamed. I pushed myself up from the rocking chair and headed for the axe, but he was too aware of me. Whirling around, he grabbed my top, dragged me back and pushed me to the floor at the foot of the rocking chair.

He stalked across the room, grabbed the axe and moved to stand in front of Mrs Waters. Without a backward glance he said to me, "Move and I'll gut you next."

I closed my eyes as he raised the axe above his head.

"Please," Odette said, "Please don't hurt my mummy."

Carl's hands froze above his head. I couldn't see his face. His breathing was ragged.

Mrs Waters turned her head and said, "Shush now, darling. It's okay. Everything's going to be okay." Her voice shook.

Carl lowered the axe and moved to Odette. He crouched in front of her and stared at her face. His expression was thoughtful. He raised his hand and stroked her cheek. In a soft voice he said, "Don't worry, honey. I'll take good care of our son. I'm taking him home with me. Me and Ivy'll look after him and I'll teach him everything he needs to know and one day he'll be just like me. He'll -"

Odette's head jerked upwards and she screamed. Carl lurched away as she launched herself at him knocking him onto his back. Straddling his chest, she raised her arm. A small blade protruded from her fist.

She smashed her hand down into Carl's chest again and again and again. He screamed and threw her off but not before she'd stabbed him three times. Clutching his chest, he reached for the axe. Odette's feet were still tied together. She tried to crawl away but he grabbed her leg and dragged her back. As his hand found the axe, I threw myself on top of his arm, pinning it to the ground long enough for Mrs Waters to smash her feet into his jaw. Odette used her blade to slash through the rope around her ankles. She pushed herself to her feet and turned, eyes huge and helpless.

"*Run*," Mrs Waters said.

Odette just stood there. Carl found his strength and threw me off. I landed on top of Mrs Waters and rolled onto my side. He grabbed the axe and raised it above his head.

"*Run,* baby!"

This time Odette listened. Carl took aim and threw the axe at Odette's retreating back. It landed behind her foot missing her by an inch, and she carried on running.

Carl swore and hesitated. He seemed to make up his mind and turned to me. I was frantically trying to untie Mrs Waters' hands. I was almost done, but he grabbed my neck and hauled me up, wrapped his arm around my neck and got me in a headlock. I struggled and clawed at his arm but there was no way I could get out of his grip. With his free hand he seized Mrs Waters' hair and dragged her across the room toward the axe, which was wedged in the floor.

Blood dripped down his jumper onto my face. He was panting hard now. Mrs Waters fought him but with her feet and hands still tied, she was powerless to do anything except slow him down. To my relief, he ignored the axe and pulled us into the living room past Maddock's and Ping's bodies. Mrs Waters inhaled a sob and he sniggered. I let my body go limp to make myself as heavy as possible but he dragged us both out of the room into the entrance hall.

He paused halfway across the room to rest and Mrs Waters came alive – thrashing and twisting and biting - and so did I. Together we managed to unbalance him. He roared and hurled Mrs Waters across the space. She fell onto her side with a gasp and tore at her binds, managing to free her wrists. I stilled as Carl's arm tightened around my throat, choking the air out of me. He lunged for Mrs Waters and she brought her feet up and smashed him in the chest. He staggered back with a cry and she ripped the rope off her ankles and pushed herself to her feet. She was drenched in her own blood.

"Go," I said as Carl reached for her and tightened his grip on my neck.

She hesitated a moment, looked at me fearfully then

staggered outside. In the pre-night gloom, I glimpsed the enclosure and the fence and the dark mass of wood beyond. Saw a white smudge that must have been Odette in the distance. I heard Mrs Waters scream her daughter's name as she stumbled into the darkness of the moor, blood trailing in her wake.

Carl cursed and hauled me toward the front door. Again, I made myself a dead weight. He paused in the doorway, swore again and spat on the ground. His breaths tore from his chest. He was clearly in pain from the wounds Odette had inflicted. I expected him to drag me out of the house and go after them, but he didn't. Instead, he kicked the door shut and dragged me into the dining hall. Pain sent waves of nausea roiling through my stomach.

"Fucking bitch," he muttered as he dragged me through the room into the kitchen. I didn't know if he was talking to me or about Mrs Waters but I stayed silent. Inside, hope flared; Mrs Waters and Odette had escaped. They'd run down the hill and get to safety. It wouldn't take them long to reach Weirlock and call the police, then the police would come and rescue me and Wren.

The thought that Mrs Waters wouldn't call the police crossed my mind but I pushed it away. No. She wasn't that far gone. She'd get me and Wren the help we needed and she'd do it as quickly as she could – as long as she survived long enough. The wound in her stomach was bad. Very bad.

Chapter Forty-Six

While Carl shouted at Wren to come up out of the basement, he grabbed hold of my wrist and shot warning glances at the kitchen knife he'd slipped between his belt and jeans.

The pain in my shoulder was increasing. Fighting had taken the last of my energy and there was no point in trying anything now, not when I was in this state. He seemed in bad shape too but if the strength of his grip on my arm was anything to go by, he was in better shape than me. I stole a glance at his chest wounds. They didn't look deep. I wondered what Odette had used on him and decided it was probably a pen knife, though where she'd got one I couldn't guess.

The blood on his jumper had dried into a cloggy mess. Dried blood smeared the side of his face and hands. It could have been his, mine or Mrs Waters'. Mrs Waters' wound was deep. The knife had still been wedged in her side when she'd run from the house. It was a miracle she'd been able to run at all. Like me, adrenaline must have kept her going. Or hysterical strength – I'd read about it once; in life or death situations mothers could somehow flick a switch and channel inhuman strength, lifting cars to save their child. But now, like me, her adrenaline was probably waning. I didn't want to consider the possibility that she and Odette might never get to Weirlock, but the idea span like a propeller blade whirring incessantly in my mind. If they didn't get to Weirlock and call the police, what then?

I gave Wren a reassuring smile but his eyes were locked on my shoulder - on the blood that soaked my T-shirt.

Carl downed a glass of water then offered Wren some.

He recoiled and slipped his hand into mine. His father shrugged and slammed the glass down on the counter making Wren jump.

"We're going," he said jerking his head toward the kitchen door.

"Where?" I said stumbling over my own feet as he yanked me forward.

He didn't answer, just gave me a strange smile.

Wren was silent, feet quick beside mine as Carl hurried us out of the kitchen through the dining hall into the entrance hall and out of the house.

Darkness was complete now, the sky starless, the wind at full force. Icy gusts whipped at my cheeks and lifted my damp T-shirt, chilling my skin. Wren squealed and I pulled him in behind me to block some of the wind.

With a wince, Carl withdrew something from his pocket. A moment later, a tiny beam of light appeared on the heather in front of his feet and he used it to guide us along the path toward the inner gate, which swung back and forth with blackboard-like squeals. The gate clanged shut just before we reached it and Carl shoved it open and dragged me through.

Wren scurried along behind me. His hand was ice-cold in mine. I glanced back at him and mouthed *okay?* He nodded but was anything but. I pulled him closer and wrapped my free arm around his shoulders. Carl looked around but said nothing.

We reached the outer fence. Carl opened it and lead us toward a white van. Dizziness made my knees buckle as he withdrew keys from his jeans and unlocked the vehicle.

"Get up," he yelled, but his words were distant, his face a blur.

I landed on something hard and smashed my cheekbone. Pain ricocheted around my face and I closed my eyes, heard something slam, felt something cold touch my cheek, then everything went dark.

*

I woke to see Wren sitting on the floor surrounded by toys. He held a red car in one hand and dully stared at it while fingering the bumble bee pendant around his neck. His face was pale but he appeared unharmed. He wore a man's jumper. The voluminous garment swamped him making him look even smaller than normal. A plastic cup filled with what looked like water sat beside a plate of biscuits next to Wren's feet on the dusty wooden floor.

I scanned the room for Carl but he wasn't there. We appeared to be shut inside a shed or outbuilding of some kind. An electric heater hummed in the corner warming the space enough to prevent my skin from goosing. There were no windows, just a few empty flower pots, a pair of soiled gardening gloves, a rusted rake and a half-empty sack of compost.

Around my shoulders lay an orange shawl covered with white cat hairs. I was shocked to see that my arm had been bandaged. I raised my shoulder the tiniest bit and pain knocked me sideways. I gasped and Wren looked up at me. Delight spread across his face and he ran over and threw his arms around my waist. I hugged him back and kissed his head.

"I'm so sorry. I must've passed out. What happened when I was asleep?"

Wren pulled away and sat cross-legged opposite me. With a frown, he whispered, "The bad man locked the door. He said he'd be back soon and he told me to be quiet and said that if I was a good boy, he'd bring me back a big piece of chocolate cake. I've never had chocolate cake before."

"How long's he been gone?"

Wren blinked at me and scratched his head. "I don't know."

"Okay. Don't worry."

"It was still dark when we got here," he said.

"Any idea how long we were in the van for?"

He shook his head and nibbled his thumbnail. Tears welled in his eyes and I reached out and grabbed his hands. "Don't worry. Everything's going to be okay. I promise. You trust me?"

He nodded and wiped his eyes with the back of his hand. "Yes, Ivy."

"Then trust me when I say everything'll be fine. Things might seem bad right now, but soon we'll be out of here. Okay?"

"But what about the bad man?"

I pulled him close. "The bad man will be gone soon. I'll make sure of it."

Wren pulled back and raised an eyebrow. "How? How will you make sure? He's strong and really bad. He's the most baddest man in the whole wide world."

I looked into Wren's eyes and smiled. "I know, but the goodies always win. It might be tricky but I'll find a way."

"Promise?"

"Promise."

"Cross your heart and hope to die?"

"Stick a needle in a fly."

Wren smiled and I pulled him in even closer, hoping that I'd actually find a way to keep my word and get Wren to safety.

Chapter Forty-Seven

Less than an hour later the door clicked and Carl stepped into the shed wearing a red jumper and black jeans into which was tucked a gun. He was clean-shaven and had tended to his chest wounds. His face was slightly grey but he looked and smelt clean. A strong wave of aftershave hit as he bent down and smiled at Wren, whose body stiffened. Wren glanced at me and I gave him a small smile. I'd coached him on how to behave, giving him three rules to follow.

One: don't argue.

Two: be polite.

Three: call him Daddy.

If Wren followed these rules, he wouldn't make Carl angry. I hoped. Of course, I could be wrong. I didn't know this man well enough to predict his behaviour. He was violent and sadistic. Wren might be his son, but that might not be enough to stop the bastard from hurting him.

Fear made my insides cramp as I imagined how far Carl's sadism might go. Horrors of what he might do to Wren if he annoyed him crawled around my head. So far, he hadn't hurt Wren, but from what I'd seen in the basement at Fairwood House and what I'd witnessed since, he wasn't beyond hurting his own flesh and blood. Maddock had been his half-brother. His family.

Maddock's dead body loomed large in my mind. Carl had killed his own half-brother.

Wren looked at me for reassurance. Inside I was screaming, but I smiled at him and said, "Be a good boy, now. I'm sure your daddy just wants to spend some time with you. Get to know you better."

I looked at Carl. He ignored me and crouched down in front of Wren. With a broad smile that lit up his eyes in a way I never imagined possible he said, "I've got you chocolate cake. Aren't I the best dad ever?"

Wren looked at me and Carl grabbed his chin and yanked his face back. "Look at me, not her."

My heart lurched as Wren whispered, "Yes, Daddy. Thank you for my chocolate cake."

Carl let go of his chin and nodded. He smiled smugly and stood up. "Good boy."

He turned to lead Wren out of the shed and Wren said, "Can Ivy have some too? Can she come with us, Daddy? Please?"

Shit. Every single part of me tensed. Carl's shoulders stiffened. He said nothing for a few seconds. I couldn't see his face, didn't know what he was thinking.

"It's okay," I said quickly, "Daddy wants to spend some time alone with you, Wren. Now be a good boy and enjoy your cake, okay?"

Carl turned and met my eyes. "Actually, let's have Mummy join us, shall we Wren? I'm sure she'd love some chocolate cake too. I'm sure she'll behave herself and be a good girl."

Mummy?

He glanced down at the gun then reached out a hand and pulled me to my feet. His hand was dry and rough. I flinched at the contact as I stood up. To my horror, he planted a wet kiss on my lips. Wren's eyes widened.

I forced a smile and took hold of Wren's other hand as Carl opened the door. Together, the three of us walked out into a strikingly sunny day. Cold air hit me and my breath misted in front of my face. I snuck glances of the area; ahead was a sandstone cottage; on either side of it nothing but fields. Further to the east stood another building, a farmhouse possibly. There were more fields to the west.

I squinted past the cottage and saw a narrow country road, beyond which ran a barbed wire fence and another stretch of fields. No houses stood opposite the cottage. The farmhouse was the only other structure in sight.

I glanced back: behind the small brown shed was a wooden fence that surrounded the back garden. The grass was overgrown and wild with weeds as if it hadn't seen a lawnmower in years. Past the fence lay more fields. We were somewhere remote, tucked away in the countryside far from other houses. I couldn't work out where we were. All I knew was that Carl had brought us somewhere far from civilisation. Somewhere no-one would hear us scream.

I squinted at the farmhouse and tried to make out if anyone was over there. I could see what looked like a tractor sitting in the field but there were no cars around. No sheep, cows or pigs. No people. To the left of the farm, a set of electrical support towers cut across the fields butchering the view. On the horizon I saw fields in varying colours rising and falling in hilly waves that were pieced together like a patchwork quilt. It was maddening. With no-one living nearby, it was unlikely anyone would ever work out what was going on here. My only hope was the road in front of the cottage. It was a narrow country road, but someone was bound to drive down it and pass the cottage at some point. How much that would help us if we were inside the house was another question.

Carl led us around the side of the cottage and opened the back door. He ushered Wren and me in first then closed and locked the door behind us all.

"Tea?" he said.

I peeled my eyes away from the kitchen counter and nodded my head at him. He smirked and set about preparing the drinks. I looked back at the counter. Wren was staring at it too. He gripped my hand and huddled in close.

Lined up on the side were four guns. All different. All

equally terrifying. Now there were five including the one tucked in his jeans.

He placed a cup of tea in my hand and tapped the gun at his waist reminding me not to do anything stupid. Pulling out a plastic chair, he sat down, placed his mug on the table and pulled out the chair beside him. He tapped the seat and told Wren to sit down. Wren did as instructed. He was so small that his feet hung a foot from the floor. He couldn't peel his eyes away from the guns. Neither could I.

"Sit," he said to me.

I sat opposite him and said, "Interesting collection."

"Thanks. It is, isn't it?"

"Yes. Where'd you get them?"

"Black market. I've got a bunch of contacts from my younger days. Networking was my forte. Oh, and a stash of money obviously. Guns aren't cheap."

I nodded as if I knew what he was talking about. "Where'd you get the money?"

Carl glanced at Wren who was still staring at the guns. "I have my ways."

I tried to look impressed then glanced around the kitchen. It was tiny and cheap but the surfaces were clean. White blinds hid the windows.

"Is this your house?" I said, "It's lovely."

Carl's eyes narrowed. He sipped his tea and winced. I hoped the bastard had burnt off his tongue. "It's a crap heap but it'll do for now."

Behind him was a closed door. I gestured toward it. "Is that the lounge?"

He nodded, got up and walked to the fridge. He pulled out a packaged chocolate cake and dropped it on the table in front of Wren.

"This is for all the birthdays I missed," he said rubbing his nose.

"Thank you, Daddy," Wren said.

"No problemo, Son. Here," he said, handing us each a fork, "dig in."

Wren frowned at the fork and said, "Can I have a plate, please?"

Carl's lips twisted. "No. You cannot have a plate. Now *eat.*"

Wren looked like he'd been slapped. He scraped a tiny piece of chocolate buttercream off the side of the cake. Carl watched him, eyes intense, jaw clenched. He handed me a fork and I copied Wren. The buttercream tasted like rancid milk but I forced myself to swallow it. Carl stood and watched us with his hands on his hips. I imagined plunging the fork into his eye, but his fingers were millimetres from the gun at his waist.

"Let's have some tunes, shall we?" he said with forced brightness.

He withdrew a phone from his pocket and fiddled about with it until Blur was playing, the sound tinny and horribly reminiscent of my childhood. Mum's boyfriend had loved Blur; he'd played it every time we'd been in the car.

Memories snatched me from the present and I was back there, in the car, hating him and wishing he was dead. It had been my eighth birthday.

On that particular occasion, he'd thrown Mum out on the street dressed only in her underwear then locked the house and taken the keys. He'd chucked me in the car and started driving. I hadn't known where we were going or why we'd left and was too scared to ask. He'd never hurt me but had threatened to plenty of times, and I'd seen him hurt Mummy.

I'd made myself as tiny as possible and stared out of the window at the world flashing by. He'd put on Blur and sung along. To me he sounded drunk, but so did the man who sang the song. The music was so loud it hurt my ears. I wanted to cover them but didn't dare. I tried to turn inside myself and think about good times before he'd come along, when Mummy hadn't been so confused.

I almost got lost in a memory when the maggots began to whisper. At first, I'd looked around the car, convinced someone else was in there with us. After a while I realised the maggots were in my head. They whispered to me, tried to persuade me to do awful things to him. I managed to ignore them for the entire journey. I dug my nails so hard into my palms that they bled.

At dusk, he drove me back home. Mum was sitting around the side of the house shivering. There was frost on the ground and she still wore nothing but her underwear. Her lips were blue and she looked like she was about to die. No-one had helped her because they were too scared to get involved. They knew what he was like.

When he saw her, he *laughed*. He didn't go to her or didn't help her inside the house. He just left her there, out in the freezing cold in her underwear.

I got in bed and waited until I heard him shut his bedroom door before I crept downstairs and let Mum inside. She was so cold she couldn't speak. I made her a hot water bottle and covered her with a blanket. The whole time the maggots whispered to me and at last I let them in.

When I was sure Mum was asleep, I crept into the bathroom and grabbed her razor then tiptoed upstairs and opened his door. He was lying on his front, snoring.

The maggots sniggered as I walked up to the bed and lowered the razor to his face. I positioned the blade in the space between his eyes and dragged it down his nose, pressing as hard as I could. Skin peeled away from the bone like a potato. There was so much blood. More than I'd expected. He woke up screaming, confused and terrified. The worms cracked up. Now, it was my turn to laugh. They danced the mambo and sang If You're Happy And You Know It when he fled the house in nothing but his Homer

Simpson boxers, clutching his ruined nose, quivering with shock and fear.

He never came back. I'd turned him into a stripe-nosed skunk. Given him his own nightmare. One he'd never forget. It was secret I'd take to my grave.

Unfortunately, it was too late to save her. Soon after, she tried to kill herself. Six months later, Grandma had her sectioned because she became catatonic...

"Ivy? Ivy? COME IN, IVY."

I re-focused on the kitchen - the guns - Carl's irritated frown – Wren's terrified face. Crumbs of chocolate cake dotted Wren's lips. Carl was holding one of the gun's that had been on the counter, a big one. A shotgun possibly.

"Sorry," I said.

"Where were you?"

"The past. Bad memories."

He nodded as if he understood and eyed me thoughtfully. He looked down at the cake.

"More?" There was a note of insistence in his tone that would be dangerous to ignore.

"Yes," I said scraping a tiny piece off the top of the cake and imagining I was scraping the fork down his nose.

Chapter Forty-Eight

For an hour Carl sat at the table with Wren on his lap showing him his gun collection. Wren was interested but scared. His fingers never left the bumble bee pendant and every few minutes he looked up to check I was still there. Whenever he looked up, Carl tensed. I longed to warn Wren not to look at me, but knew it wouldn't be wise so I just watched and listened, and took it all in.

He told Wren every detail about each gun. Sweet, innocent Wren who thought he could fly.

Would Wren think the guns were toys? Carl certainly seemed to think they were, though he clearly loved the damage they could do. His eyes shone when he told Wren a story about how he'd shot up an old fridge in a salvage yard. How the fridge had blown apart like it had been hit by a grenade – not that Wren would know what a grenade was, of course.

"This gorgeous beast's a 12-gauge pump-action shotgun. Awesome right? .22LR pistol – sweet as. Then there's this beauty: Glock 19 handgun – no-one's messing if they spot him. And, last but so not least, the pièce de résistance. Mr Colt 6920 rifle. Sexy or what?" He patted the gun in his waistband and said, "Not forgetting my mate here Sir Smith and Wesson .357 Magnum, at your service."

The silver thug of a gun looked like something out of a cartoon. Carl pulled the gun out of his belt and held it up to the bulb that hung from the off-white ceiling. Its silver body gleamed.

"This baby is the *king*. Don't worry, Son, I'll show you how to shoot him. Day's perfect. Sun's a-shining, weather's sweet. Gimme a moment to sort out Mummy then we'll set off."

"Where're you taking him?" I said trying to keep my voice even.

Carl lifted Wren off his lap and stood up. He tapped his nose and seized my elbow.

"Now that would be telling." He glanced at Wren. "Sometimes it's fun to have secrets. Right, Son?"

Wren didn't answer. He was staring at the gun collection. The Colt rifle lay inches from my hand. As if reading my mind, Carl yanked me to my feet and pulled me away from the table. My shoulder screamed in protest and I winced. He saw my pain and pulled a mock-pity face then steered me out of the room into a narrow hallway.

"He's too young to fire a gun," I said, "the recoil will hurt him."

Carl paused and shook his head. "These beauties are low recoil. He'll have the time of his life."

"He's never been outside Fairwood House, remember. He'll be terrified of everything."

He shrugged. "Kid's got to learn sometime."

"I agree, but not now. Not after everything that's just happened."

Carl laughed and smacked a hard kiss on my forehead. He led me to the front door, pointed at a door to our right and put his fingers to his lips. "Quiet now. We don't want to wake the dead."

With a smile, he opened the door and pushed me into a small, dark living room. Navy curtains were drawn across the window shutting out the sun. A horrible smell roved the air; something like gone-off chicken mixed with bleach. In the far corner of the room on top of a pine cabinet stood a TV. A navy sofa sat opposite and a pine coffee table stood beside the sofa, on which sat a lipstick-stained mug. The fireplace had been filled in. In its place, stood an electric heater. On the floor beside the heater lay a body.

I brought my hands to my mouth and stared at the old woman on the floor. She was clearly dead. Ping, Maddock and this woman. All dead. All because I'd let this monster out of his cage.

Mrs Waters was right. I should have kept my nose out. For all I knew she could be dead too and Odette could be alone in the wood, lost and terrified and too vulnerable to save herself.

I looked at him and his face blurred. Horror and anger and the unfairness of it all surged up inside my lungs, making it hard to breathe. The urge to pound my fists into his face was so strong I had to bite my lip. He frowned as if puzzled by my reaction.

"You didn't know her, so what's the problem?"

All of a sudden, I felt so dizzy I could barely stay upright. He caught me, stopped me from falling, wrapped his arm around my shoulders and pulled me in close. With his lips in my hair, he said, "Be a good girl. Don't make this be you."

A shiver of disgust rippled over my skin. He pulled me out of the room and led me upstairs. As we ascended, I stared down at the beige carpet and told myself to breathe. At the top of the stairs I registered a small landing and two closed doors. He opened a third door and pulled me inside a small double room filled with a double bed, a pine dressing table and little else.

Despite my dizziness, I looked around the room and tried to make myself focus on where I was and what was happening.

Discoloured net curtains hid the windows. They would look onto the back garden and the fields at the back of the house. The bed was made with a flowery bedspread. A Paddington Bear teddy sat between two flowery pillows. The room smelt of dust and mildew. A framed photograph of someone's family, the photo black and white, hung on the wall behind the bed. I wanted to scream and run head-first into the wall, but allowed him to push me onto the bed.

He stood over me with his hands on his hips. His face hardened. "We'll be gone a couple of hours. If you're not here when I get back, I'll kill the kid and it'll be your fault."

"Where're you taking him?"

"Somewhere we can practise undisturbed."

He leant down bringing out faces close. "Rest up, honey. You'll want that shoulder better soon 'cos when my chest's healed, we'll be christening this bed, if you get my drift."

He winked and left the room, locked the door and ran down the stairs whistling.

I waited for the front door to slam shut then tried the door, but it wouldn't budge. Panic threatened to overwhelm me. I put my head in my hands to stop the world spinning. Tears filled my eyes and I jabbed them away. I paced the room and scratched at my lips, trying to wipe away any remnants of his mouth on mine. Panic rose again and I forced myself to sit on the bed. I ducked my head between my knees and sucked in deep breaths but wave after wave of icy fear crashed into me. Digging my nails into my palms, I gritted my teeth and pushed myself up then strode over to the net curtains and yanked them apart.

The day was beautiful. The fields glowed beneath the sun. The sky was perfect.

I pictured Wren's little face and realised I couldn't give in to fear and despair. What I could do was give in to anger - surrender myself to it - let it give me what I needed.

With a scream of rage I threw myself onto the bed, pictured Carl and pounded my fists into Paddington Bear's smiling face.

Chapter Forty-Nine

Odette and I are running through the wood trying to catch up with Mrs Waters but never managing to. Beside me, Odette is a flash of red. She wears a scarlet hooded cape like Little Red Riding Hood, and instead of panting like a human, she moans like a new-born calf. Ahead of us Mrs Waters weaves in and out of the gnarly trees with the agility of a gazelle. Behind us, thundering through the gloom on four legs and laughing like a hyena, runs a hybrid creature that's half-wolf, half-Carl.

One of the creature's talons is wedged in my shoulder. The pain is continuous and scorching, but I plunge on with the sole aim of getting away from him and reaching the farmhouse where I know we'll all be safe.

Suddenly I'm stuck in a swamp and can't run. I try to shout but even that's impossible.

Odette stops to help me and I scream at her to carry on running, but no words come out of my mouth. She discards her cape to reveal her white ballerina costume. She smiles and pirouettes toward the swamp and I watch, mesmerised, unable to move, my body inching down, sludge rising over my shoulder making the talon dig in even more, the pain rising.

The beast is coming. I see its face, its white teeth flashing in the darkness. I try to scream. Instead of sound, maggots come pouring out of my mouth.

I watch - not in horror, but in awe – and a sudden calm spreads throughout my body as the maggots slither across the swamp.

The swamp stops rising and I stop falling.

The hybrid stands behind Odette laughing that crazy, high-pitched laugh. It doesn't seem to see the maggots, but Odette does. She dances back to let them pass then turns and waves happily at her mother, who's standing a few feet away in a sapphire Victorian dress, nodding and sipping tea, pinkie finger raised.

I try to get out of the swamp, but remain its prisoner; there is, however, a little wiggle room now – enough for me to wade through the murky liquid after the maggots.

Odette spins excitedly as the beast looks down and sees the grubs: but it's already too late. With wicked speed, they slither up his front legs, over his chest and into his black, gaping mouth. He rolls onto his back and writhes around in agony as my maggots work their magic.

Mrs Waters appears above me smiling, blood gushing out of her side. She helps me out of the swamp then lies down in the dead leaves and closes her eyes. Odette begins to cry and I look up to see a tree that isn't really a tree but a door, which slams shut with a bang that makes me jump -

I opened my eyes, wiped tears off my cheeks and listened, wincing at the terrible burning in my shoulder and struggling to separate my mind from the dream. Glancing down I saw that my blood had turned the bandage red. Blood was all over the bedsheets too. Footsteps sounded on the stairs. He was back.

The door opened and Carl appeared looking angry. He stormed into the room and pushed me back onto the bed. Straddling me, he stabbed a finger at my face as he spoke. "He wouldn't shoot. Said he didn't think you'd want him to. You ruined our first trip together."

"I didn't say anything to him. I didn't get the chance."

"You must've whispered to him when my back was turned."

"I didn't. I wouldn't dream of spoiling your first outing with him. I swear."

He narrowed his eyes and wrapped his hand around my neck. Lifting my head off the bed, he said, "Tell him to shoot."

"I will."

"Tomorrow. Not now. I've sent him to his room."

"For how long?"

He shrugged. "Depends."

He dropped my head and pushed himself off me. With a glare he said, "Clean yourself up. You look like shit."

I opened my mouth to beg him not to punish Wren, but realised he was probably safer shut up in a room where Carl wasn't.

The lock clicked and I was alone again with my thoughts, no plan and no weapon. I searched the room and found nothing useful. I ran over to the window and tried it, but it was locked and there wasn't a key on the windowsill.

Not ready to give up, I ran my hands under the bed frame then around the back of the dressing table. Nothing. I'd been hoping for a protruding nail. Something sharp that would do a lot of damage.

Losing hope, I collapsed on the bed and stared at the dressing table. There was no stool in front of it but there was a mirror. I stared at my shadowed eyes, at the bloodshot whites and the dead colour of my skin. I thought about Grandma and what she'd do in this situation.

With a surge of adrenaline, I picked up the mirror and carried it over to the corner of the bed. Throwing caution to the wind I smashed the mirror down onto the bed post. It splintered on impact and a good-sized shard fell to the carpet next to my foot. I grabbed it and stared at the lethal tip.

I might have just given myself seven years bad luck, but seven years bad luck was better than seven more seconds with that psychotic bastard.

Chapter Fifty

"You need a shower," he said tossing me a towel, "There's a first aid box in the cabinet. I bought you a toothbrush. Clean up then come downstairs."

He wore fresh clothes and held Wren's hand. I tried to catch Wren's eye but he was staring at the gun in Carl's waistband. To my relief, he had no bruises anywhere. Carl had bought him new clothes. He wore jeans, a green jumper and trainers. It was the first time I'd seen Wren in modern clothes. It made him look even more vulnerable.

In the bathroom, I immediately locked the door. Bending over the sink, I gorged myself on water then sat on the edge of the bath and took a moment. Wren wasn't hurt. That was all that mattered. I pulled the shard of glass out of my jeans. Using it would be a huge risk. I'd have to make sure Wren wasn't around and that we had a quick, easy exit out of the house.

The smell of frying onions drifted up through the house. I unrolled the towel and found a pair of lace knickers, ripped jeans and a low-cut pink top that looked like it would be a size too small. No bra, but I could wear my current one. There was no way I was going braless.

So I had new clothes too. Whoop-de-doo. At least I could get out of my blood-soaked T-shirt. I peeled it off my body and chucked it in the bin.

The shower curtain was mouldy but the water was hot and felt good - as long as I kept my shoulder away from the spray.

In the first aid box I found a roll of bandage, some tape and a pack of painkillers. All bandaged and dosed up, I got dressed then checked the cabinet but found nothing of any use. Music blared through the floor; Blur again. I tensed and hid the piece of glass in the back pocket of my new jeans. With a deep breath I opened the door and walked down the stairs.

Carl was spinning around the kitchen with Wren in his arms. To my surprise, Wren was smiling and for a split second seeing them together like a regular father and son made me feel strange, then I was slammed by revulsion at the sight of his hands on Wren's small body, and rage that I couldn't act for fear of Wren getting hurt in the crossfire.

I dragged my eyes away from Carl's smiling face. The guns still lay on the counter, a constant reminder of his insanity. I flashed back to the horrific comic strip he'd graffitied on the wall in Fairwood House. Through a host of memories, I watched him carry Wren around the room, singing and laughing.

Seeing me in the doorway, he stopped dancing and raked his eyes over my body. He wolf-whistled and said to Wren, "Doesn't Mummy look good?"

Wren nodded. Carl put him down and told him to sit at the table. He gestured for me to do the same. I took a seat and watched him serve up fried bacon and onions on toast.

"Isn't it bizarre that this is what I've been craving for the last seven years? This and a Macdonald's strawberry milkshake," he said.

He took a seat beside me and placed his hand over mine. "Before we eat, let's say Grace."

I raised an eyebrow and he burst into laughter. "Only kidding."

He ate like a starved man. I wasn't hungry but needed the energy so forced myself to eat. Wren didn't touch his food. I mouthed at him to eat but he was staring through me at the guns on the counter.

"Eat up, Son," Carl said through a mouthful of food.

Wren's eyes shifted and locked on Carl's. Carl's hand paused halfway to his mouth. He frowned and leaned forward. In a low voice he said, "Eat."

"It's good," I said.

Wren stared down at his plate then looked up at Carl again. In a voice far older than his years he said, "You're the bad man Mrs Waters locked up in the wood but you're my daddy. That's why she hates me. She hates me because I'm bad like you."

I held my breath, tensed to defend Wren should Carl attack, but he merely smiled and shook his head. "You're not bad and neither am I. Mrs Waters is a sad, confused woman, but you don't ever have to see her again because you're with me now. We're finally together and nothing and no-one can break us up."

Carl got up from the table and collected the guns. He carried them out of the room, yelling over his shoulder for Wren to stay in the kitchen with me while he 'cleaned up' the living room. I assumed that meant get rid of the body.

I crouched down in front of Wren and pulled him in close. Wren's arms wrapped tightly around me.

"You two look cosy," Carl said dragging a black bin liner across the room. "Help me with this, will you Mummy?"

I took the other end of the bagged body. My pulse quickened and I shivered violently. Carl dropped his end with a thud and unlocked the back door and we carried the old woman's corpse out into the back garden.

Carl jerked his head at the shed and I helped him carry the body into the small wooden building, feeling the whole time like I was watching myself from the outside. Like it was another me depositing a dead woman in a shed, another person helping a murderer discard his victim's corpse.

"What're you going to do with her?" I said.

"I thought she'd go well with some fava beans and a nice Chianti."

I resisted the urge to hit him. Just. My fingers moved for the glass shard in my back pocket. I slipped my thumb and fore finger inside my jeans as Wren appeared in the garden.

"What are you doing Daddy?"

"Taking out the trash," he said with a smile.

"Oh."

"Go inside. We'll be in in a minute."

Wren turned and ran back inside the cottage. I wished he would make a run for it. The back door wasn't locked. He could sneak out when Carl wasn't looking. A car was bound to come along these country roads, and the driver would see him, help him, question him, find out everything...

Carl handed me a petrol can and ordered me to pour it over the body. I stared at the can. Told myself not to think about what I was doing. Carl's hand hovered above the gun in his belt. "Do it. She's already dead."

I didn't bother trying to explain to him that that wasn't the point.

I began to pour, telling myself I was watering a plant not pouring flammable liquid over a corpse.

After I'd covered the bag with petrol, I stood back and Carl used a few matches to ignite it. The bag caught fire and within seconds the toxic smell of burning plastic floated into the air followed by the stench of burning flesh.

Carl slammed the shed door shut, grabbed my elbow and dragged me a short distance away, close enough that the heat made my skin sting. I tried to go back into the house, but he wrapped his arm around me, pulled me into his side and nestled his face in my hair.

As if we were watching a beautiful sunset, he oohed at the flames and marvelled at the funnel of black smoke that rose into the sky like a tunnel to hell.

"Old goat had to go," he said.

I licked my lips. Swallowed. "Who was she?"

"My great aunt. Pushing eighty. Deaf as a post and

crippled with arthritis. I did her a favour."

"Won't someone come?" I said.

He shrugged. "Maybe, maybe not. She was a witch. I'll deal with it if the time comes."

"How exactly?" I said.

"We won't be here for long," he said leading me back to the house.

My fingers twitched. I thought about the shard of glass. Hesitated too long. His hand rested on the gun in his jeans. He tapped the cold metal. Glanced down at it to remind me.

"Good girl. Now hurry inside and finish the dishes."

Chapter Fifty-One

I still had my shard of glass and I clung onto that fact all night. The shard was under the pillow, my fingers poised an inch away ready to grab it if he came in and tried to attack me.

By morning I was a nervous wreck. A nervous wreck with a small pointy bit of glass to use against a sadistic murderer with a gun collection. It wasn't an even battle. I might have the element of surprise on my side but Carl had the power. He was stronger than me and he possessed a proper weapon. If I didn't pick exactly the right moment to attack, he would easily overpower me. All it would take was one squeeze of the trigger in my direction and I'd be dead, and if I was dead there would be no-one to protect Wren. I couldn't let that happen. Obviously, the thought of dying was like plunging my face into hot coals, but the thought of Carl hurting Wren was worse. It was better that I was alive than dead, for Wren's sake, even if it meant suffering at the hands of a sexual predator like Carl Maddock. It didn't mean that I wasn't going to try to use my glass blade; it just meant that I had to choose the perfect time to use it, and when the time came, I had to be willing to kill.

I'd slept in my clothes, too terrified to sleep uncovered, so the moment I heard movement, I got out of bed and hurried to the door. Placing my ear against the wood, I listened. The piece of glass was in my back pocket. I heard the shower go and relaxed, thinking that he wasn't coming to let me out of the room yet, but a couple of seconds later Carl unlocked the door and stepped into the room pointing a gun at me.

"Morning, honey bun. Sleep well?" he said, raking his eyes across my chest. He grabbed my wrist and pulled me out of the room.

At the foot of the stairs he lifted a purple fleece off the banister and handed it to me. "We're going outside for shooting practice."

I pulled on the fleece and he shrugged on a leather jacket that still had the tag on.

He grabbed my arm and pulled me down the hallway into the kitchen and out through the back door. The day was overcast and drizzly, too cold to be out for long.

"Where's Wren?" I said.

"His room. I told him to stay put for a bit. Said I'd call him when breakfast's ready."

He led me to the burnt remains of the shed and positioned me in front of the charred heap. Kneeling down, he rummaged through the rubbish and found a blackened watering can which he handed to me.

"Hold this out to the right. Don't move."

Panic almost choked me but I managed to say, "No. You can't. What if you hit me? Who'll look after Wren?"

"I will. I am his dad after all. Now stay still and shut up. I'm a good shot but I'm not perfect yet."

He turned and strode back to the cottage. When he was about fifteen feet away, he raised the gun.

"Don't move," he said.

I froze and loosened my grip on the watering can. If he hit it, it would, I hoped, be less painful if I wasn't holding it tightly.

"Ready?" he said.

I nodded and closed my eyes. My heart slammed and my knees shook. This was next level madness.

He fired. The bullet hit the watering can, blowing it out of my hand and sending black pieces of metal scattering into the air around me. I opened my eyes, which were watering from the pain running up and down my arm. He beamed, proud of his shot.

"Move back five paces and pick up something else. Smaller this time."

I didn't move. "What's all this practice for?"

He laughed and shook his head. "Listen to you, Little Miss Nosy. Why're you so curious? It's not like you can do anything to stop me."

I tried to work out what to say, but couldn't.

He ordered me to move back again and told me to pick up another target, this one smaller.

Heart smashing against my ribs, I bent over and found a piece of charred wood that was only a fraction smaller than the watering can.

"*Smaller*," he shouted.

I picked up a smaller piece of wood, backed up five paces and held out the target.

"Above your head this time," he said with a grin.

The sadistic bastard's enjoying this.

Icy drizzle soaked my hair and seeped through the fleece making me shiver, but I forced myself to stand dead still, raised my arm above my head and closed my eyes, hoping and praying he wouldn't aim too low. A sudden breeze howled around me and I opened my eyes and watched, terrified the wind would throw him off.

He raised the gun a second time and took aim. He fired and missed. I felt the bullet whiz past, far too close.

"Fuck. *Again*."

He raised the gun, took aim and fired; this time the bullet hit its target, splintering the wood. My shoulder screamed. I felt dizzy and tottered to the side. He frowned and shouted at me to pull myself together, go back another five paces, pick up something even smaller.

Fighting the urge to throw up, I walked forward and picked up a small piece of charred wood then walked back to where I'd stood before, hoping he wouldn't notice, but he gestured for me to back up, so I inched back further and further until my spine hit the fence. He gave me the thumbs up then cracked his neck and shook his arms, limbering up for the shot.

Dread flooded my body. I held the piece of wood next to my side and prayed he would hit his target, not me. Every part of me wanted to drop the piece of wood and run.

He reached the cottage and took up position, and I sucked in a breath and squeezed my eyes closed. Pushing my fingers into my pocket, I wrapped them around the shard of glass.

I steeled myself for the shot and opened my eyes, swallowing a scream as Wren appeared by the back door with Carl's Glock in his hands.

Carl raised the gun and so did Wren. I stared at Wren and began to shake my head and as I did so, Carl realised I wasn't looking at him and turned to look over his shoulder.

I ran forward as he turned to face his son.

"Put it down," Carl said dropping the gun to his side.

Wren's arms shook but he didn't lower the gun.

Chapter Fifty-Two

I tripped and fell to my knees. Carl raised his gun and pointed it at Wren.

"Drop it, Son. You don't need to do this. You're not a bad boy. Listen to me. Drop that gun and come over here."

Wren took a step closer to his father. His arms trembled.

I pushed myself to my feet and ran forward. "Wren – no."

He turned his little face to mine and gave me a small nod then turned back to face Carl.

"If you don't drop that gun in three seconds, I'll shoot," Carl said, his tone hard.

Silence spilled around us. I looked at Wren and tried to tell him with my eyes to drop the gun, but he wouldn't look at me. His face was so white, his body so small, the gun so beastly in his tiny hands. He was just a little boy. An innocent, sweet, little boy. And he was suffering all because of this monster.

Anger like I'd never known ripped through my chest making me feel like I was being torn open by a giant claw. Wren should not have to be doing this; I should have beaten the bastard by now; I should have protected him, got him away, kept him safe. I couldn't let the bastard win. I couldn't let Wren ruin his life by shooting his own father. I had to do something. I had to do it now.

Sweat blinded me. I blinked.

Wren's arms drooped. Carl smiled at his son. "Come on now, buddy. Give the gun to Daddy, there's a good chap."

Wren's chin wobbled.

The maggots screamed. Pain pulsed in my heart and rage

tore through me. With a scream I launched myself onto Carl's back and wrapped my arms around his neck. He thrashed from side to side and I stabbed at him with the glass and missed. He roared, ripped my hands away and threw me to the ground. My injured shoulder took the brunt and I screamed and tried to get up but he kicked my chest and yelled at me to stay still.

It was over. I'd tried and failed. Just as I'd tried and failed before. I hadn't been able to save my mum and now I couldn't save Wren. I couldn't even save myself.

He aimed the gun at my face. "This is all your fault. I never should've brought you here. You're the reason he's doing this. You've twisted his mind against me. You've all twisted him against me. You, Harriet, Maddock – you're all in it together."

I brought my arms up and covered my face with my hands. This was it. I'd fought and lost. Grandma's face appeared – I saw Wren running and laughing - a red-bricked house on a nice street - Ralph sitting in his study tapping at his laptop - and me, standing at the front of a classroom, teaching. This was what I should've had but never would. I moved my hands away and stared at Carl as he moved his finger to the trigger.

He smiled and took a step closer. His tongue flicked out and licked sweat off his upper lip.

I held my breath. Carl seemed to have forgotten about Wren, but I hadn't.

I dived onto my front as Wren fired.

The bullet exploded from the gun and skimmed Carl's arm. Wren stumbled backwards and fell onto his bottom and the gun span across the ground, lost in the wild grass.

Carl roared and swung the gun back towards Wren and I screamed and reached forward helplessly – too far away to save him - and a blue figure barrelled into Carl's chest, knocking him to the ground.

I stared, too shocked to do anything as Ralph attacked Carl. A moment later, Ping launched herself on top of them and began to claw at Carl's face.

I scrambled to my feet.

"Find the gun," I said to Wren, who immediately got on all fours and began to hunt for it. I ran over to him and searched the ground for the Glock but it seemed to have vanished. A cry made me spin around to see Carl raising the gun towards Ralph's face. Ralph grabbed his wrist and Ping tore a chunk out of Carl's cheek with her nail. With a groan, Carl brought up his feet and slammed them into Ralph's ribs. Ralph cried out and rolled onto his back, leaving Ping and Carl wrestling.

"You killed my husband!" Ping screeched.

She tried to claw at his eyes but he smashed the gun into her head and threw her off with ease. He laughed as she cradled her head in her hands. He got to his feet and aimed the gun at Ping then turned the gun on Ralph who was on his knees struggling to get up. I froze and pushed Wren behind me.

"Get back inside, Son," Carl panted.

Wren clung to the backs of my legs. I felt him shake his head.

"Now!" Carl shouted.

"Ivy?" Wren said.

"Do as he says, Wren. Everything's going to be okay."

"But -"

"Go," I said.

Wren sniffed and let go of my legs. I turned and watched him run back inside the house.

"That's better," Carl said, smearing sweat off his upper lip. "Now, all of you, get on your knees."

I glanced at Ping. She mouthed 'sorry'. Ralph started to get to his feet and Carl strode up to him, held the gun an inch from his eye and screamed, "ON YOUR KNEES!" He waved the gun around wildly, swinging it from my face to Ping's then back to Ralph's.

"All of you. On your knees. NOW."

I dropped to my knees beside Ralph and he slipped his hand into mine. Ping crawled through the wild grass and knelt beside me. Her hand slipped into mine. Only now did I notice her face was splattered with blood.

"Good. That's better," Carl said. He stood completely still. For a long time, he stared down at us. The wind whipped our hair about our cheeks, stinging our skin, turning our lips blue. Ping's eyes never left Carl. I could feel them burning into him, her rage hot enough to flush her cheeks in spite of the cold.

"How did you find us?" I whispered.

"Maddock tell me about this place. Ralph drive to house. See me and -" Ping said.

"I thought you were dead," I interrupted.

"No. Just pretend. Lie still. Maddock – he save me."

I squeezed her hand.

Carl fired his gun into the air and said, "No talking. Let me think."

"You can't get rid of three bodies on your own," Ralph said.

"Shut up!"

"Ralph's right," I said quickly, "you can't possibly cope with it all on your own. And the police will find Maddock's body at the house and it won't take them long to work out that you're here and -"

Ralph said, "The police are already on their way."

I couldn't tell if he was telling the truth; I prayed he was.

Carl turned a slow smile on me. "You know what? You're right. That's why I'm going to let you live, honey. You can help me get rid of their bodies just like you helped me with my dear old aunt. The question is: who shall I kill first?"

He walked around to stand behind us. The wind whistled

and heavy rain began to fall.

"Eeeny, meeny miny mo, who will be the first to go?"

"Don't do this," I said.

Carl laughed and whispered into my ear, "Looks like I'll be keeping you around after all."

Ping's hand was trembling. Ralph's shoulders shook. Our eyes met. He looked terrified.

Carl moved to stand directly behind Ralph. He raised the gun and pushed the tip into the back of Ralph's head.

I began to cry. Ralph raised his chin and stroked the back of my hand with his thumb.

Carl said, "Ready to find out if you've been a good boy or a bad boy, mate?"

I glanced at Ralph. Silent tears trickled down his cheeks.

Ping muttered, "Bastard."

Carl whirled around and strode back to stand behind Ping. He pushed the gun into the back of her head and said, "You shouldn't have said that, bitch."

He pulled the trigger. The bullet exploded from the gun. I expected Ping to drop to the ground, but she remained upright. Carl laughed manically. He'd fired the bullet into the air above Ping's head. She began to sob and he moved back to stand behind Ralph.

He blew imaginary smoke off the end of the gun.

"This time it's for real," he said. "Say goodbye to your boyfriend, honey."

Something in his voice had changed. This time, I knew he was going to do it.

"I don't know who the fuck you are, mate," Carl said, "but this'll teach you to mind your own business."

I turned around, sensing something behind me. A blood-stained figure drifted down the side of the house, dark hair covering most of her face. Carl put his finger on the trigger. I stared, unable to peel my eyes away as Odette walked up to Carl's broad back.

In her hand, she held a knife.

In my head, the maggots cheered.

Carl grinned at me. "Watch and learn, honey. Watch and learn."

His eyes widened as he registered that I was looking at something behind him, but it was too late.

Odette stood on her toes and plunged the knife into his neck.

Ralph, Ping and I shot away from Carl as blood spurted from the wound and he dropped to his knees. The gun fell from his hand and he clutched frantically at his neck, but blood gushed out between his fingers. He tried to speak but no words would come.

Odette moved to stand in front of him. She tilted her head. For a split second she was the spitting image of her mother and a look entered her eyes that brought her to the present for the first time since I'd met her. In a small voice she said, "You hurt me. You killed my mummy. She died in my arms. You did this to yourself."

The knife fell from her fingers. Tears streamed down her cheeks and spilled onto the ground blending with the rain and the blood. Ping rushed forward and wrapped her arms around Odette, who fell to her knees and began to cry.

A moment later, Carl stilled. His eyes glazed over and he fell face-first onto the blood-soaked grass.

Wren ran out of the house and stared at his father's body. I started to walk to him, but Odette looked up.

"Wren?" she said softly.

Wren looked up at her. For a long time, they stared at each other. Odette crouched down and stretched out her arms. "Baby?"

Wren glanced at me then back at Odette. I nodded.

He stared at her and said, "Mummy?"

Odette beamed. Tears shone in her eyes.

"Are you really my mummy?"

"Yes, baby bird."

Wren looked at me. I smiled. He smiled back, walked across the wild grass and allowed Odette to pull him into a cuddle. He buried his head in her neck and she kissed his head and whispered something that made him smile.

I looked at Ping. She was hugging herself and crying, but the faintest of smiles touched her lips.

Ralph wrapped his arms around me and I pressed my face into his chest and told him he was an idiot for coming to save me. With a gentle finger, he lifted my chin and kissed me.

The maggots fell silent, and I knew, at last, they had gone.

Epilogue

Eighteen Months Later

Wren fidgeted with his navy bow tie and wrinkled his nose.

'No fiddle,' Ping said, slipping an ivory stiletto onto my right foot.

I straightened and looked at my reflection, shocked to see how curvy I looked. Ping looked pretty in her blush-pink dress, but even concealer couldn't mask the shadows under her eyes. She suffered Maddock's loss in silence, but grief shadowed her like a second skin.

'You both look perfect,' I said, beckoning Wren in for a cuddle. He was as cute as a puppy in his tiny suit.

'Careful – dirty hands!' Ping said.

Wren halted a step away from me and I grabbed him. He smelt clean and fresh. 'I don't care. I'm already a sweaty mess. Wonder how Ralph's bearing up in this heat.'

Grandma rushed into the room, wiping sweat from her brow. 'It's time – oh, wow - darling, I…' For once, she was speechless. Her eyes welled and she dashed them away with her lace handkerchief.

'Already?' Butterflies swarmed in my tummy and I grinned to mask the nerves.

'I wish Mummy was here,' Wren said.

Ping gave me a look and I bit my lip.

'You'll be together soon, darling. The house is almost ready and Mummy's going to be allowed to leave the hospital next month. Now, try to think about all those yummy sweets you'll get after the boring part. Remember the pick and mix trolley?'

Wren smiled, but his mind was elsewhere. He was staying with a lovely foster couple who were already in their seats along with the other fifty guests, waiting for me to stride down the aisle in all my bridal glory. Once Wren had given the ring to Ralph's best man, he'd take his seat between Jade and Joe Harris. Ping would sit with them too. She was one of my bridesmaids. Over the last year, we'd grown close, meeting up for coffee then visiting Wren at his temporary home in Wells, or Odette at Willow Ward Hospital. With her savings and the money Maddock had left her, she'd bought a small flat in Frome and now worked at Longleat Centre Parcs as a housekeeper.

Odette had made remarkable progress and was now lucid and stable. Sadly, she'd been too ill to attend her mother's funeral, but I'd returned to the moor with her six months later to spread Mrs Waters' ashes. Harriet had been a complicated person, but ultimately a hero. I would never forget her.

Wren was now a child who smiled and laughed and ran about with other children playing imaginary games consisting of astronauts and aliens; a little monkey who loved to talk and play practical jokes. The only thing he was missing was his mummy. But they would be together again soon. Sooner than he realised.

Grandma air-kissed my cheeks, murmuring about not ruining my make-up, then tottered off clutching her handkerchief to her chest. I slipped my hand into Wren's and Ping took her place behind my best friend and chief bridesmaid, Annalise, who had moved back to England two months ago - to my absolute delight.

'Ready?' Ping said, giving me a rare grin. She passed my bouquet over.

I took the flowers from her and nodded. Wren looked up at me. 'I love you, Ivy, but I love Mummy more.'

'I know, sweetie. I know.'

Led by Annalise, we left the hotel room and emerged into the gorgeous grounds of Widbrook Grange. The sun was high, the sky clear, the rose-scented breeze light and pleasant.

Ralph's parents had funded the wedding, and we were planning on honeymooning in Thailand when we could afford to. I had just completed my teacher training and was due to start my Newly Qualified Teacher year in September. Since the dreadful events of eighteen months ago, Ralph and I had barely spent a day apart. It was funny how much we'd bonded in such a short space of time. Shared horror seemed to have glued us together. I'd even told him about the maggots.

The theme music to *Top Gun* drifted out of the barn across the rose bushes and Annalise turned around to share a knowing smile. Ping rolled her eyes at us.

Our little procession reached the barn and Ralph's dad appeared at the entrance.

'You look stunning, dear,' he said, linking arms with me.

'You don't look too bad yourself, Bob.'

He chuckled, reached across me and said to Wren, 'First, I think there's someone who'd like to say hi to you, young man.'

Wren frowned and looked at me. I winked.

Odette appeared behind him beaming from ear to ear. She ruffled Wren's hair, and he looked around, did a double take, glanced at me then squealed and threw himself at her. She knelt and held him tightly, dropping little kisses on his ears and neck.

I felt myself tearing up. Ping's hand found mine. Her eyes were bright and shiny.

Odette's gaze met mine and she mouthed, *Thank you.*

She extricated herself gently from Wren's grip, slipped her hand into his and gave me a tearful nod. She had lost her mother, but she had her little boy back.

I ushered them forward and, together, mother and son led the way into the barn.

When, at last, I saw Ralph standing at the front of the barn looking like the cat with the cream, I burst into tears; tears of love and hope, sacrifice and survival. Tears that would bond us forever.

Acknowledgements

Thank you to my dad for being such a brilliant Alpha reader and promoter, and to my mum for her constant support. My husband Tommy deserves immense thanks for such astute proofreading and insightful feedback. Thanks so much to Victoria Hyde @Instabooktours for her wonderful work in helping to spread the word, and to Olly from More Visual Ltd for another cracking cover! I'm so grateful to my Beta reader, Vix, for her excellent insights, and to every reader and blogger who has read this book and taken the time to share their views. A final thanks must go to Edgar Allen Poe and Henry James for inspiring this story with their unforgettable tales.

ABOUT THE AUTHOR

Abby Davies was born in Macclesfield in 1984 and started writing 'thrillers' when she was seven.

After reading English Literature at Sheffield University and training to be an English teacher, she wrote novels in her free time and attained an MA in Creative Writing.

She was shortlisted for the Mslexia Novel Competition in 2018 and longlisted for the Blue Pencil Agency First Novel Award in 2019. Her debut *Mother Loves Me* was published by HarperCollins in 2020. *The Cult*, also HarperCollins, came out in 2021. *Arrietty* was released in July 2023 and her fourth thriller, *Her No.1 Fan*, came out in September. *The Girl Who Heard Maggots* is Abby's fifth novel.

She lives in Wiltshire with her husband, daughter and two crazy cocker spaniels.

She loves chatting to readers and reading reviews, so please do get in touch/share on Amazon, Instagram, Twitter and Goodreads.

Find out more about Abby and her books at

www.abbydavies.com
Twitter: @Abby13Richards
Instagram: @abbydaviesauthor

Milton Keynes UK
Ingram Content Group UK Ltd.
UKHW010642271123
433342UK00001B/8